BEEFCAKE

&

Retakes

JUDI FENNELL

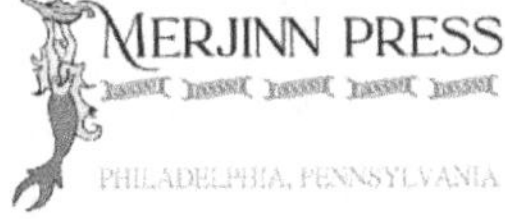

MERJINN PRESS

PHILADELPHIA, PENNSYLVANIA

To My Kids
It's all for you. Everything.

Books By Judi Fennell

Royally Sunk
In Over Her Head
Wild Blue Under
Catch of a Lifetime
Love on the Rocks
~Making Waves ~ outtakes compilation

Bottled Magic
I Dream of Genies
Genie Knows Best
My Fair Genie
~Your Wish Is His Command ~ outtakes compilation

Once Upon A Time Romance
Beauty and The Best
If The Shoe Fits
Through The Leaded Glass ~ prequel

BeefCake, Inc.
Beefcake & Cupcakes
Beefcake & Mistakes
Beefcake & Retakes
Beefcake & Snowflakes
Sweet as Candy (short short)

Manley Maids
What a Woman Wants
What a Woman Needs
What a Woman Gets
What a Woman
What A Guy Wants

We were supposed to be forever.
Then I made sure we weren't.

Juliet Chambers has spent seven years wishing she could go back and do it differently.

Tanner Wentworth has spent seven years trying to forget her—and failing.

When Juliet's grandmother falls ill with a single wish—to see her favorite couple happy together—Tanner agrees to play the happy husband one last time. It's the only way to get everything he's been waiting for.

One last performance, pretend to be happy, and they all get what they want.

The problem is…
pretending is starting to feel a lot like remembering.

He never expected one retake to change everything.

***

"*Beefcake & Retakes* hit me in the gut. The best stories take you on a journey through the emotions, and *Beefcake and Retakes* did that. I couldn't put the book down."
~ Renee N., Amazon

Prologue

I now pronounce you man and wife. You may kiss your bride."

Tanner stared at the woman before him. *His wife.*

How the hell had he gotten himself roped into this?

"Tanner?" Juliet said his name so softly with a little curl on the end to make it a question.

He didn't know how to answer her.

"Uh, you may kiss the bride." The Justice of the Peace coughed as he said it.

Yeah, yeah, Tanner knew the drill. He just didn't know *why* he was standing here having to do it.

But he leaned in anyway, intending to make it nice and quick.

Juliet made it more than nice and definitely not quick.

Damn her.

She knew just how to kiss him. Knew just how to get the heat started in his groin. Knew how to wrap her sexy-as-hell body around his and send all the blood rushing south.

Damn her.

Tanner speared his hands into her hair as he thrust his tongue into her mouth. She wanted to make him hot and horny as hell? Fine. Then she better be ready to deal with the consequences because, as his wife, she'd be dealing with a *lot* of consequences.

No she wouldn't.

Tanner wrenched his mouth from hers, his breathing ragged, and he looked into those blue eyes he'd lost himself in before. Back when he'd believed in love and happily-ever-afters between them.

God, he was such a schmuck.

"May I be the first to offer my congratulations?" The damn Justice just wouldn't get off the married-for-love kick. Of course, that'd been *Tanner's* stipulation. Bad enough he had to do this; he didn't want people knowing the real reason he was doing it.

So long as Juliet did.

He pulled his fingers from her hair and grabbed the marriage certificate from the clerk. There. Done. Next.

Luckily, he also remembered to grab his *wife's* hand before striding out of the courthouse office with a brief— very brief—wave to their respective families.

He dropped her hand the minute they were outside.

He had to, for his own well-being.

Because every time he touched Juliet, his heart ended up getting ripped to shreds.

Juliet had to run to keep up with Tanner. Not that that was anything new; she'd always been trying to keep up with him. From the first moment she'd laid eyes on him—okay, maybe not then, given that she'd been two weeks old, but ever since she'd been old enough to notice him—she'd been running after him.

It'd started with hide-n-seek, and had progressed to skateboarding and bike-riding and swimming. She'd had to keep up with him her entire childhood because he'd been her best friend. Their parents had been best friends, their ranches butted up against each other, and Tanner had been larger than life.

'Course, that body was big enough as it was. Tanner had the build of a linebacker, the abs of a swimmer, and the face of a Greek god. He'd been beautiful to her since puberty and the feeling had only grown with age.

They'd been the golden couple. Homecoming king and queen. Best-looking. Most likely to succeed. The yearbook staff had even added his last name after hers under her senior picture because *of course* they would get married.

"Tanner, wait."

He didn't even break his stride. "We're on a schedule."

No, *he* was on a schedule. He was always moving these days, always busy. It was to avoid spending alone-time with her, she knew that. He thought so little of her that they never had a chance to catch a breath together lately.

Tonight would change that. This next week would change it. She'd used the only thing she could think of to get some alone-time with him and she wasn't proud of it. But dammit, they needed to be alone. To have time to talk and sort out what had happened—the scene she'd set up for when her father would walk in…

It'd gotten them to the courthouse and on the plane to Fiji where Daddy had shelled out a fortune for the honeymoon hut on the water. If she had to take her husband to the ends of the earth to get some time alone with him, then that's what she'd do.

"Tanner, please. I can't run in these heels."

"So take them off. They don't look like they're designed for walking anyway."

She choked back the angry retort. She didn't want to start their honeymoon with a fight. There'd been too many harsh words between them already.

She took a few extra seconds out of their "schedule" to remove the shoes, then ran after him, wishing she'd trained for that half marathon Tricia had tried talking her into.

She made it to the limo a few seconds after he'd opened the door for her, barely enough time for the frown to form.

"The plane's not going to wait, Juliet."

Actually, it would. Her father's money said it would, but she wasn't going to argue with him.

He pulled the door shut behind him, then took out his phone the minute the driver pulled away from the curb.

He was on the thing the whole damn way to the airport, through security, and right onto the tarmac. He even had it on when the flight attendant handed them the champagne.

"Mr. Wentworth, we'll be departing shortly," she said when he waved for her to put the flute on the table between them.

Tanner punched another couple of letters into his text or email or, hell, maybe he was just playing some stupid game so he wouldn't have to talk to her, but then he turned off his phone.

Finally. Juliet couldn't hold back her smile. Their honeymoon could finally start and the healing could begin.

But then Tanner stood up.

"Tanner? What are you doing?"

"Hang on, Juliet." He stuck his phone in his pants pocket and headed toward the cockpit.

Juliet stared after his broad back that tapered so incredibly nicely down to a narrow waist. Tanner's looks and physique were just icing on the cake of the man she'd fallen in love with so long ago—

The same man who was getting off the plane.

Chapter One

Seven years later

The man had a beautiful body.

And Juliet Chambers-Wentworth remembered every single ridge, plane, and muscle. Especially how it'd been wrapped around her—how *he'd* been wrapped around her—the night she'd set him up to trap him into marrying her.

"*That's* him? Are you *kidding* me?" Her friend Sandy took a sip of her drink as they sat in the dimly lit dining room of Tanner's gig, BeefCake, Inc. "No *wonder* you want him back."

Her husband had an amazing body and knew what to do with it, but, no, that wasn't why she wanted him back. But she'd let him and everyone else think so. Because it was convenient. Because it worked.

Because the truth was something too heartbreaking to think about.

The dancers up on the stage hip-actioned their way into a straight line, all the black pants with the silk stripe down the side just itching to come off. Juliet had seen enough strip shows to know what was coming, and she'd seen enough of Tanner beneath his clothes to know what was coming, but still, when it did, when they ripped off those Velcro-ed pants, her heart fluttered like it had the first time his pants had come off.

"Sweet mother of God." Sandy fell back against her chair, tossed the straw from her drink onto the table, and guzzled the rest of it down. "Please tell me he knows what to do with that."

Yeah, Tanner knew. Juliet's thighs tingled in remembrance. So did another part of her. And her breasts ached. There hadn't been anyone since Tanner. Eighty-seven long months of no-interest-in-anyone-else-induced celibacy. Probably not a good idea showing up here like this. Not when she had to do what she had to do.

The six oiled-up, muscled guys on stage, each one as delicious as the other, swiveled around, their hips and other, um, parts, ensuring that no one was looking at their faces.

But Juliet was. She was watching Tanner's every expression. Watched him look at the audience but not really see them. Granted, the stage lights probably had a lot to do with that, but when she looked at him in comparison to the rest of the dancers who were trying to interact with the audience, to make that connection and zero in on each woman to create the fantasy that they were dancing for her alone, Tanner didn't have it.

Until he saw her.

She knew the minute he did. He missed a step. Tanner never missed steps, not in dancing, not in life, not in the romance department—until *she* had, and it'd been the biggest misstep of her life. She'd lost him.

But now she needed him back.

"Uh, did he see you?" Sandy leaned over and whispered in her ear. "He's staring right at us."

Juliet swallowed. She wasn't ready for this. She'd thought she was, but she wasn't.

Tanner's eyes narrowed and he quickly got back into step with the other guys, but he didn't stop staring at her, with his mouth a flat line—those gorgeous talented lips that could curve into the most beautiful smile right before they delivered the most cutting remarks of her life.

His broad chest and even broader shoulders glinted in the stage lights. He'd waxed his chest. Not that she minded, but she had enjoyed curling her fingers in the just-enough amount of hair he normally had, all golden blond like the rest of him.

The scar was new. She winced when she saw it. Looked like an appendectomy scar. And she hadn't even been told.

Well, what could she expect? She was his wife in name only. Though if that had been an emergency appendectomy, she could have been his widow and she'd never have known.

She shivered. She couldn't think about a life without Tanner in it. Even if he was a thousand miles away.

He'd let his hair grow. Wouldn't his father have something to say about that if he saw him… But then, his father had always had a lot to say about Tanner.

Hers, too.

Juliet shut off those thoughts. Her father was the main reason she was here and she didn't want to think why.

Another reason would be the person staring at her from across a dozen stage lights.

The solo dances started. Tanner was in the background, hips rotating, abs clenching, a muscle in that square jaw of his keeping time with the music. He was distracted. She could always tell with Tanner. She knew every one of his moods, had for the whole twenty-nine years she'd known him. There'd never been any question in her mind who'd she'd end up with in life. The Chambers and the Wentworths. They went together like peanut butter and jelly, though her father would have a coronary if she used such a mundane comparison. But the Chambers and the Wentworths had been friends socially and partners in business for three generations. She and Tanner were the first two to join the families.

Until she'd made the fateful decision that had landed them here.

"So come on, Juliet. Spill. You can't tell me that

whatever you two fought about can't be cleared up with a conversation. I mean, look at that, will you?"

She *was* looking at it. At him. That was the problem. She should have remembered how she turned to mush around Tanner. The hell with their families' wants and needs; what about hers? She'd been fantasizing about Tanner her entire teenage, college, and adult life, and when she'd finally gotten him to the altar—er, Justice of the Peace—it'd been a fantasy come true.

For about an hour until he'd gotten off that plane.

"Oh *baby*!"

Sandy whooped beside her when Tanner hung his thumbs where a belt buckle should have been but wasn't and did enough of a two-step to get every woman's mouth watering. Then he rotated slowly, the skintight spandex shorts hiding n-o-t-h-i-n-g from anyone's eyes. Jesus, she could tell his religion in those things.

And then he shook his ass, and oh, man, did the crowd go wild. Sandy was slapping her on the shoulder so hard Juliet had to move her chair or she'd end up with a bruise.

"Please tell me he has a brother. A cousin? Hell, I'll take his pool boy."

Tanner didn't have a pool boy. Not anymore. He didn't have anything. Not since his father had gambled it all away—and hers had picked up the pieces.

One more nail in the coffin of their marriage.

Tanner swung his hips and shook his ass so hard he would've worried about throwing his back out if he didn't want to lay one more sin at Juliet Chambers' feet. What the hell was she doing here?

Little Miss Juliet Chambers, spoiled beauty queen. He'd given her a second chance when she'd begged him, thinking she'd changed.

He'd been wrong.

Again.

He slapped his ass then, knowing women found it sexy. He posed, flexing just enough to keep their interest—and their screams—then he rotated slowly, giving them all a good look at the abs he worked out two hours a day, and the pecs he could make dance like his grandfather had taught him. He'd always laughed, but the women? They screamed.

He held another pose, making eye contact—or so they thought—through the smoky stage lights, winking a few times. At any woman but Juliet.

She was watching him, though; he could feel it. He'd always felt her eyes on him. From the moment they'd decided to be each other's first kiss, he'd always known when Juliet was looking at him.

He'd looked at her just as much. The woman was gorgeous, and unfortunately, she knew what effect she'd had on him.

Well no more. He could stare at her for the rest of the night and it wouldn't erase the disillusionment he'd suffered at her hands.

Juliet was a piece of work. He'd never seen it before, never realized how selfish and shallow she was until the moment he'd found out—

Shit, he missed a move. Tanner pulled his head back into the routine and got in sync with music. He wasn't about to let Juliet Chambers-Wentworth—and he cringed when he attached his name to hers—disrupt one more part of his life. Forty-five days and then she'd be gone for good.

The final stanza of the song started and Tanner tilted the cowboy hat down over one eye, all part of the routine. It worked every time.

Did it work on Juliet?

Why the hell did he care?

He turned around again, his ass front and center. That was truly his money-maker and normally he used it as such. Tonight, he was shaking it for all the wrong reasons.

Let her eat her heart out. If she'd only kept her secret

to herself, he'd never have known and Juliet could have had him tied around her little finger for life.

He bent his knees and pelvic-thrusted as if he were pole dancing, playing with the waistband of the shorts. He had the banana sling on under them; the temptation to just rip them off and flaunt exactly what she was missing out on a really strong temptation.

She'd destroyed what they could have had. First, with her lie, then with coming clean about it. All while he'd still been reeling from the worst shock of his young life.

He could never forgive her for putting him through not one loss, not even two, but so many he'd lost count over the years.

The catcalls kept coming, so Tanner kept working the imaginary pole, flashing his signature smoky-eyed gaze back over his shoulder. He knew the power of that look; knew the tips it would bring in, so when he turned around and slid forward on the stage on his knees, hat in hand, he wasn't surprised to find it filling with bills.

Eat your heart out, Juliet.

Chapter Two

"Hey, Tan, there's a hot chick out here to see you."

"I'm busy."

"Dude, she's *hot*. As in smokin'."

"Still busy."

Adam shook his head, muttering as he walked away. Tanner shrugged. The guys ought to be used to it. He never picked up one of the guests—Gage and Bryan's cardinal rule on the job. Once they were in street clothes in someone else's club, however, anything could happen. And it often did. But not with him. Juliet had put her brand on him as securely as that wedding ring he'd pried off his finger not five minutes after she'd put it on him. But he was still married and the thing about Tanner: he actually lived by his word. No subplots, no subterfuges, no little side plans.

No, he laid his cards out on the table. And in forty-five days, he'd toss a big check on top of them and get her—and her father—out of his life for good.

Gage stuck his head in the dressing room. "Hey, Tan—"

"Not interested."

"Good. You know the rule."

Gage was one to talk. He'd made a beeline for Lara one night at a bachelorette party and that'd been it for the guy. But the partners didn't have anything to worry about in that department when it came to him.

"However, she says she knows you and isn't leaving until you come out. We don't need a scene."

Tanner exhaled and lost count of the tens he was unfolding from the Stetson. One of his better hauls, so of course Juliet would interrupt. "Fine. I'll be right out. Let me get dressed."

Gage, thankfully, didn't ask any questions, and nodded before pulling the dressing room door closed.

Taking another breath, Tanner stood up and undid the towel from around his waist. At least Gage had given him some warning so he wasn't meeting Juliet for the first time in seven years with barely anything on.

Though she'd certainly seen enough from the audience.

He wondered what she'd thought, watching him dance for other women like he'd once danced for her.

He'd once done a lot of things for her, and with her, and to her… And it'd all been built on a lie.

Tanner shook off the bad memories. He'd put it behind him and moved on with his life; Juliet was part of the past and in another six-and-a-half weeks, that's where she'd stay. He already had the papers being drawn up.

"Yo, Tan. The blonde. If you're not interested, can I get her number?" Markus walked in their shared dressing room, whipping the stark white towel off his dark body way too far from his clothes for Tanner's liking. Markus was always willing to prove the stereotype. Well, with everyone but him.

Tanner chuckled. Markus had seriously been bummed that he wasn't the biggest one in the club and bitched at him constantly that he was wasting the opportunity.

"You don't want her number, Markus. Trust me. I've got it and it's not all that it's cracked up to be."

"I didn't say I wanted to marry her, I just want to, you know."

Tanner looked away before Markus gyrated. He'd seen it more than he cared to.

He pulled the t-shirt over his head, then punched Markus in the bicep as he headed toward the door. "You'll thank me for it one day, bro."

"I'd thank you for it *today* if you'd just give me her number."

"Not happening," he said, pulling the door closed behind him. Markus was a friend and he wouldn't sic Juliet on his worst enemy.

"Hello, Tanner."

She was standing at the bottom of the steps leading to the stage.

Damn, she was pretty in this light without the smoky dark lighting of the club that'd thrown shadows on her face.

Juliet had always been gorgeous. Big smile, big blue eyes, big blonde hair, big boobs, tiny waist. She was the quintessential Texas beauty queen. Which she'd been. They'd been the perfect couple.

Then she'd blown it.

"Didn't expect to see you for another month and a half."

"A month and a half? Why? I could've shown up anytime."

"But you haven't." He put his cowboy hat on his head as he passed her, symbolic and practical all at the same time. He didn't have to look at her, and it let her know he didn't want to. He took the stage steps two at a time. Easier to leave through the club than answering the questions from the guys in the back.

"Tanner, we need to talk."

He kept walking downstage. "*We* don't need to do anything, but if you feel the need, I can't stop you. It's a free country."

He jumped off the stage, then turned around to make sure she could get down.

Damn his innate chivalry.

And damn the fact that touching her still had the ability to send molten lava through his veins.

He helped her off the stage then let go of her arms, stepping aside to let her pass.

She turned around and blocked his path between the tables. "Can we go somewhere and talk?"

"No." He skirted a table and chose another route to the front door.

"Tanner, please."

He stopped. Dammit. When her voice got soft like that, as if she were going to cry…

God, he was still a schmuck when it came to Juliet. "Juliet, let it go. We've got another month and a half, then it'll all be over. I'm using my trust fund to pay off my father's mortgage to your father and then we can finalize things."

"I don't have a month and a half."

He spun around, looking at her. *Really* looking at her. She didn't have a month and a half? Why? "What's wrong with you? What do you have? Is it curable?"

That beautiful bow-shaped mouth twisted sideways, her naturally-perfectly arched eyebrows veeing toward the bridge of her nose, a look that would make other women look, well, if not ugly, definitely not their best, but for Juliet, it was just one more expression on her beautiful face. One he'd learned to read years ago because he'd stared at her for hours. Days. Weeks. Months. He'd never gotten tired of looking at Juliet.

"What are you talking about, Tanner?"

"You. You said you don't have a month. What's wrong with you?"

Her expression changed into a smile just like that. As if she'd rehearsed it—

God damn it. He'd fallen for it again.

"You're not sick at all, are you? You just wanted me to stop and listen to you. Well, you can forget it, Juliet. I'm not falling for your moves again. Fool me once, shame on you, fool me twice, shame on me, fool me a third time? Just take me out and shoot me."

"Tanner, hang on. I didn't say I was sick. You jumped to that conclusion."

"Sure. Blame it on me. Why should today be any

different?" He took the cowboy hat off and raked his fingers through his hair. He had a damn headache and he'd only been around her for less than ten minutes.

"Tan, please, just give me a chance to explain—"

"You're about ten years too late for explanations, Juliet. Look, my lawyer will contact yours the end of next month." On his birthday. Luckily, he'd been born at nine in the morning, so her lawyer couldn't take issue that he wasn't actually thirty until the middle of the night. This would all be wrapped up nice and easy by lunch and he'd have the best birthday celebration of his life that night. Juliet Chambers-Wentworth and her father would be out of his and his parents' lives for good. He wouldn't have a dime of his trust fund left, money that was supposed to pay for the master's degree he was painstakingly working through as he earned the cash, but it'd be worth it to be free.

"*I* have a month and a half, Tanner, but my grandmother might not."

Oh hell. Tanner gritted his teeth and stopped walking. Juliet's grandmother had been as unwitting a player in this whole mess as he'd been. "What's wrong with Nana?" He fell into the name too easily, but she'd been like *his* grandmother since he hadn't had any grandparents since third grade.

"She had a stroke."

"When?"

"Two weeks ago. She's not doing well."

Tanner pinched the bridge of his nose. He hated that Nana was going through this, but seriously, why couldn't it have happened two months from now when his nightmare was all said and done?

Aw man, that was shitty of him. He didn't wish it on her at any point. His anger at Juliet shouldn't lessen his humanity.

He turned around. "I'm very sorry to hear that."

"Thank you. You know she still cares about you."

Tanner didn't answer. Despite what Juliet had done, her grandmother had always been kind to him, and as a prospective family member back in the day, he'd realized he could have done a lot worse than having "the matriarch," as she called herself, in his family. "So what do you want from me, Juliet? Why come here now?"

Juliet looked around. The guys weren't here, but they were listening. He knew them. He also knew his reputation. The fact that he had a woman here asking about him… And the fact that she was about to spill the beans over what their relationship truly was—

"Come on." He grabbed her hand, ignoring the shooting spark of desire that sizzled from his palm right up his arm, over his shoulder, and down into his abdominal cavity where it was working on some very hardened nerve endings. He didn't need the guys overhearing whatever it was Juliet was going to tell him. Because the guys had never seen him with a woman—and wouldn't they be surprised to find out the one they did finally see him with was his wife.

Chapter Three

There was a limo parked out front.

Of course.

"Your father knows you came to see me?" Tanner jerked his head toward the limo whose headlights were glaring through the pouring rain.

"Actually, no. He doesn't. It wouldn't go over well."

Understatement of the year.

He so didn't want to do this, but once again, it didn't seem that he had a choice. "Ready to make a run for it?" He wasn't exactly looking forward to being in such a confined space with her, but if they were going to have privacy, this was about as private as they could get without heading to someone's hotel room. And given that he didn't have one and he wasn't about to step foot in hers, the limo was their only option.

He yanked open the door for her. "So how'd you get to borrow his car and driver?"

"Actually," she slid into the dimly lit interior, "this isn't Daddy's. I flew here and rented it."

Tanner sat on the back seat and pulled the door closed behind him. "You know, there are these things called taxis. Much cheaper. Your father's going to love getting this bill."

She tapped the divider that separated them from the driver and the car pulled out of the parking lot. "I pay my own bills."

Uh huh. With her father's money. And the money he

sent her. She might not be the wife he wanted, but she *was* his wife and no one could say he didn't support her—right up until the day he'd turn thirty and kick her and her father out of his life for good.

"I wanted to be able to talk to you instead of focusing on driving."

"So talk. I don't have all night." Actually, he did. Sad state of affairs, his life these past few years. All work and study made Tanner a very dull boy. But it sure beat the so-called excitement he'd had when Juliet had been part of his life.

He could do without that particular brand of excitement.

Juliet reached for the wine bottle in the built-in ice bucket on the car's interior, along with a wine glass hanging upside down from the rack attached to the roof. "Would you like some?"

Tanner uncorked it for her with the corkscrew that was on his side. "No." He needed his mind to be sharp when he was dealing with Juliet. Blonde bombshell she might be, but there was definitely a brain in her head. "Come on, Juliet. This could have been a phone call. And when it'd happened, not two weeks later."

She took a too-long-to-be-called-a-sip of the wine that had him wondering what this was about. Juliet had never been a big drinker.

"I know. But I need to ask you a favor, Tan."

"A favor? Me? Why would you think that I'd agree, and what the hell do you have to ask me that you can't ask any of the hundreds of people working for your dad?"

"Because you're the only one who can do it." Juliet finished the wine, which worried Tanner.

"What's going on, Jules?"

She sighed and set the wine glass down. "It's…" She sighed again. Blinked a few times. "Nana isn't… I don't know; it's like she's… like she's given up. She just sits in her hospital room and stares out the window. She talks about my grandfather and my mom as if they're still here, and it's just…"

Tanner's chest got tight. Juliet's mother had taken off when Juliet was a baby for a child-free life in Europe with a rich playboy she'd met God-only-knew-how, so Nana, her father's mother, had raised her. Her mother had been a sore spot in Juliet's life, one she rarely ever spoke about. The fact that she even mentioned the woman spoke volumes.

"And my dad… It's killing him. I see it when he thinks I'm not looking. He barely goes to work anymore and, well, Tanner, I just think if I could give them something to hope for that Nana would perk up. Have a reason to fight, you know?"

"I'm not following you." Because his mind was still reeling. He'd walked out seven years ago and never gone back; he shouldn't have expected everything to stay the same, but he realized now that he had.

"I need your help. Since we're technically still married, it makes sense. I can't pull this off with just anyone and have her believe it."

"Pull what off? Believe what?" The minute the question left his mouth he knew the answer. "You want me to pretend that we're happily married?"

"Yes."

"No one's going to buy it, Juliet. I haven't been around for the past seven years; who do you think will believe that we suddenly reconnected and want to spend the rest of our lives together?" Even as he said the words, that old feeling suffused his chest cavity. He'd wanted nothing more when he'd been a teenager than to grow old with Juliet.

And then it'd happened. She'd gotten pregnant senior year and they were putting together a wedding. He'd been terrified about having a child at their ages, but the joy of being able to call Juliet his wife, of living with her and sleeping with her and seeing her over the breakfast table the rest of his life had overridden his trepidation and the sadness at having to give up his scholarship to play ball.

Surprisingly, though, he'd actually been happy back then. But eleven years was a long time and he couldn't remember what happiness felt like because, in the intervening years, he'd tried to forget everything about her. How she'd looked in the first wedding dress he wasn't suppose to have seen but had when he'd peeked through her bedroom door as she'd modeled it for her friend, Tricia.

She'd taken his breath away, as had that precious bump in her belly he'd glimpsed when she'd peeled the gowns' sleeves off her arms and stepped out of it.

His baby.

He'd been so happy. *They'd* been so happy. Life would have been a bed of roses…

If only she hadn't lost the baby.

To this day, the thought of that moment, when they'd known they'd lost Keegan and Tanner had been terrified he was going to lose her too, had the power to bring him to his knees. He'd loved them both so fiercely and when his son had been born too early and not breathing, Tanner hadn't known what to do.

There Juliet had been, looking dead herself, all hooked up to tubes and monitors and IVs in the ugly cloth gown where there should have been a wedding dress… He'd walked around in a haze, questioning everything he'd thought he'd known about life. About how they could have seemingly had it all only to lose it in the space of a few hours.

He'd held her hand as she lay in that hospital bed, counting every breath she took while people asked him about funeral services and caskets and names and headstones. All he'd wanted was for his Juliet to wake up and tell him this was all a bad dream.

Only… it'd been a nightmare when she *had* woken up and she'd had been so inconsolable that she'd blurted out that she'd gotten pregnant on purpose, derailing his life for her own selfish reasons and trapping him into marrying her right out of high school.

And then, unbelievably, four years later, he'd fallen for her lies all over again.

He shook his head, more to get rid of the memories he never wanted to think about again than to tell her *no*. But tell her *no* he would. Forty-five more days and then he'd never have to think about the most painful thing in his life ever again.

"What makes you think your grandmother will even believe it? Your father sure as hell won't."

"They will because they want to. It's all Nana used to talk about; seeing me happily married with a family of my own. Obviously, I'm not going to ask you to go that far, but just come for a little while. Give her some hope. Let her get better. Then, when she is, we can tell her it isn't working and we can move on. But if I tell her we're getting a divorce now, that *will* kill her."

"How about if I delay the divorce instead?" The thought socked him in the gut. He'd geared himself up for the idea of ending their marriage once he paid off his father's debt; he didn't want to prolong it. But if that would help Nana out…

"That's where we are now and it's not helping her. I've tried to come up with something else, Tanner, but I can't. Would it really be so bad to do this?"

On so many levels. "I'm sorry, Juliet, but I can't lie for you. I *won't* lie for you."

"It's not a lie, Tanner—"

"Oh yes it is. We are not happily married. We're *barely* married, a fact that I intend to fix in six weeks."

Juliet was silent, her blue eyes filling with tears.

Tanner hardened his resolve. He was not going to fall for tears. She wasn't going to manipulate him that way ever again. He'd become immune to a woman's tears in the years since he'd last seen her.

The limo pulled up to a curb and the driver stopped. "Where are we?" Tanner looked out the tinted windows but couldn't see anything in this weather. He wouldn't put it past her to have them at the fanciest hotel in town—and have her father show up at just the right, er, *wrong* time.

Again.

Which was how she'd gotten him to marry her the second time, when they'd actually gone through with it. Her father had been so angry at the scandal surrounding Juliet getting pregnant in the first place, then the stillbirth two days before the wedding, the cancellation of that wedding, and Tanner leaving town the day after Keegan's funeral, that when Mr. Chambers had walked in to find him and Juliet in bed four years later—

Tanner had considered himself lucky that the guy hadn't pulled out a shotgun.

He had, however, pulled out a pre-nup and the name of the attorney he was going to use to call in the mortgage on Tanner's father's property if Tanner didn't do the right thing this time.

So Tanner had had to agree. He'd signed the papers they wanted, had put his foot down about a big wedding, and tried to make the best of a situation that wasn't exactly bad, but hadn't been optimal.

Until he overheard Juliet admit to Tricia that she'd set them all up to make it happen.

Fool him twice.

A third time was *not* happening.

He reached for the door handle. He'd rather face the rotten weather than one of Juliet's schemes. "I'm sorry about your grandmother, Juliet, but lying won't make her better."

"Tanner, please." She put her hand on his arm as he went to get out. "Please do this for her. Not me. Her. Please, Tanner. She loves you. Always has. Considered you the grandson she never had, and all this time that we've been separated, she still considers you family. She just needs something to hope for. That's all. Just for a little while, I promise. It will help her, I know it will. Please, Tanner. For my grandmother? For Nana?"

He wanted to say no so badly. Didn't want to do this.

But how could he refuse? It wasn't as if he'd have to live this lie for the rest of his life and if it would help Nana…

He opened his mouth to say yes when Juliet put a hand on his arm.

"I'll throw in your father's mortgage if that will help your decision."

He froze. "The mortgage? You'll wipe the slate clean?"

She nodded. "Whatever it takes. You do something for my family; I'll do something for yours."

He'd have his trust fund back. He could finish paying for school, which meant he could quit dancing, and he'd have money to offer Bryan and Gage to be a third partner. They'd been talking about wanting to expand BeefCake, Inc., but cash flow was tight, and with each of them having gotten married recently, they weren't too keen on racking up a chunk of debt. With his money, that could happen for all of them.

Nana, him, Gage, Bryan, even Juliet… It was a win for them all. There was only one decision he could make.

"Fine. I'll do it." After all, it wouldn't be for very long. He'd go there, play the part, Nana would get better, then he could leave with his father's mortgage paid off and his trust fund intact. What could go wrong?

Chapter Four

Everything was going wrong.

The story was out, and he was in Texas, two things he'd worked hard to not have to deal with over the past seven years. Yet, thanks to Juliet—once *again*—his life was no longer his to control.

Shit.

He'd had to tell Bryan and Gage so they could cover his shifts. They'd put two and two together and come up with a close enough approximation to the truth that Tanner hadn't denied it. And when he'd told them he'd wanted to partner with them… They were just as in favor of him going to Texas as Juliet was.

Then there was his landlord. She knew something was going on because she'd overhead (eavesdropped) him telling the mail carrier to forward his mail, so of course there was a horde of questions from her.

There would be hordes more once he showed up in his hometown.

He looked out the window as the plane taxied to the terminal, bringing him back to the scene of the crime. And, yeah, it was a crime—the pregnancy had robbed him of the chance to play ball in college.

When he'd found out the truth, the bitterness had almost killed him. If only she hadn't done that their lives would never have taken the turn they did. And who knew?

They could've been very happily married right now with a couple of kids.

And to top it all off, everyone in town knew every miniscule detail of the worst part of his life. He and Juliet had been everyone's idea of the perfect couple. Even his, so he hadn't wanted to face the stares and the gossip, not to mention Juliet, by coming home during college—from his second-choice school. Sure, he'd played ball, but not where he'd wanted, and it hadn't gotten him anywhere close to the pros.

One more sin to lay at the feet of the woman he'd been forced to marry.

The one who was waiting for him as he exited the airport. Damn. He'd wanted more time to prepare. This past week he'd been too busy with finals and working and making arrangements to be gone so long that he hadn't had that chance. Seeing her again was a double-edged sword—she was so beautiful he ached with want-ing her when he looked at her, yet seeing her held such painful memories he never wanted to look at her again.

"I would've met you at the ranch, you know." He tossed his carryon into the back seat when she pulled a Mercedes sedan up to the curb. No limo this time. Surprise, surprise; she'd gotten her way so there was no need to bring out the big guns.

He shook his head. Only in Juliet's world would a Mercedes not be considered a big gun.

She put her purse on the floor behind her seat as he sat in the passenger seat. "I remember you and airports. I'm not taking any chances."

He set his cowboy hat on the dash while he buckled in. "If you think you're going to make me feel guilty for that, I'm not."

"Guilty? Why should you feel guilty? You sent your wife on a honeymoon by herself. Least you could've done was arranged for someone else to meet me there. It wasn't exactly a ball of laughs all by myself."

"Yes, because we were going on a honeymoon to have a ball of laughs. After coercing me into marriage. You really think it would've been any better if I'd been there?" He pulled his hat onto his lap.

"It would've been nice to find out."

"Oh no, Juliet. You don't get to pull that with me. The only reason we were married was because of your little 'surprise.'"

"The only reason?" Juliet tilted her head to the side so her hair hung over the one shoulder, leaving the other bare. For him to nibble on in the old days. But these were the new-and-improved days and he wasn't going back.

He didn't answer her—the question didn't require an answer. Instead, he picked up his cell phone and opened his email. His banker, his lawyer, the guy he had looking into a few venues for him to help Gage and Bry expand the business… He had enough work to keep him busy the entire ride home so he wouldn't have to deal with her.

When they got there, however, was a whole other story.

He was ignoring her. Juliet would never get used to it. Tanner had never ignored her. Hell, he'd always been Mr. Attentive until—

She hated thinking about it. Yes, she'd made mistakes. Huge ones. But not out of malice. She'd just been so scared he'd find some other girl at college and forget all about her. She hadn't really thought through the decision to get pregnant on purpose; she'd certainly never expected he'd have to give up his scholarship. She'd just thought she'd go along with him to school and stay in a tiny apartment while he went to class and played ball. She hadn't known about a morals clause in his contract, and she certainly hadn't expected her father to be as insistent on a wedding before the baby's birth as he'd been. Heck, everyone knew that Juliet Chambers and Tanner Wentworth would be together forever. It was as inevitable as breathing. They'd get married later.

When he was finished with school and they could have a proper wedding and a proper house and a proper family.

But then she'd lost Keegan and had a few complications herself. Which was why she, in her weakened state with crazy hormonal emotions, had dropped that little bomb about getting pregnant on purpose.

Tanner had seen it as the ultimate betrayal. She'd thought it was the ultimate sign of her love for him.

Granted, looking back over a decade later, she understood that it'd been an incredibly selfish and thoughtless thing to do for all of them, the baby included. But when she'd tried to apologize, Tanner wouldn't hear her. And he definitely wouldn't forgive her, though she wasn't so sure that was for the pregnancy and not the miscarriage.

Tanner had wanted that baby.

She pulled into traffic. "We have to go over our story."

"Jesus, Juliet, do you lie to everyone or am I just the lucky one?"

She counted to ten before she answered. She'd given Tanner incentive to do this for her, but he could walk away from it in a heartbeat because of his trust fund. She was the one who needed him, not the other way around.

History was repeating itself.

"Look, Tanner, Nana isn't stupid. We have to make this work. Our stories have to be perfectly in sync or we're just going to cause her more heartache."

"Correction: *you're* going to cause her more heartache. I'm not the one who came up with this idea, and frankly, I'm not so sure I should stay with it. What might seem like a kindness to you could be so much worse if the truth comes out."

"That's why we have to make sure it doesn't. We have to know exactly what we're going to say and be believable."

"Oh trust me, Juliet, your acting chops are the best. Just be careful not to get into a crying jag and your secret should be safe. Me? Well, I'm not an actor, but for Nana, I'll do my best. I don't want to hurt her anymore than you do."

Juliet's stomach dropped. She'd really wanted him to have some semblance of feeling left for her. She'd hoped he had. That maybe, in doing this for her grandmother, it could be good for them. It could show him that he did still love her, and she'd get the chance to show him she'd changed.

And she had. Watching him get off that plane, leaving her to go to one of the most romantic places on earth by herself, had made her face the truth.

As had the pity from the concierge, housekeeper, and the wait staff. She'd spent the first two days in the hammock overlooking the ocean in a drunken mai-tai haze. The next two had been full of self-recrimination, and the final three had been a time of reflection. Of figuring out what she wanted to do with her life—a life that wasn't going to include Tanner.

Oh, she was planning to get him back, but as a woman he'd want to be with, not the insecure girl who'd tricked him not once but twice. If she was going to end up with Tanner, she had to be worthy of him.

So she'd gone to college. Nana had been supportive, but her father had been skeptical; Juliet had never been one for academia. But she'd buckled down and gotten not only her bachelor's degree, but also an MBA in the past seven years.

It couldn't have come at a better time. She'd been learning the ropes when Nana had had her stroke, and now Dad wanted to—and could—be there for his mother. So *she* was now running the family businesses. Oil, cattle, transportation… She'd immersed herself in every aspect so much that her friends were surprised to learn she was still in town because she'd become a recluse—even more than she'd been when Tanner walked out—pouring over contracts and spreadsheets and balance sheets.

She'd found Tanner's father's mortgage that her father had bought from the bank—a few days before he'd caught the two of them in bed together. She'd cringed; it'd given him the perfect bargaining chip. And sure enough, it'd worked; Tanner had married her.

And then left her.

She didn't blame him. No, this was all on her. And therefore, it was up to her to make it all right.

But right didn't mean losing Tanner from her life. They belonged together and if she'd only had faith in what he'd felt for her back then, they would be.

Well she had that faith now; faith that what he'd once felt was still there and all it'd take was for him to see that she'd changed.

"So what's our story? How are you going to explain the past seven years of silence between us?"

Juliet merged onto the highway and kicked up the Mercedes' speed. "Your name wasn't spoken all that much at home."

"Yeah, I'm sure abandoning you at the airport endeared me to your father and grandmother."

"They don't know about that."

He turned in his seat and arched an eyebrow. "You didn't tell them?"

"It wasn't exactly my greatest moment in a career of shining moments when it comes to our relationship, you know?"

"Oh I don't know, Jules. It was good for a while."

Before she screwed it up. He didn't say it. Then again, he didn't have to; it hung between them like a third passenger.

But the fact that he remembered there'd been good times was promising. It gave her hope—when hope was pretty much all she had to go on.

"So what'd you tell them when I didn't come home with you?" He fiddled with the brim of his black hat.

He looked so damn good in cowboy hats. He'd had a favorite one back in high school—worn so often it'd practically been bleached by the sun to match his hair. He'd been ready to toss it then, said it'd looked too feminine, but she'd told him it looked like gold—a crown for her prince. He'd given it to her.

She still had it.

"I told them that we needed some space. That the pain of what we'd gone through and the years you were at college were hard for us to work through. That we needed time."

"Seven years? What'd they say when I didn't show up for the holidays? When I never called?"

Juliet cringed. "Um… you actually did call. And I visited you for the holidays. In whatever country you were working in."

He turned in his seat. "You lied. Again."

"I was protecting them."

He pointed the cowboy hat at her. "You were protecting yourself."

Yeah, that too. But not her reputation; that'd been tossed into the mud when she'd gotten pregnant. No, she'd been protecting her heart because if she had everyone thinking that she and Tanner were working things out, maybe they could.

"You haven't changed a bit."

"Yes, I have."

He exhaled and strummed his fingers on the top of the hat as he looked out the window. "No, you haven't. Still manipulating people and situations to best suit yourself. Case in point." He drilled her with those gorgeous blue eyes she'd dreamed about forever. "If this weren't for your grandmother…"

"I know. I understand. And I appreciate it, Tanner. I really do. But I have changed."

He looked back out the window, a muttered, "Yeah, well I'll believe that when I see it" beneath his breath.

He would see it; she'd show him.

"So what's the plan? We kept our reunion secret from everyone why?"

She'd given this story a lot of thought and one thing when creating a lie; it was best to stick as close to the truth as possible. "We needed to work things out. To find ourselves outside of what happened between us. That's why you went away; too many people know about us here."

"And you didn't come with me because…?"

"Because I went to school."

"What?" His head swiveled around to face her. "You went to school? How are you going to pull that one off, Jules? There are, you know, tuition bills that don't just go away. Degrees that can't be faked if someone looks closely."

"I went to school. Actually got a degree. Two."

"Two. You." He arched his eyebrows. "You went to college."

"Hey, just because I made some stupid decisions doesn't mean I am stupid. I'm actually pretty good academically when I put my mind to it. I'm not an airhead." It'd given her no small amount of satisfaction to prove that. And not just to herself.

"Never said you were." He stared at her. "You really got a degree?"

She nodded, glad that this wasn't a lie. "Bachelors in Economics and an MBA in Finance."

"*You* have an MBA."

"Yes, me. And it's a good thing because now I can run the business while my father takes care of Nana. He's semi-retired."

Tanner stared at her a few more seconds before he shook his head. "I'd never have put you down for running the empire."

She smiled at the nickname they'd called her father's business. Jointly, their families had had a cattle-breeding partnership for generations, but her father had wanted more so he'd branched out. She and Tanner had joked about it every time Dad had come home with a new business venture.

They'd also enjoyed a few of the business-venture perks—namely the cabs of more than a few of the trucks when there'd been no place else to be alone together.

The memories stirred that same heat that thoughts of Tanner had always ignited. Even when he'd left her, all it took was one memory of his smile and she'd want him again. That had never gone away.

He hadn't changed a bit. Still as gorgeous, still as big, still as strong and charismatic as he'd been when she'd fallen in love with him so many years ago.

"Dad wasn't exactly excited to put me in charge, but his CFO had a family emergency so there was no one else he trusted enough." He'd been planning for Tanner to be that person, but, thanks to her, that hadn't happened. She'd *had* to step in and help out. "And this way, he can look over my shoulder in a way he wouldn't be able to with another employee while allowing that person to actually run the business."

"I thought you didn't like the business."

She shrugged. "I didn't know what I wanted to do with my life beyond being your wife. I've had to decide."

Though she still wanted to be his wife. In every sense of the word.

Juliet glanced at him out of the corner of her eye. God, she could remember as if it was yesterday what it felt like to be enveloped in his arms. To have him rest his chin atop her head and hug her to him. How he smelled, how he felt. How he tasted…

Yeah, not going there. It'd been seven years since that'd happened between them—and four years before that. Good thing she had a very good memory.

If only he didn't.

Tanner shifted in his seat and rested his hat on the bend in his knee. She wanted to brush the hair off his collar—to run her fingers through it. It was longer than when he'd lived here and she liked it.

Then again, there wasn't much she didn't like about Tanner. Even his stubbornness in believing the worst of her. Tanner had a very strong moral code and she appreciated that. Had learned the value of having one.

So once this subterfuge for her grandmother was over, she'd never tell another lie again.

But she'd also never have Tanner again.

Unless she could prove to him that she'd changed.

<h1 style="text-align:center">Chapter Five</h1>

Y ou haven't asked me why I'm working in a strip club." He hadn't said anything for the past half hour—didn't know what to say, but it hit him that she hadn't laid into him about his choice of employment.

Which was ironic given the fact that *she'd* been the one to get an MBA. Oh, he was working on one, hence stripping for tuition and living expenses since he hadn't been able to count on using his trust fund. The hours fit his schedule and the pay was good. As for the working conditions and the guys… He'd be lying if he said it wasn't fun. Gage and Bry ran a classy place so there was no stigma to working there. And if he'd wanted chicks, they would've been lined up at his dressing room door—well, maybe not there since the club had the no fraternization rule, but more than one phone number had made it into his g-string with the dollar bills.

Too bad he hadn't worn the g-string when she'd shown up—though, actually, he was glad she hadn't seen him like that. He wasn't embarrassed about what he did but there was something about someone he'd been so intimate with seeing him do publicly what he'd done in private that had made it uncomfortable.

But Juliet just shrugged at his question—unusual for her. For all that they'd be inseparable in high school, Juliet had always been jealous. He'd liked it back then. Before he'd

33

realized it'd meant she was insecure about their relationship. That she was so unsure that she'd do something foolish like get pregnant on purpose to make sure he stayed with her.

If she'd just asked him, he would have told her he loved her. Hell, he *had* told her he loved her. Hell, he told anyone who'd *listen* that he loved her. He'd heard the things people said about him all the time: that he was gorgeous, the All-American boy, a dreamboat, every girl's fantasy; he could have had any girl he'd wanted. He got it that his looks worked for the opposite sex, but the thing was, he'd only wanted Juliet. And he'd been just as much in awe of Juliet choosing him as she'd been that he'd chosen her. The difference was that he'd believed her when she'd said she'd love him forever.

He ran his finger along the brim of his hat. If only she'd had the same faith and trust in him, the last eleven years would have been so different.

"I don't have any right to have any say in what you do for a living. I realize that." She pulled into the left lane to go around the driver in front of them, gunning the engine to do so.

Tanner was surprised; Juliet had always been afraid to drive on the highway. Said the speed scared her, so she'd always insisted that he drive.

Then again, that'd been when they were in high school and then for the two weeks it'd taken her to convince him to take her back to bed after college and the three months they'd been together before the rest of it had happened.

Not that he'd needed all that much convincing. Losing the baby had bound them together and he'd wanted to forgive her for getting pregnant because, in the end, after four years away from her, losing both of them had been too hard. Juliet had been his life, his future. Keegan a bonus. So he'd wanted to make it work with her. Had actually hadn't minded that her father had caught them that night and had been so adamant about them getting married—right up until he'd overheard her tell Tricia what she'd done.

He'd felt like a commodity. A piece of meat. It'd killed every soft emotion he'd felt for her.

Or so he thought.

He glanced at her. At that perfect profile. At the way her lips curved up in a natural smile. The high cheekbones, the long lashes Nature had gifted her with that so many women pasted on. The just-right wave to her long blonde hair that he remembered trailing over his thighs when she'd gone down on him—

Shit. He didn't need to remember that. Had tried to block it out and had succeeded. Or so he thought. All it took was a half hour in her presence and he was back to imagining her naked.

"What, exactly, are you planning to say about me showing up now? And where am I supposed to stay? I'm not staying at the ranch with you."

"No, you're not. I don't live there anymore."

"I'm not staying with you, period, Juliet."

"Tanner, you have to if we want to make this look real."

He didn't want to make it look real. He wished to God he'd never agreed to this. "How's Nana been since last week?"

Juliet glanced at him and the smile she gave him sucked the wind right out of him. Time had filled out her face, making the transition from girl to woman stunning.

"When I told her you were coming, she perked up. Insisted we bring her home. We have visiting nurses, but she refused round-the-clock care. 'That's what your father is for,' she says. But she's so excited to see you. I knew this was a good idea."

"You told her? What if I hadn't gotten on the plane at the last minute?" Like he'd thought about doing.

"You wouldn't do that. I knew you'd come."

It'd be easier to get angry if she had a smug look on her face, but she didn't. Because she didn't have to—he *had* come; there'd been no other option because he'd given his word.

"I thought we'd get you settled in at my place, then go visit this afternoon. She tires easily and the best time is around three, right after her nap. Mornings are tough with the nurses and bathing and trying to get some food into her, then Dad likes to take her on a walk around the gardens out back. He brought in a landscaper to plant more of her favorite roses, and added a concrete path so he can push her wheelchair easily. Remember how she loved her garden?"

Another memory torpedoed to the surface. They'd made love in the potting shed a few times. When Nana had moved in, she'd done some redecorating on the inside and the outside of the house. The gardens were her pride and joy. She'd been adamant that the landscapers not touch her flowers, so when she'd left the house to run errands, the garden shed was the one place he and Juliet had known they wouldn't get caught. Their favorite picnic blanket had seen a lot of action inside that place, and to this day, Tanner couldn't smell the scent of roses without remembering that shed.

It'd killed him more than once over the past seven years.

"Don't they find it strange that I'm coming back now? Why wouldn't I have come back right when it'd happened? That doesn't show me in a great light."

"I told them I didn't tell you. That I wanted you to want to be with me for me, not because of Nana."

"The exact opposite of the truth, Juliet. Which, I believe, is called a lie."

Her fingers tightened on the steering wheel and a muscle ticked in her jaw. She took a few seconds to answer him. "It's a lie for a reason, Tan. Look, I'm doing this because of Nana. You told me what you're going to do on your birthday—I could have just waited another month and a half and gotten the money for the mortgage and the divorce papers and let it all go then. Do you think I like seeing you, knowing what you think of me? After all we'd meant to each other and I screwed it up, do you really think I'd put myself in this position if it weren't important? Nana has done so much for me; this is something I can do for her to ease her worry. If I could have manufactured another husband out of thin air, trust me, I would have. It would have been a lot easier on me than dragging you back into my life."

She was lying through her teeth. Again. But this lie was about self-preservation. She could no more pretend to be with another man—let alone *be* with another man—than she could forget Tanner. He was everything to her. Always had been and, she realized, always would be. What they'd had—before she'd messed things up—had been the stuff fairy tales were made of.

Unfortunately, her name wasn't Cinderella and the only mice she'd seen were definitely not working on her behalf.

She wanted the happy ending. She wanted Prince Charming.

She wanted Tanner.

The thing was, she should probably feel guilty about using Nana's health, but she didn't. It was what her grandmother wanted for her. Where Dad had hated Tanner from the moment he'd learned about her pregnancy, Nana just wanted her to be happy, and she knew that Tanner made her happy. And Tanner was good, and kind, and moral. That was why he'd left; he'd felt betrayed. Lied to. Couldn't trust her. All things she understood.

The irony being that, where her mother had betrayed her father by leaving, Juliet had done the same thing to Tanner by trying to hold onto him. She didn't like the comparison to the worthless piece of air that was her mother at all. It'd been that, as much as a necessity to do something with her life, that had gotten her to apply for college. She was *not* going to be like her mother; Juliet had to become her own woman and someone Tanner could trust.

Which is why she hadn't told him about Nana's stroke when it'd happened. She hadn't wanted him to think she was using her grandmother's health for her own purposes, but when Nana wasn't making progress, Juliet had started to think she'd have to. Then Nana had said she'd wished Tanner could come back to ease some of Juliet's burden, and it had given her a legitimate reason.

"So then why am I here if not to make your grandmother happy? Jesus." He exhaled and raked a hand through his hair. "This is lies on top of lies and I'm not going to be able to remember which is which to keep it all straight. You might regret this, Jules."

He slipped into his nickname for her so easily. She'd never let anyone shorten her name like that—except him. He usually said it softly into her ear when they were making love, or in a crowded place when he wanted her to know he was thinking about making love to her.

Too bad that wasn't on his mind now. She would definitely be up for that.

"I said that we're working things out. So just act in Nana's best interest and you'll be fine, Tan. We want her to think we're reconciled and happy so that she can get better. This really scared all of us and we don't know how much time she has left."

His fingers tightened on his knee. "Jesus, Jules. I'm sorry."

"Thanks." She gripped the steering wheel a little tighter, his apology filling her with a warmth she was going to miss when this was all over. She had to remind herself that this was only pretend. Temporary. A lie.

But if it gave her grandmother hope so she'd get better, it was worth it.

And if it got Tanner to stay, even more so.

***

"Are they here yet?" Penelope Chambers slipped her false teeth into her mouth and slid them in place with her

38

tongue. She wanted to be ready for Tanner's visit. It had to go well. "Burt? What did Juliet say?"

Her son looked up from the tray table he was fixing for her. She'd finally had a reason to get out of her darn sick bed. It'd taken Juliet long enough to take the darn hint…

"She said she was just pulling up to the airport. Give them some time, Mother."

"I might not have time." Penelope looked away from her son. Guilt wasn't a fun emotion, but someone had to do something for this family and, God help her—and He was, she was surely convinced of it with this little ol' TIA—it was going to be her.

That'd been her argument with Dr. Jackson, and while he hadn't agreed to lie, he'd promised to keep his doctor-patient confidentiality oath front and center in his mind when dealing with her family. It was the only way she'd been able to milk her pitiful recuperation drama this long.

As *if* a little blip could keep her down. Ha. She still had a lot of living left to do. And she was just the *teensiest* bit peeved that her own family didn't know that about her. Still, it'd given her the perfect opportunity to play the invalid so Juliet would finally get off her duff and go after her own husband. Those two would never work things out if they weren't in the same place.

"Give them an hour or so. Depending on traffic, the drive could take a while, and then they're going to drop his things off at Juliet's house and then they'll be here."

"I don't see why they couldn't stay here."

"Look, Mother. I know you're excited that Juliet and Tanner have worked things out, but I'll reserve judgment. That boy has let my daughter down more than once and I don't trust him not to do it again. We can use the distance."

"You're too hard on him." Though Penelope certainly understood why. But Tanner wasn't Elaine, thank-God-for-small-favors. Her ex-daughter-in-law was in a league all her own.

"Apparently I wasn't hard enough. Otherwise he would have been here for the past seven years instead of wasting both their lives."

Penelope settled her skirt over her knees again. She was of the mind that the past seven years were a waste only in that Juliet and Tanner hadn't had more children, God-rest-little-Keegan's-soul. But thirty wasn't too old these days, and the growing up Juliet had done in the interim was worth every bit of the loneliness. Or at least a good portion of it. Penelope didn't wish her granddaughter ill, but Juliet had needed to learn to do something other than traipse after Tanner as if he were a god. Women needed to stand on their own two feet, not ride someone else's coattails. Or snuggle up inside of them like that whore of a mother Juliet had had.

Penelope didn't mince words. Well, when she thought them, that was. When voicing them… that was a whole other matter because there was no sense hurting Burt's feelings more than Elaine already had. Penelope had known from the first time she'd met the little gold-digger that it'd only take someone with more money to come along and she'd be off. Thank God—again—the tramp had left Juliet behind. It'd given Penelope the daughter she'd never had.

And she was proud of the woman Juliet had become. And of her son for allowing it—something else her TIA had hurried along since he'd been so hung up on Elaine abandoning them that he'd protected Juliet from any harsh reality of life he could. He hadn't done either of them any favors, so Penelope had had to when this opportunity presented itself. That Tanner was being dragged into this was a bonus—one he'd see when he learned to appreciate the Juliet he would come to know instead of the child he'd left behind.

Penelope ought to know; she'd put her William though his paces before she'd finally settled down with him. And look at the ride they'd had. It might not have been as long as she would have liked, but in every other aspect, her marriage had been perfect. Sometimes delayed gratification made the final outcome worth it.

Now if only she could get out of this damn wheelchair. Already, the past week had made her antsy, but she'd suffer through it to give Juliet and Tanner the time to figure out they were meant to be together.

Well, whatever it took, she'd do. Because *this* time around, there wasn't going to be any courthouse quickie— she wanted to dance at their wedding.

Chapter Six

"Ihis is your place?" Tanner looked at the tiny stone Cape Cod whose driveway Juliet had pulled up in. Juliet was the grandiose ballroom-type girl, not something that would fit in her childhood bathroom. "It's not much bigger than your grandmother's garden shed."

Shouldn't have said that.

The atmosphere in the car changed instantly. They were both remembering that garden shed—and they both knew the other one was thinking the same thing.

Tanner jerked the handle. "It's locked."

"Huh? Oh." Juliet scrambled for the release latch. "Here you go."

He grabbed his hat and his bag and got out of the car into the thick heat. There was a storm coming; he could smell it. Felt it in the air—hot and sultry, things he didn't need to notice with visions of the garden shed and Juliet on top of him dancing around in his head.

And now he was going to go into the tiny house in front of him with the woman next to him and have to pretend that he felt nothing for her—all the while pretending *to* feel something for her so her grandmother wouldn't suspect they were lying.

Shit. This gave him a headache.

Juliet unlocked the front door and stepped inside.

Tanner took a deep breath of hot air and followed her.

The temperature dropped a good twenty degrees inside which gave him goose bumps—ones that had nothing to do with the fact that Juliet's arm brushed his as she shut the door behind him.

"You can have the guest bedroom. Obviously." She darted a glance at him then tucked her hair behind her ears.

The memory of her doing that when she was embarrassed washed over him as if he'd seen her do it yesterday. Damn, he'd forgotten just how well he did know her. And just how much he remembered. Like that birthmark on the inside of her right thigh that looked like a lip print. Her grandmother had said an angel had kissed her when she was born; he and Juliet said it was an X-marks-the-spot Nature had left for him to find.

Shit. Now why'd he have to go and remember that?

He allowed his bag to hang in front of him, hoping it'd shift his dick enough to let go of the memory and quiet down.

No such luck.

"It's, uh, over there." She pointed toward the room on the left side of the living room/dining room combo they were standing in. At the back, a half-wall separated this area from the tiny kitchen that was just big enough for the standard appliances and about two feet of counter space.

"Guess you don't do much entertaining here." The words popped out before he could stop them. He meant entertaining as in parties, but if she took it to mean something else, yeah, he'd like to know that, too. Juliet *was* still his wife and he'd honored their wedding vows the entire time they were apart.

He wasn't quite sure why he had since he hadn't planned to stay married to her and had made her no promises when he'd left, but he *had* made those promises before God and the Justice, and he was nothing if not a man of his word.

But that meant he'd been frustrated for a really long time, and here he was in his wife's home, wondering if she'd *entertained* anyone else here.

"I really don't have time to throw parties. I studied all the time I wasn't in class so I could graduate as quickly as possible with both degrees. Then I had to learn the business, and now, with what's going on with Nana and the demands at the office, I really don't have time."

Didn't answer his question about dating, but what was the answer going to do for him? If she *had* dated someone, the guy wasn't here so he obviously didn't mean enough to her to be that guy. And the fact that Tanner was here…

Hang on. He didn't *want* to mean that much to her anymore. They'd outgrown each other. Their relationship. Their marriage. They were both going to have to move on, and once the divorce was final, Tanner *could* move on and be free to pursue whatever—and whoever—he wanted without worrying about breaking his vow.

Isn't divorce breaking it though?

It would be if he'd entered into the marriage of his own free will, but he'd been put up to it at a metaphorical gunpoint. When it was over and done, he'd be over and done with Juliet.

The thought burned its way through his chest. "Where's my bathroom?"

She pointed to a door on the right. "*Our* bathroom is through there."

"You only have one?"

"Up 'til now, I only had one person here. I guess I could rent a port-a-potty for your stay if you like, but you'll have to use the hose out back for a shower—and I don't have hot water out there."

It wouldn't matter; he'd be taking cold showers the entire time he was here anyway.

Share a bathroom with her? God help him. He remembered every one of her lotions and soaps and shampoos. They all smelled like bluebonnets—a scent that had significant memories attached to it for both of them and a certain field…

Staying here was becoming a worse idea by the minute.

"I put new sheets on the bed and a set of towels on your dresser." She slapped her hands to her side. "So if you want to go freshen up or relax or take a nap or anything before three, you can."

"What are you going to be doing?"

"Me?" She practically squeaked the question.

Hmmm, despite her outward calm, he'd bet Juliet wasn't as comfortable sharing her home with him anymore than he was sharing it with her.

"I have some contracts to go over."

"You're going into the office?"

"Oh no. The house might not look like much, but it's wired for high-speed Internet. I do a lot of work from home."

Great. He wasn't going to get much of a break from her if she didn't leave the house.

Then *he* would.

"I should have rented a car at the airport and driven here. Where's the closest place to get one?"

"You can borrow mine. I trust you to take care of it."

Was there a hidden meaning to that statement? Tanner wasn't sure. But then, the Juliet he'd grown up with hadn't known the meaning of the word *subtle* when it'd come to the two of them. She'd been all-in from the first time they'd looked at each other that way. He'd never had to guess what she was thinking or feeling. He especially never doubted how she'd felt about him so he couldn't figure out why she had doubted him.

He shook his head. It didn't matter now. That Juliet no longer existed. This Juliet, the one who'd grown up, gone to college—gotten an MBA before him—he didn't know her. For all that he'd said she hadn't changed, she had in some things. Juliet the Prom Queen wasn't going to buckle down and run Daddy's company; she was going to marry someone who would, and she'd spend the money by going to lunch and shopping with her girlfriends.

And he'd been ready to sign on for that.

Tanner shook his head. God, how naïve he'd been back then. He'd had his head in the clouds.

Now it was firmly back on earth. "But what if you need it?"

"Tanner, where do you need to go? Are you planning to look up all our friends and hang out for hours on end like we used to?"

That thought hadn't even crossed his mind. He hated that people knew what had happened between him and Juliet. He hated that they knew he'd been poised to go big in football and then hadn't. That he'd had a son… and then hadn't. "I don't like being stuck. If I want to run out, I want to run out."

"Okay, okay. We'll stop in town on our way home from the ranch later. For now, if you want to go anywhere, use my car." She tossed him the keys. "I've got reports to go over."

And just like that, she left him standing there as she headed into what he assumed was either her home office or her bedroom or both. Whatever it was, it was around the corner and she was gone from his sight.

He felt the lack immediately.

And he hated that he did. He'd worked hard at getting Juliet out of his head. Actually went a day or two now without thinking about her. Well, not lately because he had the daily countdown going on that guaranteed he'd think about her, but for the past few years, yeah. He'd managed to not think about her a lot.

But when he *did* think about her…

Tanner plunked his hat on his head then hiked his bag, *purposely* hitting himself in the nuts. That'd teach his dick to get all happy thinking about Juliet. Fantasizing about her was one thing; being in proximity to her and hoping something would happen was insane. She'd messed up his life enough already. In thirty-eight days, he was getting it back.

Chapter Seven

She wasn't giving him back.

Juliet leaned against the doorframe to her office and counted to ten. Slowly. She needed to get her heart rate under control so the blood would stop rushing to her head—and other parts. Her body needed to calm the hell down.

She couldn't believe he was in her house. What it felt like to have him *in* her house. She'd always enjoyed the coziness of this place—had wanted something small and intimate after the sprawling ranch she'd grown up in. The one where she'd planned to live with Tanner. This place was as different from the ranch as could be. But then she'd brought him here.

At over six feet tall, Tanner filled her living room. Though, honestly, Tanner could be four feet tall and his charisma would still fill it. He had always owned whatever room he'd walked into. She'd forgotten that. Or rather, she hadn't forgotten, she just hadn't remembered it until he'd been standing here.

He belonged here. With her. In this space. And *not* in the bedroom across the hall, but here, in the room off her office with her king-sized bed—the one her grandmother had bought them for their wedding that she hadn't been able to part with. Stupid, really, because Tanner had never slept in it.

Maybe that was why she could.

Juliet took another shuddering breath. Good lord, this was going to be difficult. She had to pretend to him that his presence didn't drive her wild, but she had to prove otherwise to her grandmother. And both of them knew her so well, she hoped she could pull this off, both for Nana's sake *and* her own.

Well, and Tanner's as well. She'd made him happy once; she could again. But it was going to take a lot more than come-hither looks under her lashes or sexy sashays or cute clothing that teased at what it hid—

Though why not take advantage of what she already knew caught his attention?

Tanner might think he hated her—might *actually* hate her, she was forced to admit—but everyone knew physical attraction didn't always listen to the dictates of the heart and mind. Physical attraction had a mind all its own and if that was what would get him to see her again, notice her, she'd be a fool not to use it.

She'd stopped being a fool seven years ago.

She pushed off the wall. She hadn't thought much beyond their cover story and getting him here, but now, the reality of having him in her home, day in and day out, was starting to sink in. If she wanted Tanner back—and there was no question that she did—she had one last chance. She couldn't blow it.

Tanner blew out a breath as he tossed his hat onto the dresser then dropped his bag onto the bed and sat on the edge of the mattress.

The place *screamed* Juliet.

Nothing so overt as putting her picture all over the place—Juliet wouldn't do that; she wasn't stuck on herself. No, the room had that Juliet feel, because she'd decorated it as if she'd known he was going to come here.

His favorite shade of blue had been the slate blue of her

eyes. Yes, he'd actually said those corny words to her, but they'd been true. The comforter was that exact shade. The hardwood floors were the color of the floors in his bedroom growing up—where they'd snuck her into more times than they should have risked. The chair in the corner looked like the one in his parents' den, and the pictures on the walls were of the Guadalupe Mountains he'd fallen in love with on a camping trip freshman year. The room was masculine without being overtly so, yet still felt as if it belonged in a woman's home. Juliet's home.

He should have stayed in a hotel. Should have insisted that they both stay there if she wanted everyone to think they were together. He would have rented a suite with a connecting door—one that would have stayed locked. He didn't need this temptation. Then again, Juliet, to him, was walking temptation.

He fell back onto the bed and looked at the ceiling. She'd covered it in textured wallpaper and painted it light pewter—like his mother had in the guest bathroom.

Either Juliet had planned to bring him here for a long time, or she really liked this décor.

He wanted to think it was the latter because the former would mean she was up to her old tricks of lying to him.

He rubbed his eyes with a thumb and forefinger, wincing. He still couldn't believe how she'd lied to him. How she'd struggled to hold on to him when all she'd had to do to keep him was love him and be honest with him.

He sat up. Not going there. It was done. Over. He'd hoped to end the marriage without having to see her again, but he had a soft spot for her grandmother, so here he was. He'd deal with it.

Smacking his thighs, Tanner stood. He wasn't about to take a nap with Juliet across the hall. He had no idea how he was supposed to sleep here tonight. That ought to be fun.

Not.

He moved his bag onto the dresser—he wasn't going to

put his clothes in the drawers, still holding out some weird hope for a miracle that would keep him from having to stay here.

Get a grip, Wentworth. You're stuck for the duration.

Damn it—his heart actually leapt or fluttered or whatever the hell that feeling was when he thought about being stuck with Juliet. Time was, he'd wanted nothing more.

Damn it. History couldn't repeat itself; Juliet was bad news and he needed to just let her go.

Let her go.

The words sounded harsh. Painful.

Empty.

He shook his head. Needed to clear it. He'd go splash some cold water on his face. His wrists. Back of his neck. *His dick.* That'd wake him up. Get him out of this stupor. Had to be all the traveling. He'd gotten up God-awful early this morning to get here at a reasonable hour.

He dragged his hand along the half-wall by the kitchen and walked around to the sink. Closer than the bathroom, and therefore, not as close to Juliet.

"Hey, Tanner." Juliet came around the corner from her room just as he splashed water on his face. Which meant he missed and ended up wearing most of it on his head and dripping down his back. Ah, well, nothing like cold water to dissipate the heat she dragged into the room with her.

Well, in theory it did.

Juliet's legs in those shorts, however, brought the heat roaring back.

She was all leg. Golden skin, shapely calves and thighs… She hadn't lost that cheerleader look.

"You *could* use the shower, you know." She smiled at him, the dimple off the corner of her right lip making an appearance.

How many times had he kissed that dimple? Traced it with his tongue—

"I, uh, didn't want to disturb you. By having the water running, I mean."

"Oh, that's okay. It wouldn't have bothered me."

They were making banal conversation over water. Someone needed to say something to move it along or they'd start counting the rises in her popcorn ceiling.

"Did you want to tell me something?"

"Oh. Um. Yes." She crossed her arms and cocked her hip to one side, a move Tanner well remembered.

She'd thought it was a serious look for when she had something important to tell him, but, really, it was sexy as hell the way her hip curved to the side and her crossed arms accentuated her small waist—and the breasts above them.

He'd wisely never told her what that move did to him. "And… what is it?"

"Oh. Right." She gave him a fake smile. It was her cover-up smile, when she needed to think an answer through.

"Come on, Juliet. What is it? No need to hem and haw. This is me, remember? I know all your tricks."

"This isn't a trick, Tan. I was just coming to look for you because my dad called. Nana wants to know when we're coming over. We should get going."

"Oh. Okay. No biggie. Let me just, uh, change my shirt." He reached over his head and tugged the collar at the back of his neck. "Wet."

She licked her lips. Dammit. Why did everything have to be filled with sexual innuendo? There were times when they'd been together that they'd actually had fun without every syllable being sexually charged.

Of course, there'd been just as many, if not more, laden with it. Or, most times, downright lust. Juliet had never been shy about making love with him.

God damn it. He was never going to get through this if he brought everything back to sex.

"Tanner?"

He blinked, clearing his focus.

Same Juliet. Looking way too gorgeous in her shorts and scoop-necked t-shirt. The woman made a burlap sack look good. "Yeah?"

"Your shirt?" She twiddled her fingers at him. "You were going to change it? We don't have a lot of time before Nana starts fading. I'd like to get there while she can talk to you."

"Oh. Right." He cleared his throat and walked around the kitchen counter to head into his room.

He shut the door behind him, making sure it stayed closed. He didn't need to undress without the buffer of a door between them. Granted, it was a hollow-core thin veneer of a door, but the visual was enough of a barrier.

He hoped.

Too bad there wasn't a barrier between them in the car. If it wouldn't have entailed too many explanations— excuses—he would have sat in the back. He didn't want Juliet to know she still got to him. That'd be all he'd need; Juliet thinking they could pick up where they'd left off.

Stuck on yourself, are we, Wentworth? Maybe she *doesn't want* you *anymore.*

Well there was a sobering thought.

He glanced over at her. Funny to see her in the driver's seat; he'd always driven. Of course, more often than not, it'd be because she'd had her hands on his thigh and wanting to move elsewhere. Tanner had learned to drive real fast all those years ago.

But now her hands were firmly on the steering wheel— where they ought to be—and she was navigating the Benz like a racecar driver. "When you'd start driving like this?"

"Like what?" She swung her head to look at him then back to the road, her hair swishing around her shoulders.

Juliet's hair was incredibly silky. The gold strands used to catch beneath her as he'd pounded into her—

Dammit. He really needed to get his mind off sex with her.

"Like you're late for a doct——er, driving like a bat out of hell." He'd caught the word before it was all the way out but the damage was done. As if they needed an all-too-harsh reminder of the day they *had* driven like a bat out of hell to get to the doctor's when she was losing the baby.

Juliet cleared her throat and roared the engine as she jumped into the next lane over. "I have a lot to do these days and not enough time to do it. I should probably move closer to the office, but I don't want to give up my home."

"It's a nice house. Not what I would have thought you'd go for, though."

"Yes, well, like I said, I've changed a lot since we were last together. Surprised even myself at times."

Just like she was starting to surprise him.

Chapter Eight

Hi, Nana. Look who I brought." Juliet stuck her pageant smile on her face and swept into the living room. She'd be dammed if the mention of the awful doctor's appointment would ruin her day or even have an inkling of thought in her grandmother's day.

Damn Tanner, though. Less than an hour and he'd had to remind her about one of the saddest days of her life and the fact that she'd created the situation to begin with by poking a hole in the condoms.

God, what she wouldn't give to have a do-over of that moment. Seventeen and stupid, that's what she'd been. A mistake she'd been paying for for the last eleven years.

"Tanner!" Nana pushed on the wheels of her wheelchair and propelled herself toward Tanner.

"Nana, be careful. We don't want you to overexert yourself." Nana had been so weak and Juliet had worried that Tanner's appearance might be too much of a shock. It's why she'd told her he was coming beforehand, but she hadn't expected Nana would try to move her wheelchair. She hadn't had any strength since the stroke. Luckily, her mind and her coordination hadn't been affected, but still… Nana wasn't exactly a spring chicken. She had to be careful.

Which was why, whatever pain Tanner's visit would cause Juliet—or rather, whatever pain his leaving would cause her—it was worth it to see that spark in Nana.

That'd been the hardest part of this—Nana had grit, something Juliet had always admired about her. So, to see her in her hospital bed and now, here at home, not recovering like they'd hoped… She couldn't lose Nana, too. Not yet.

That was why she'd gone to see Tanner. It'd taken Nana's health to get her to finally get the courage to face him.

She hadn't been able to do so before because he'd end things between them. Any contact would be the impetus he'd need, so she'd waited until just before his birthday. She knew about his trust fund and she knew the mortgage on his parents' place was what had gotten him into the marriage. It wasn't hard to put two and two together.

And while Nana's health was her excuse, the reality was, she'd wanted to see him and had been looking for an excuse. One last time. That's all she'd wanted.

Well, not quite all. *You'd like to stay married to the guy—and make it a real marriage. Not this name-only crap.*

They'd been too good together for that.

"Hi, Mrs. Chambers." Tanner strode into the room, all Texas big and hunky. He was the quintessential All-American guy, filling the stereotype as well as he filled out his jeans.

She should *not* be looking at his jeans. Especially after that thought.

Hell, she shouldn't be *having* that thought.

"*Mrs. Chambers?*"

Nana pushed herself to standing and Juliet almost fell to the floor in shock. Must be an adrenaline surge because of her outrage or something. Nana needed help just to sit up whenever Juliet was around.

"Why, Tanner Wentworth. You stopped calling me Mrs. Chambers in fifth grade and I'm not going to let you revert back to it. Mrs. Chambers is my mother-in-law, God rest her soul, and you know it."

Tanner's smile was every bit as devastating as Juliet remembered. "I'm sorry, Nana."

"That's better. Now give me a hug like you mean it."

Words Juliet wanted to say to him herself.

"I'm so glad to hear about you and Juliet." Nana patted Tanners' biceps when he released her from the gentle hug.

Tanner had always known his own strength. When Juliet had needed him to be tough and strong, he had been. When she'd needed him to be gentle he'd done that, too. And she wasn't talking about sex. Well, not totally.

Oh, hell. This was going to be a lot tougher than she thought to pull off. And she didn't mean pretending to her grandmother—no, there was no pretense there. She wanted Tanner back. Pretending to Tanner that she didn't, *that* was going to be the true test.

"You're looking well. I see living up north is agreeing with you." Her grandmother cupped his cheeks and Juliet had to look away. Nana loved him so much—had since the first time Juliet had told her she wanted to marry him back when they were nine. Then again at twelve. And thirteen. And pretty much every year since.

"The winters took some getting used to, but I don't miss the heat."

"But you've missed Juliet, so you'll just have to get used to the heat again." Nana reached behind her for the chair.

Tanner helped her into it.

Juliet tried not to sigh at the tenderness he had for her grandmother. He was such a good man and she should never have doubted him.

"Would you like some of that cheesecake you love? Ermalinda made it when she heard you were coming."

"That'd be great. Thanks." Tanner had always loved Ermalinda's cheesecake. To this day, their housekeeper wouldn't tell them the recipe, but she'd make it for special occasions, and she considered Tanner's return one indeed. She'd loved him as much as the rest of them had.

Another person's whose hopes would be dashed when he eventually left.

"Tanner." Dad walked into the room and held out his hand. "Thank you for coming."

Kudos to Dad for saying that. He hadn't been thrilled with Tanner walking out either time and was only suffering through being polite for his mother's sake. And Juliet's. But if he knew Tanner was going to be leaving again, he probably wouldn't be quite as civil.

Juliet would deal with that when the time came. Right now, she needed everyone's reactions to be as real and as normal as possible in the scenario she'd created.

Now if she could just get her own under control.

"Juliet, honey, would you ask Ermalinda to bring the cheesecake?"

"No need, *Señora*. I heard the car arrive." Ermalinda walked in with the pizza-sized dish that she baked the cheesecake in. No one knew how she cooked it so evenly in that big pan, but the results were always the same: amazing. "Miss Juliet, if you could get the dishes and lemonade, *por favor*?"

Nana had always been *Señora*, while Juliet had always been *Miss Juliet* since Ermalinda had started working for them after… well, after Nana had come to live with them. And even after Juliet got married, she'd still been *Miss* to Ermalinda.

Sadly, that's what she'd felt like to herself, no matter the fact that her driver's license still had *Wentworth* on it.

"Sure." She shook off the sad mood, headed into the kitchen, keeping an ear on the conversation. Tanner was here now and that was what mattered.

Well, that and getting him to stay.

"Seven years is a long time," Nana, never one to mince words, said to him. "Have you seen your parents yet?"

"Not yet."

Tanner's voice was strained. He'd been at odds with his parents ever since he'd found out about his father's gambling. Thank God Tanner's grandfather had set up the trust that no one could touch because Mr. Wentworth had owed everyone, putting her father's and his joint business venture at risk. Dad had had to bail him out, taking the mortgage on the Wentworth ranch as collateral.

But he'd done it to help his friend, not keep him under his thumb. Granted, it'd helped put an end to Mr. Wentworth's access to the business accounts, but when Tanner had found out—and when Dad had used it as leverage to get him to marry her—things had become strained not only between her father and Tanner, but also Tanner and his dad. He'd said more than once that he was paying for the sins of his father through his feelings for her.

And she'd made it possible.

"I'm glad you and Juliet have worked out your differences. Losing a child is never easy and I know the situation hasn't been optimal"—there went Nana with her knack for understatement—"but there is so much love between you two and always has been that I knew you'd work it out. I'm just glad I was able to live to see it happen."

Juliet gripped the tray of lemonade, dishes, and glasses harder as she headed back into the living room. That was why she'd had to do this; she'd been so scared Nana would die. She couldn't take another loss.

Tanner cleared his throat. "I'm very sorry to hear about your stroke. Juliet didn't tell me until last week."

"I know. I wouldn't let her. You two needed to figure out your relationship for yourselves, not because of me. You're *not* doing it because of me, are you, Tanner?"

"Mrs. Chambers—I mean, Nana." He took Nana's hand in both of his. "I'm doing this because of Juliet. Make no mistake about that. This is all about Juliet and me."

Damn, the man was good, saying so much her grandmother wanted to hear but meaning something completely different to her.

Dad, however, was looking at Tanner with narrowed eyes. Granted, he'd been looking at him that way ever since they'd gone from childhood friends to ones with benefits, but her father was shrewd. He might be upset over his mother's stroke, but when it came to other matters, he was still as sharp as a tack.

Great, now she was going to have to ramp up her disinformation game to convince him, too, that she and Tanner were madly in love again.

So she set the tray down, then walked over to Tanner to put her hand on his shoulder. She'd been looking for an excuse to touch him again. She'd always wanted to touch Tanner. Hold his hand, rub his back, lean against him... Before, she'd never needed a reason and had always been touching him. It'd been as natural as the love she'd felt for him—and had turned her on every time.

This time was no different.

Tanner tried not to flinch when Juliet's hand landed on his shoulder. It was hard enough to pretend to be the happy husband back for round three when he wanted to walk out of the room and never see any of them again.

Nana wasn't making this easy, and anger was radiating off Juliet's father in waves. Not that Tanner could blame him, but the guy needed to revisit the situation and see that it was his daughter who'd created it not only with the first set-up but the second as well.

Yes, Tanner probably shouldn't have given in and taken her to bed after college, but he'd been trying to put his heart back together and Juliet had known just how to draw him in. She always had, from that first kiss in the barn when he'd tried so hard to stay away from her, but she'd been having none of it. Then there were times when she'd pulled him into the truck cabs and the back room at the warehouse with her when there'd been no other place else to go.

His body heated at the image of her straddling him in that office chair, the thought of getting discovered as thrilling as the act they were doing.

God, he'd loved her once.

Her fingers squeezed his shoulder as if she was reading his mind.

She squeezed again. Two more times.

Oh, right. Their signal.

Shit. He didn't want to remember that. Didn't want to do this, but her grandmother would notice—her father would, too—if he didn't, and he'd come here to play a part for a sick woman, so play it he'd better.

He reached up and grasped Juliet's fingers in his, tapping them against his shoulder three times like they'd done for years. Everyone knew it was their signal, their "I love you" taps. They'd started it in high school and it'd been one more part of their cute-couple arsenal that had put them on the homecoming court and awarded them the prom crowns as well as Cutest Couple in the yearbook.

He'd thrown his yearbook away when he'd moved out.

Thankfully, Ermalinda passed out the cheesecake then so he could release Juliet's fingers. He took the plate, not having to fake his gratitude. For many reasons. Ermalinda's cake really was amazing. She'd told him she'd bequeathed the receipt to him in her will. He'd told *her* that he never wanted to have the recipe so she would just have to stay around so she could make it for him forever.

He'd missed her. He'd missed all of them, actually. But if he had come back, he would've seen Juliet. It'd been hard enough to stay away from her halfway across the country; forget it halfway across town.

And what about halfway across her house?

Yeah, that wasn't going to be easy.

"So what have you been up to, Tanner?" Juliet's father asked.

Juliet choked on the lemonade.

He ought to tell the guy the truth. Let them all know he was stripping for a living. He wasn't embarrassed about it, but they would be and it wasn't fair to take his anger at Juliet out on Nana. Though, actually, Nana had always called it like it was; she might get a good laugh at what he did.

Mr. Chambers, however, would be horrified.

That was almost enough incentive to tell them.

But Juliet was the one he'd wanted to have know what he did for a living. He'd like to know what she really thought about it. She'd been all cool in the car, saying she didn't have the right to have a say, but he knew her. Hell, it was half the reason he'd started doing it initially. She'd pulled her stunt because she'd been upset that other women wanted him? He hadn't given her reason back then, but now was a whole other matter.

Probably childish, but the job paid really well and let him live his life. And he had the added perk of knowing it'd bug her—though fat lot of good it'd done him when she hadn't even known until she'd shown up in the club.

She'd watched him; he'd felt her eyes on him. He'd always known when Juliet was looking at him. Had it turned her on?

On second thought, maybe he didn't want to know what Juliet thought.

"I'm in land acquisition." Well, now that he was going into business with Gage and Bryan he was.

"That's new." Mr. Chambers glanced at Juliet before looking at him.

Tanner kept his features composed. He and Juliet should have gone over that aspect of their story, but it was too late now.

He was supposed to have gone into business with her father. The joining of two ranching properties. Mr. Chambers was pro-active when it came to growing the business, and he'd wanted the person who'd take over upon his retirement to have a vested interest in seeing the ranch and other industries do well.

Truth be told, Tanner had looked forward to working with Mr. Chambers. To growing the business for his own children and grandchildren. Children that had been on hold since Juliet's "little ploy."

Tanner's breath caught in his throat and he had to cough it out. He could never get through thinking of his son without that skipped heartbeat. As if one of his had been taken from him.

"What projects do you have going?"

He focused on the question and shoved the awful memories to the back of his mind. It was the best way to deal with them. "A couple commercial properties. They're in the prelim stages at the moment." Very prelim.

"I'd be interested in hearing about them." Mr. Chambers actually lost the gruffness to his voice that'd been there ever since he'd first confronted him about Juliet's pregnancy all those years ago.

"I'm sure we can work something out." Tanner nodded at him, the implication being that he'd be around to talk about the projects.

"You were always such a go-getter, Tanner." Nana patted his knee, sending guilt shooting up through his heart. "You've done this family proud."

In another life, those words would have meant something to him. But now… They were based on so many of Juliet's lies Tanner didn't feel as if he had a rightful part in any of this.

So he just smiled and bit into Ermalinda's cake, saluting her with his second forkful. *"Maravillosa como siempre, Ermalinda."*

She beamed at him and dropped a kiss on the top of his head as she took Nana's plate which had a decent portion of the pie gone. From what Juliet had said, he'd thought Nana was withering in bed, so to see her in the living room with a decent appetite was a good thing.

It also made him wonder if Juliet had overplayed the seriousness of Nana's illness.

He winced. A stroke at any age was nothing to make

light of. He should be thankful Nana was able to be out here—and he was. But he hated that he had to wonder at all.

"Juliet's not doing so badly in that department either," Mr. Chambers said, taking the seat beside her and patting her hand. "She's done a great job running the business while, well, while I've been taking care of my mother."

"I'm just sad it's taken this to get you to slow down, Burt." Nana's voice was sharp. "I've told you for years that Juliet was more than capable of taking care of things."

"Yes, Mother, you did."

Mr. Chambers' voice was soft in a way Tanner had never heard. But maybe that was because he'd been the recipient of a sharp, questioning tone from the man.

"So, Tanner." And there it was: that tone. "You are planning to stay this time, aren't you? That's why you came back, right?"

"I came because it's time Juliet and I did something about our marriage." And if that gave Mr. Chambers hope it was because the man wanted to find hope in that statement. But Tanner was going to do his damnedest not to lie to them. Didn't mean he had to come clean with the whole truth, but he wasn't going to lie outright if he could help it.

"Marriage isn't easy, son. You have to be committed to making it work." Mr. Chambers crossed his arms and sat back. From what Juliet had told Tanner over the years, her father had been devastated by his wife leaving. It'd hardened him, so when he'd insisted that Tanner marry Juliet—both times—it hadn't been an arbitrary thing. He'd expected Tanner to marry her and stick around.

Tanner had been all for it—until he'd found out what Juliet had done.

"Daddy." Juliet settled on the arm of Tanner's chair. "You don't need to say things like that."

Because she didn't want to risk Tanner's reply.

She'd caught the double entendres in his responses to her father; she didn't know how many of Dad's comments

Tanner could take before he'd reveal the truth, and that was something she couldn't have. Nana had such a smile on her face and was more alert than Juliet had seen her in the last three weeks. And even before the stroke.

"Perhaps I do, Juliet. I've kept quiet for too long. Maybe if I'd said something sooner, we wouldn't have had to wait until *now* for you two to put everything back the way it should be."

Tanner tensed beside her. Yes, his patience was nearing its end. And she couldn't blame him, not really. He was doing this because he loved her grandmother, *not* because he loved her. Of that she had no illusions.

Once upon a time, yes… He'd loved her enough to have done anything for her. Well, except get engaged. Said they were too young. He'd had college and hopefully a pro career, and he wanted to wait until he could do it the right way.

As far as she'd been concerned, the right way had been to put a ring on her finger—she wouldn't have cared if it'd come from a caramel-corn box—but he hadn't seen it that way. What she'd seen was that he hadn't wanted to claim her. She'd also seen the way the other girls looked at him. She'd watched them touch him as they'd walked past him. Tanner was a god among the Texas gods and every girl had wanted him, especially her.

She'd chosen the wrong way to go about keeping him and she'd been regretting it for years.

Yet here you are, doing something similar again.

No, this wasn't a similar situation. She hadn't lied about Nana's condition. This truly, first and foremost, was about bringing Tanner back to comfort her grandmother. And if she'd had to lie to Nana, well, she'd done it with the best of intentions. Nana would understand when the truth eventually came out, but Juliet was counting on Nana being back to her feisty self before that happened.

Dad, on the other hand…

She'd deal with her father later. But *she* would deal

with him, not Tanner. Tanner's responsibility to her ended the day he'd asked her to marry him the first time. He'd loved her and had been doing the right thing by her. But then he'd overheard her with Dad, and things had gone down the proverbial toilet—and that was all on her.

"Dad, Tanner and I are adults now. You don't have to fight my battles anymore."

"Love shouldn't be a battle." Nana and her words of wisdom. She reached out a hand to each one of them, one less shaky than it'd been in days. Having Tanner here *was* a good thing. "Take care of each other, you two. Be kind. Look at the bigger picture. The one before Keegan came along. Where you were going, what you were doing, who you were becoming before circumstances forced you to make hard decisions no one should have to make, let alone kids your ages."

Juliet slid an arm around Tanner's shoulders. It was the most natural movement in the world to her.

Obviously not to him, however. He tensed, but then he moved a hand to her knee, squeezing gently, and it was almost as if... as if he'd wanted to.

"Don't worry, Nana. Juliet and I will make things as they should be."

The words would have made Juliet smile if she hadn't heard the "You owe me," he whispered as he stood up to help her grandmother back to her room.

Chapter Nine

So how'd you get into, strip—er, dancing?" Juliet tried to keep the first words spoken between them in the twenty-two minutes since they'd left her family's ranch light because the silence was getting to her. And because she wanted the answer. When she'd learned he was a stripper, she'd wanted to hurt something. He was still her husband and all of that gorgeousness was hers—even if only for a little longer.

It was so ironic it made her want to cry. The one thing she'd feared—women wanting him—was now what he did for a living. Karma was a bitch.

"I needed to make money quick. It paid the best, and the hours ended up being a good thing. It allowed me to go to school during the day. I have one more semester and my thesis left for graduation and not a student loan in sight. That was important to me." Tanner didn't like to owe people— he'd said it more than once when he found out about his father.

"And now you'll use your degree to run the club?" If that was all he'd be doing at it, she could rest somewhat easier, but if he still danced...

She'd wanted to climb on that stage and toss a blanket over him. Then she'd wanted to drag him to a hotel room and show him just what all those movements in his tight, barely-there clothes did for her.

Juliet adjusted the air vent on the dash, upping the A/C while doing so. The close confines of her car weren't helped by thoughts like that when he was sitting next to her.

"I'll help run them. If we're going to expand, we're going to need to train staff."

"Train them? You're going to teach guys how to dance?"

"Hey, it's not just about getting up there and wiggling your hips. We have routines, we create personas, we work on projecting to the audience. This isn't some dive bar with blue lights and smoky air. You saw BeefCake, Inc. It's a high-brow place. We're talking about increasing the menu options, so we're going to need high-end chefs. It takes money and effort to run a classy place. I don't plan to lose my investment and neither do Gage and Bryan. They have families to think about."

She wished she did. What she wouldn't give for a family with Tanner.

She couldn't think about that now. "Then why have you been sending me money, Tanner? You could have used it for school and have finished already."

"You're my wife."

As if that had made a difference in the past seven years... But she bit her tongue. They were having a nice conversation; she didn't need to blow it. "I haven't touched it, you know. The money. I, um, didn't need it and it didn't feel right taking it from you."

"It's yours. I take care of what's mine."

She so wished she was his in every way that mattered. "I'd like to donate it if you don't want it back."

Tanner shrugged and looked out the window. "It's yours. Do what you want with it."

"I was thinking of giving it to Children's Medical Center." The words came out softer than she'd intended.

Tanner shifted to look at her. "In his name?"

"Of course."

He blinked then looked away. Juliet had to look away so she wouldn't drive off the road. And because she didn't want to see the pain in his eyes.

"I think that's a good idea." Tanner's voice was every bit as soft as hers had been.

Juliet concentrated on her driving, the silence now thicker than it'd been before. More uncomfortable.

After a block she couldn't take it. He was thinking about Keegan; she was thinking about Keegan. Those thoughts were always painful, and if she and Tanner were going to move forward with their lives, they had to focus forward. Keegan would always be in her heart, but she couldn't let the loss color her future—or keep her in limbo any longer.

She straightened her back and cleared her throat. "So, um, managing a strip club is a bit different than going into business with my dad."

He exhaled and drummed his fingertips along the top of the door by the window. "It's lucrative, it's enjoyable, and I like the people. Beats hanging in an office forty-plus hours a week."

She glanced at him. "Gives you time to do other things."

"What are you asking me, Juliet?"

The one burning question she wanted the answer to but didn't know how to ask. "Do you… is there… I mean—"

"What? Spit it out. This is me, remember?"

As if she could forget. "Is there someone… special?"

It took him two blocks before he responded. "You want to know if I have a girlfriend?" He shook his head. "Come on, Jules. We're married. I wouldn't do that."

It was the answer she wanted, but the accusation in his tone hurt. "It's an honest question. I mean, we haven't been together. It would be understandable if you'd, you know, gone out with someone."

After all, he had dated in college; it'd been the main reason she'd set up the scene for her father to find them. Her heart had been broken to find out he'd had other relationships and she'd had to make sure that never happened again.

God, if only she could take back the mistakes she'd made. Tanner certainly hadn't needed much convincing to get back into her bed; it probably would have only been a couple of months—if that—before he decided to make it permanent. If only she'd waited, but then, patience had never been her strong suit.

"I made a vow, Juliet. I take my vows seriously. My word is my bond." The implication being, rightfully so, that her word wasn't worth anywhere near what his was. "Why? Have you?"

"Hardly." She hadn't been able to. It'd taken her a while to want to be able to move on after he'd left her on the plane, and she'd built a wall around herself to deal with everyone's questions. And of course, since he'd left her right after the honeymoon—she'd kept the little *nugget* to herself about going there alone—he'd come out looking like the bad guy if she told people. For all that she'd been upset with him, she hadn't wanted him to be painted that way, so she'd jumped through hoops explaining his absences to her friends, most of whom figured out she wasn't telling the whole story. But that hadn't been anyone's business but hers and Tanner's, and she wanted to keep it that way. Plus, if they *could* work things out, she didn't want anyone to hate him.

No, there'd been no desire to date, especially right after Tanner had left. Then she'd been in school and learning the business… and her heart just hadn't been in it. Her heart would always be with Tanner and she didn't know how she was supposed to find someone else after he divorced her.

Her stomach clenched. She didn't want to think about that.

A sign in the entrance to the shopping center on her left caught her attention and gave her the perfect excuse to change the subject.

"Do you mind if I stop here?" she asked as she turned into the parking light.

"Not as if I'm in any hurry." He turned slightly, resting his right arm along the top of the door and his left along the top of his seat, his hand gripping the top of hers. She liked her sporty Benz, but she'd bought it when he hadn't been in her life. And now with him back, the car was much too small with him in it.

She zipped into one of the parking spaces closest to the pet store. "I'll probably be a bit. Want me to meet you somewhere or call you when I'm done?"

He looked at the store. "You don't have a pet."

"Not yet." She got out of the car.

Tanner climbed out as well and squinted at the sign. "You're getting a kitten? Just like that?"

She didn't know why he sounded so surprised. She loved animals. They'd talked about getting a dog together. That'd been the plan before they'd started to have babies.

She hadn't been able to bring herself to get a dog since he'd left. But a kitten she could do. Especially a rescue. And having it in the house would give the two of them something to focus on besides each other and the past.

"I've been thinking about getting one, and then I saw the sign. Seems like destiny to me."

Tanner shook his head as he caught up to her at the door. "You really haven't changed, have you? Always impulsive."

For a second, that comment hurt. But then it made her angry. "I seem to remember you liking when I was impulsive. More than a few times."

She flung open the door and strode inside, not caring if he followed her or not—as she tried to outrun the memories of when she *had* been impulsive.

Funny, but one of those times *hadn't* been when she'd poked the holes in the condoms. That moment had been well-thought out and planned. Right down to sterilizing the pin she'd used so they wouldn't catch anything. Well, anything but a baby.

God, she'd been so naïve. So self-centered.

So young.

Well she was older now and if she wanted a kitten, she was going to get a kitten and he couldn't stop her.

Yeah, that's sounding older.

Ignoring that little voice, she headed toward the woman at the counter in front of the pens. "Hi. I'd love to take one of these cute little babies home with me."

"And we'd love for you to." The woman handed her a form. "We'll need vet references first, though."

"Vet references? But I don't have a vet because I don't have any pets."

"Then we'll need to do a home evaluation."

"You mean, as in you'll come to my house to make sure it's safe for a kitten?"

"Yes and that you aren't overrun with cats. That it's a healthy environment. That sort of thing."

"I guess you get some unsavory characters, huh?"

"When we offer pets for free, we want to make sure they're going to a safe and loving home."

Juliet sighed. "So I guess that means I can't take one with me now."

"I'm sorry, not today. It's another part of the evaluation profile. If you're serious about adopting one of our babies, you'll understand."

"Oh I do. It's just… I wanted to take one with me now."

"We can use my vet." Tanner came up behind her and pulled out his phone. "He's out of state, but I'm moving back to town. He can vouch for me."

In a move that shocked Juliet, Tanner put a hand on her waist. She just hoped her mouth didn't fall open. Helping her was the last thing she expected from him.

"That's very generous of you," said the woman, "but we'll need a reference from where the kitten is actually going to live."

"Ah, perhaps I didn't make myself clear. I'm moving in with my *wife*." He emphasized the word by tugging her against him.

Good thing, because she need some sort of crutch to keep her upright.

"Oh, well that's different then. If you could just complete this portion of the adoption form." The woman pointed to the right side marked, *Co-Sponsor*.

The irony of him co-signing for a pet for her when they only had a month and a half left of their marriage wasn't lost on Juliet. She would have cried if it wouldn't raise too many questions—both from the woman in front of her and from Tanner.

"Certainly. No problem." He squeezed her shoulders. "Juliet? Okay with you?"

"Um, sure. That's a great idea." She probably put too much happiness into her voice, but the woman would expect her to be more than fine with it since he'd just said he was moving back. She didn't need her getting suspicious because suddenly Juliet wanted this kitten with every bone in her body. And she hadn't even picked it out yet.

Tanner finished his portion then handed her the pen. "Here, babe. Fill this out so she can call Dr. Bingham while we go see which one wants to come home with us."

Juliet took the pen in boneless fingers, the "us"es and "we"s that were flying out of his mouth sending her nerves into a tailspin. Once upon a time, she'd deserved those "us"es and "we"s and hadn't really appreciated how valuable they were.

She knew now.

She filled out the form, laughing inwardly at her shaky handwriting, then signed it at the bottom beside Tanner's signature. *Juliet Wentworth.* She'd long ago deleted her hyphenated maiden name—a necessity Tanner had insisted on when they'd filled out the marriage license. Probably to let her know they weren't truly the team they would have been when she'd been eighteen and had covered her notebook with flowery *Juliet Wentworth* signatures in every color of her Sharpie rainbow. But after he'd left, she'd wanted some connection to him, so she'd dropped the *Chambers* and had enjoyed being a Wentworth. Some people might have said it was masochistic, but she'd wanted a part of Tanner with her and his name was the only option she had.

"All right then," the woman said when Juliet handed her the form. "I'll just make the call and we'll get the ball rolling."

"Ready, babe?" Tanner's arm slid back to her waist and he steered her around the registration table to the pens of kittens.

"Uh huh." Hey, she was just happy some sound came out.

But when she got to the pens, the "Awww"s came out.

"I want to take them all home with me." She tucked some hair behind her ear as she bent down to pick up a little gray fluff ball. "Look at how cute."

She brushed the kitten's cheek with hers as she looked at Tanner—and her breath caught at the way he was looking at her…

Oh my.

Juliet didn't glance away. She knew that look. Cherished that look. *Wanted* that look.

Which of course, was why *Tanner* suddenly looked away.

She almost dropped the kitten. Apparently, Tanner wasn't as immune to her as he'd like her to believe—which could have some very interesting ramifications.

Chapter Ten

What the hell was *wrong* with him? He couldn't want Juliet again. Just because she was all sorts of sexy with that smile on her face as she held the kitten against her cheek, reminding him of the night he'd tossed a fake fur blanket onto his bed after his parents had gone out, fully intending to give Juliet a first time she'd never forget. The fur had been the same color as this kitten and Juliet had purred into it after they'd finished making love before he'd gathered her in his arms and held her 'til their breathing had returned to normal—well, as normal as his had ever been around her. Yeah, it'd been a first time *neither* of them would forget.

Though he'd sure like to.

He didn't need thoughts like that undermining his plans. He wanted out of the marriage so he'd never have to wonder if she was playing him again or what she was going to come up with next. Or when she'd let him down again.

He certainly wouldn't have to be tortured by being near her and wanting her and not being able to have her.

You might be able to have her—

"I think this is the one I want."

Her voice was husky and he knew she'd picked the gray kitten for the same reason he wished she wouldn't.

He cleared his throat and stepped back, wanting to just get the hell out of the store, but he wasn't going to ruin this kitten's chance at a good home merely because he couldn't get the thought of Juliet naked on his bed out of his head.

She'd looked so beautiful then with the soft, sated smile she'd always worn after that night when they made love.

She'd been a virgin—they'd both been virgins. That first time... It'd been awkward but so filled with love and lust that they'd worked out the logistics.

He couldn't stop the smile and had to bite his lip to keep it from covering his face. Oh, yeah. They'd definitely worked out the logistics.

"I take it that smile means you agree?"

So much for that.

He shook himself mentally and got his head back to the present. Remembering the first time he'd made love to this woman was counterproductive to his plan for being here. He'd already let his hormones rule him when he'd returned after college and look how well that'd worked out for him. "It's your cat. If you like that one, get it."

A look flashed over her face. He knew that look: hurt. Hell, he knew every one of Juliet's facial expressions. From the day she'd caught the baseball he'd hit during a pick-up game at the park, he'd paid attention. She'd gone from being his friend to being female at that moment, one that was etched in his mind because it'd been so profound. Profound enough to shape the next twenty years of his life.

Juliet nodded and tucked the kitten into the crook of her neck beneath the fall of her hair as she headed back to the woman at the counter. He'd always loved Juliet's hair. Soft and silky, long enough to get caught beneath her when he was on top... He'd loved threading his fingers through it afterwards with her head on his chest, her little puffs of breath skittering across his nipples, keeping the sensations of their lovemaking going.

God, he'd loved making love to her. She'd never held back. Had given him everything. Why in the hell hadn't she trusted in what he'd felt for her to let nature take its course?

She would have ended up with exactly what she'd wanted if she'd done nothing but love him.

And he would have had exactly what he'd wanted.

He watched her with the woman. Juliet was never still; some part of her was always moving. Her hand as she was talking, her toe tapping, her hips shifting as if she were dancing to music only she could hear. He'd loved to watch her.

He swiped a hand over his face. Some things hadn't changed.

She glanced at him with an unguarded smile and it literally took his breath away. Juliet had always been so open, so honest, every emotion showing on her face. She couldn't hide what she was feeling from him—or so he'd thought.

That was why her betrayal had hurt so badly. He never would have thought her capable of something as devious as rigging a pregnancy or setting the scene so her father would find them in bed together. Obviously, he didn't know the woman he'd married as well as he thought he did.

But you want to.

That damn little voice. It always popped in when he didn't want it to. When he'd be fixing breakfast in his apartment and it would wonder if Juliet was making those smiley-face pancakes she used to make him after football practice. Or when he'd be making his bed and remember her bending over the one in his room. Or the way her face lit up when she'd see him. Every time he looked in the mirror, he'd see Juliet's face staring back for a second, but it was long enough to keep him from forgetting.

Looking at her now, how her right hip was cocked up, her toe tapping enough to shake her butt, he knew he'd never forget her.

Jesus. He wanted to.

Then she turned around again with a smile as big as the state they were in. The Juliet Smile he'd dubbed it. Everyone had called it that in high school. Juliet was known for that smile—and everyone knew that he was the reason she smiled like that.

It hurt. It physically hurt to see that smile on her face again, when what they'd had hadn't been enough for her before.

Still, she practically skipped over to him with that smile, her blonde hair swishing behind her as if they were sixteen again.

"She's mine! Your vet gave you a great reference and the lady said we can take her home now." She grabbed his arm just like she used to, and for a minute, it felt as if they were back in high school. Back before Keegan, when the world was full of possibilities for them.

Then the kitten meowed, crashing them right back to reality, and Juliet pulled her hand away so fast it was as if she'd been burned.

No, that was him.

"Congratulations." He tried to inject some warmth into his words because he was happy for her. As much as she'd hurt him, he could never hate Juliet. He just couldn't ever trust her again. "Do you have a name?"

Juliet held the kitten up, nose to nose with her. "Not yet. I'm trying to figure out what she looks like."

"A cat."

"Funny." This time, she swatted his arm and it made everything okay again.

"So I guess you're going to need some supplies."

"Oh, gosh, yes. Hadn't really thought about that. Litter, food, some toys."

"A bed. Bowls. A scratching post."

She cocked her head. "You sound like you know about cats. Is that why you have a vet?"

"Had. I had a cat. Buddy. He adopted me one day. Kept showing up on my doorstep. Wouldn't shut up until I opened the door, at which point, he dashed inside and no amount of coaxing could get him out. I guess Buddy had had it with winter and rain and being chased by other cats and he wasn't giving up his safe and warm new home for anything.

Thankfully, Dr. Bingham made house calls, which is how she knows that I have a safe environment for cats."

"So who's watching Buddy now?"

Tanner pointed up. "He died about six months ago."

"You didn't get another one?"

Tanner shrugged, not really wanting to go down this road. Losing things he cared about was tough so why put himself in that situation again on purpose? "Not the right time. I only had Buddy because he found me. With my lifestyle, pets aren't really a good idea. But he was happy enough."

He looked around and spied a big-ass bag of cat litter. He really didn't want to talk about losing Buddy. It shouldn't hurt so much to lose an animal he'd only had for three years, but it had. And it'd brought back painful memories. Sometimes the joy of having someone to care about was offset by the pain of losing them—pain he knew firsthand. "Here, I'll get the litter. I'm assuming the woman made recommendations for what food to buy?"

"Yes. I'll look for that."

"Okay, I'll pick up the scratching post and the bed, you do the food, bowls and toys, and we'll meet at the registers in ten."

"Race you."

She got that damn impish smile and took off before he could reply. Not that he needed to; she knew he couldn't resist a dare.

Images of claiming his victory—or losing to her because the prize was the same—flashed through his mind. Juliet beneath him in the football stadium that one night. Another time in the meadow at the far corner of their ranches. They were never sure whose property they'd been on that time, so they'd had to move around a few times that afternoon to make sure they christened both pieces of property. The land they would unite with their marriage.

Technically, it was united now. He'd hadn't really thought about it since getting off that plane. No, he'd hit the tarmac and hadn't looked back—as he'd been doing for the past seven years.

She'd never contacted him. Not that she could have, he supposed. His parents knew how to get in touch with him—well, they had his home address. He hadn't told them what he was doing for a living. Didn't want to scandalize them.

It was funny that he'd gone into dancing. Juliet had been the one to teach him to dance. To listen to his body's rhythm and move to it. The rhythm that she'd put there.

So, yeah, he channeled her when he'd danced in the beginning, before he'd worked out his routine. Before he'd been comfortable. He'd channeled their time together, what it'd felt like to shimmy up against her. Remembering how she'd turned him on as she'd glide against him. He'd hated remembering, but his moves drove the club's patrons nuts—he was the highest tip earner. A couple of the guys said it was because of his junk, but Bry had said he worked the crowd like a pro. Like a natural.

Loving Juliet had been the most natural thing in his life.

Jesus. He had to snap out of this. He was here for one reason and one reason only. Then he could get the deed to his father's ranch, give Juliet the divorce papers, and he'd be gone. For good this time. There was nothing left for him here anymore, because all of it was tainted by the memories of Juliet.

"Tanner Wentworth, please report to checkout. Tanner Wentworth, please report to checkout."

Juliet's impish giggle followed at the end. No matter how stern she tried to sound, that giggle gave her away.

She'd won, dammit. While he'd been standing here, paralyzed by the memories of the past, Juliet was moving full steam ahead into her future with her kitten… and without him.

For some reason, even though that's what he wanted, the idea hurt.

Chapter Eleven

What do you think about Buttercup?" Juliet set the bowl of water on the mat in her laundry room.

Tanner handed her the food bowl. "She's not yellow."

"Duchess?" She stood up and brushed off her hands.

He cocked his head—because the kitten wanted to lick his neck. "The cat was white in that Disney flick."

She ran her hand over the kitten's back. "How about Beauty?"

"Try Beast instead." Tanner tugged the heathen's claws out of his neck as he handed her back to Juliet.

"She just wants some lovin' is all." Juliet took the fuzzball from him.

"She might have better luck by sheathing her claws." True in so many aspects of life...

Juliet hunched down to put the kitten on the mat by the food. "Do you think we should move the bowl away from her litter box? What if cats don't, you know, like to do that near where they eat?"

Tanner hefted the container of litter onto the bottom shelf in the closet so Juliet could handle it after he left. "Can't help you there. Buddy wasn't all that finicky. As long as he had food, he didn't care where I put it. Probably was just grateful he didn't have to fend for himself."

Something Tanner could relate to since he'd left.

Jesus. He didn't need to go down that path. He also needed to get out of this laundry room. It was too damn small and Juliet's perfume was too damn powerful.

Was she trying to kill him?

"So what's the verdict? Beast?"

Juliet rolled her eyes. "I'm going to have to think about it a little more. See what she looks like." She stroked the kitten's fur. "What would you like to be called, baby?"

She'd stroked him and called him *baby* once upon a time.

He really needed to get the hell out of this laundry room.

Juliet let out the breath she'd been holding when Tanner left the laundry room. She'd never thought of it as a particularly small room, but with him in here… Yeah. It was. And she didn't mean just physically. Tanner's essence filled the room. She could still smell the soap he used—he didn't do cologne. He didn't need to.

She'd never done perfume either, preferring the lotion he'd bought her after they'd made love in a field of bluebonnets. They'd stumbled upon it at the mall and he'd used his pizza delivery money to buy it for her. She'd long ago used up the original tube, but had kept buying it. Scent was a powerful reminder and she'd never wanted to forget that afternoon in the field or what life had been like when Tanner had loved her. Now, maybe the scent would help *him* remember. So she'd given herself a couple of extra applications this morning and hoped for the best. Unfortunately, so far, she didn't see any sign that he'd even *smelled* the scent, let alone remembered it.

But she wasn't giving up. He was here, he was in her house, and if she ever had a chance of winning him back, this was it.

***

Two hours later she doubted winning him back would ever happen. For it to, he'd actually have to be around her. But while she and the kitten had been hanging out in the living room playing with an exhaustive amount of toys— she'd gone on a similar buying binge when she'd stocked Keegan's nursery, which had been a real heartbreak to clean out—Tanner hadn't left the guest room once.

She tossed the plastic ball with a bell in the center for the kitten to go after and the little thing scampered off, following the ball as it rolled—oh no. There was an opening at the end of the bookcase that she hadn't realized was big enough for not only the toy, but also a kitten. And, of course, the kitten slipped through.

"Oh, no! Come back here!" Juliet climbed off her backside and crawled over to the bookshelf, grabbing the feather toy on her way. Maybe she could coax the kitten out with it.

A couple flicks of the feather by the opening got a paw out and a blue eye blinking in the darkness, but the opening was big enough for Juliet to get only her fingers through. No way to reach in and pull the kitten out.

Food. That was always an incentive. And not that dry stuff she'd bought; desperate times called for desperate measures.

Juliet opened a can of tuna. No cat could resist tuna.

Except this one apparently. The paw disappeared the minute the tuna showed up and so did the blue eye.

"Come on, baby." Juliet took some tuna on her finger and stuck it into the opening.

Not even a lick.

"Okay, let's try something else." She headed back to the kitchen and grabbed a piece of cheese.

She got a sniff this time.

A smear of butter got a lick, and a piece of ham got her finger nipped.

But the kitten wasn't coming anywhere near the opening. Not that Juliet was going to be able to get her out even if she did. The little Houdini was going to have to walk out on her own.

Juliet flopped back onto her butt after sprinkling some of the dry food in a path away from the opening. All that did was get the paw out to scrape the closest pieces inside.

She crossed her legs and plunked her chin into her palm. "Why was it so easy for you to go in there but too hard to come out?"

"You're talking to the wall?"

Of course Tanner would catch her not at her best: when she'd been bested by a kitten. "I'm talking to the kitten, but I can't tell if she's listening."

"You do know she can't understand what you're saying, right?" He hunkered down next to her. "Ah. She found a hole."

"Is that what that is? I thought it was a pinprick, but somehow she managed to squeeze through."

"Cats are like that." He peered into it. "It doesn't go anywhere, does it?"

"Go any—? Oh no!" Juliet jumped to her feet. "That's the outside corner of the house. If there's an opening—" She ran out the front door.

Great. Just great. If this kitten escaped, she'd be one more thing Juliet loved but couldn't manage to hold onto.

She ran to the corner, running her palm over where the siding met the foundation, prying her fingers under it, feeling for a hole.

So far, so good. At least she didn't have a basement to worry about.

She tried the other side, running her fingers under the edge of the siding, prying the vinyl back as much as possible, but she couldn't feel any opening. It all seemed intact.

Standing up and brushing the hair out of her face, Juliet tried to catch her breath. She needed to calm down. She was overreacting. It was just a kitten stuck in a corner. She'd figure something out.

She headed back inside—and found Tanner on his stomach, a screwdriver in his right hand, his left next to the opening.

"Come on, sweetheart. It's okay. You don't need to be afraid. I've got you," he crooned to the kitten.

And just like that, Juliet was transported back eleven years to when he'd held her after she'd given birth to Keegan and their world had come crashing down around them. She'd cried—God, how she'd cried—and Tanner had been there, crying with her, holding her, soothing her. Promising her there'd be more babies. That they'd get through it together.

She'd held on so tightly to him—her anchor in the floundering ship of her life then. But he hadn't known then what she'd done. Hadn't known that it was her guilt as well as her grief consuming her. She'd had to come clean. Had had to tell him to absolve herself of the guilt of creating Keegan before they'd been ready.

And then everything had gone to a worse depth of hell than she'd even imagined had existed.

"Come to papa, baby."

His words—they hit her in the gut. Ripped it to shreds. *Baby. Papa.* Those were such special words and she'd made a mockery of them.

She reached for the back of the chair and lowered herself into it, trying not to cry.

Yeah, that didn't work. She couldn't *not* cry. For all that she'd lost. That *they'd* lost. What she'd cost Tanner.

She was crazy to think he'd even want to give them another try. She couldn't understand why he was even here. If he'd been the one to ask her for help, after having done what she'd done, she might have told him to take a flying leap, regardless of the pain he was going through.

Tanner was a better person than she was—as evidenced by the kitten crawling out of the hole and curling into his palm.

"That's it, baby. I've got you."

His hand looked so big compared to the tiny kitten. So big yet so gentle.

How well Juliet remembered those hands on her. And she didn't mean in a comforting way, though they had been that, too. But no, she was remembering those hands running all over her. How he'd touch her face so gently, cup her breasts, grip her hips, slide between her thighs—

She had to close her thighs then. Clench them against the ache that always started when she remembered making love with Tanner. Even when she'd seen him dancing in that club, she'd been turned on though she'd known he hadn't been dancing for her. Everything Tanner did turned her on. Right down to crooning to a kitten.

"You might want to find a board or book or something to put in front of this hole, " he said, not turning around as he continued to pet the kitten. "Now that she knows where it is, she's going to want to keep going back."

If that kitten was smart, she wouldn't move from where she was right this minute.

"Good idea." Juliet stood up and headed toward her garage. She had some wood scraps out there, and it'd give her time to regroup. She hadn't expected to be assailed by memories every second she was around him. Had hoped that they could focus on the future, but their past kept overwhelming her.

Six minutes later, she was back with a couple of scraps, some screws, the cordless drill, and some stain.

Tanner was on the sofa when she walked in. "Here, you take the kitten and I'll patch that hole," he said.

"I can do it. You play with her." She wanted to focus on something besides him and if he was sitting in front of her, she certainly wasn't going to be paying attention to the kitten.

She lined up the scraps, chose the best fit, then drilled some pilot holes into the bottom of the bookshelf to start the screws.

All in all, it took her about ten minutes to close up the hole and put the first round of stain on—and then protect that stain from curious kitten paws with a fence of books around it.

"I didn't know you knew what a drill was, let alone how to use one."

"There's a lot you don't know about me, Tanner. I told you; I'm not the same girl you married." *And left*, but she wasn't going to add that. For all that it hurt her, she really couldn't blame him for leaving. Especially because she blamed herself.

She brushed the carpet fluff off her thighs, then picked up her tools. "I'll be right back, then I'll start dinner. I was thinking ribeye on the grill?"

"My favorite."

She knew that. But that wasn't why she'd chosen it. The last thing she wanted was to be in the kitchen with him, doing something domestic. The patio was a safer place to be. "There's beer in the fridge if you want to grab one. You can put the kitten in the laundry room. Just close the door so she can't get out."

"I don't think she's going anywhere." He held up his hand. The fluff ball was curled there, her tail over her nose, purring away.

Lucky kitten.

"Okay, then hang here and I'll get you a beer. Looks like you're on cat-sitting duty." Which would keep him out of her immediate vicinity while she made dinner.

She gave him the beer she'd stocked specially for him, handed him the remote, then fired up the gas grill. She prepped the ribeyes with butter, garlic, and sea salt, grabbed some asparagus and lemon, and slivered some onions with a few potatoes which she set in a pan of oil on the side burner of her grill. She'd never had to learn to cook elaborate meals with Ermalinda and Nana around, but since moving out, she and the grill had become close friends. Something else that had changed about her.

***

Twenty   fighting-with-herself-to-keep-from-going-inside-with-Tanner minutes later, she carried the serving platter in from the patio. "Food's ready."

"Guess I'll put her in her bed in the laundry room. She's out for the count."

"Okay, I'll set the table."

It was all sounding way too domesticated. What should have been.

What should be.

Juliet set their plates across from each other, ignoring the temptation to put them catty-corner to each other where their legs could accidentally brush beneath the table as she would she done if they were in this house together for the right reason.

Hell, if that were the case, she wouldn't have been outside firing up the grill when she could have been inside firing up their bedroom.

Your *bedroom, Juliet. Let's not get carried away here.*

Too late.

He walked into the kitchen, his khaki shorts hanging low on his hips.

She cursed herself for noticing.

"Something smells good," he said.

For a second she thought he was talking about her, and she sort of skipped over to him with a smile on her face—but then realized he meant dinner.

"You have cat hair on your, um, nose." She brushed it off, keeping that smile plastered to her face so he wouldn't know what she'd thought or the truth she'd realized. Thank God for all those pageants she'd been in; the experience came in handy for maintaining her poise in awkward situations, and she'd just avoided a doozy.

"Better get used to it. You're going to have it all over the place. That's the one thing I don't miss about Buddy."

"Don't you get lonely? I hate coming home to an empty house." The words slipped out before she could stop them. She didn't like how much they revealed about her life. But it was true. She hated coming home with no one here. Hated being here by herself.

"I'm rarely home. Working the hours I do, I'm there pretty much just to sleep. It was nice having Buddy, but I also felt guilty about leaving him. I don't need that in my life."

The guilt or the leaving part? Juliet didn't ask; didn't want to hear him say "both."

She sprinkled salt and pepper on the home fries, then handed him the platter. "Here you go. Ermalinda taught me to make them just how you like them."

"Man, I haven't had these in years." He took the platter and shoveled a decent amount onto his plate.

"Why not? You love home fries."

"But my waistline doesn't." That didn't stop him from picking up a forkful and slipping them past his lips.

Lips that had kissed hers. That had trailed along her body—"There's nothing wrong with your waistline."

Dammit. Her mind was preoccupied so it wasn't monitoring what her mouth said.

But it was true. She'd noticed that when she and Sandy had been at the club. Just one detail among many.

"That's because I haven't had these." He raised his second forkful, thankfully, not turning the comment to what, exactly, she *did* notice.

Which had been a lot. Tanner had always been in good shape—okay, great shape—but nothing like he'd been on that stage.

As he was, sitting across from her.

His t-shirt fit a little bit snugger than it had in the past. His calves were a little more defined. His butt—dear God, his butt—was a little firmer and rounder, and his face… These past seven years had carved maturity and life experience onto chiseled cheekbones and a jaw that looked to be made of granite. Tanner had matured so well and so sexily it was all she could do to stay on her side of the table. But stay she would. She needed to earn the right to touch him like she used to.

God, she was such an idiot for not believing in him. For not trusting him. But she'd listened to the girls in school moon over him. She'd heard them talking when they hadn't realized she was listening—or maybe they had—about how he'd go off to college and forget about her. How the cheerleaders and other college women would be throwing themselves at the hunk on the football field. Juliet had had no reason to doubt it because girls were throwing themselves at him in high school—when they knew she and Tanner were a couple. What would it be like when a campus full of women *didn't* know Tanner was hers? And when she wouldn't be there to tell them.

She'd had to *make* him hers. In a way no one could deny.

Tanner sliced into the steak. "Wow, Juliet, this is awesome."

"Thank you." She cut into her own, but she wasn't hungry. Not for food. Not when he was in the same room.

This had been a bad idea. She should have invented a convention he'd had to be at or a business trip to Europe or a deadline he couldn't miss instead of talking him into coming here. She loved her grandmother, but the heartache that would follow him leaving was going to last a lot longer than it had last time because seeing him again wasn't like ripping a bandage off—this time, it was taking the scars with it.

"Do you keep in touch with anyone from the old crowd?" he asked.

She knew he didn't because they all asked about him when they saw her. Which wasn't a lot. She didn't like to answer the questions. There were only so many conventions and client meetings he could be at before they got suspicious.

"I see them at times. Matter of fact, when they heard you were coming, they asked if we could get together."

Tanner was silent through three more bites of his steak. And another helping of home fries. "There will be a lot of questions about why I'm here. We don't want the truth getting back to your family."

"Actually..." She stabbed her steak a little more forcefully than necessary.

"Actually what?"

"Well, I couldn't tell Dad and Nana one thing and everyone else another."

He propped his elbows on the table and covered one hand with another, letting the fork dangle downward. "You lied to our friends."

At least he was using the collective *our*. "Not exactly."

"Is this like the pregnancy *not exactly* being an accident?"

Ouch. "I didn't lie to them, Tanner. I just... made myself scarce. When I do see them I say you're out of town working. Which isn't, technically, a lie."

"Not technically, no. But implied... yes. Yet now they know I'm in town." He set his fork on the plate and intertwined his fingers. "Why, Juliet? What can you hope to gain by lying this time?"

"I told you, Tanner, this isn't about them. It's about Nana."

"So everyone thinks I haven't been around long enough to get together for *seven* years? They aren't stupid, Juliet. The only one you're fooling is yourself."

And she wasn't even fooling herself. She couldn't, not when she'd had to construct an elaborate story to keep up the pretense. There were the trips out of town she'd made, pretending to meet him. All the studying that had been the perfect excuse not to be around him. Then she'd started working and anything other than weekend visits weren't possible. She'd covered for herself, but that was because she knew there'd be an end in sight with his birthday. And end she really didn't want.

"It's only for a little longer. Just 'til Nana gets better." The words squeaked out between the tears clogging her throat. He'd leave then, and the dream she'd carried in her heart these past seven years would go with it.

But if there was one thing Keegan's death had taught her it was that strength of will couldn't fix everything. That sometimes, it just wasn't up to her, no matter how hard she wished or what she did to make things go her way. Tanner was his own man. Had his own mind. His own heart.

"And she *is* getting better, Tanner. I haven't seen her in a chair since before she went into the hospital, never mind standing. And to leave her room to be with us? She had to have been so excited because I usually visit with her in her room. And that piece of pie she had? I think that's the most she's eaten at one sitting since she came home. I told you this would be good for her. I can't regret it. I just can't."

"I'm glad to hear you see improvement." Tanner speared another helping of the ribeye and chewed slowly, looking at her as if he had something on his mind.

She wanted to be that something.

"I want to see them."

She dropped her fork. She hadn't seen that one coming. "Who? Our friends? But we'll have to keep the pretense going."

Tanner shrugged. "I can't undo what you've already done and I'd like to see everyone. I'm back now, for however long, and I'm going to need something to do besides staring at these walls and rescuing that cat from holes in them."

She could think of a few things they could do…

"And with you at work, I might go stir crazy. I'd like to reconnect. Maybe I'll get a job."

"Stripping?"

He arched an eyebrow, a move she well remembered. Especially for how sexy it made him look.

Not what she should be thinking about.

"No, not *dancing*. Though… actually, Maybe I could scout a couple of locations for Gage and Bryan to see if it'd make sense to open a location here. Maybe we can get into franchising."

If they hired guys like the ones she'd seen dancing with him that night in the club, yeah, franchises would be a good idea. And there'd definitely be interest around here— especially if he was going to be doing some dancing.

She didn't want to think about that.

"So I'm going to need a car. We forgot to get one."

"I'll have one of the fleet cars sent around. We don't use them all that much."

Silence came crashing down again.

They'd used a couple of fleet cars a few times. And not for driving.

Tanner swallowed the piece of steak and washed it down with his beer. Then he placed his knife and fork on his plate, leaving a few home fries left. "Thanks, Juliet. This was good. But I'm beat. I'm going to grab a shower and turn in."

He stood and it was as if he took the air in the room with him. She'd always loved how big he was compared to how small she was. It'd made her feel safe and protected.

But now, as he headed into the kitchen to wash his plate then put it on the drain board, giving her a small nod as he headed toward his room, the differences in their sizes just made her feel insignificant.

***

Penelope transferred from the horrible wheelchair to the rocker in front of her bay window after Juliet and Tanner left, chuckling that she'd kicked them out because she was "tired."

She was so far from tired she'd consider running a marathon if it meant she wouldn't have to be in that chair again, but these things must be handled delicately. She couldn't recuperate too quickly or people were going to get suspicious.

She chuckled. Even Burt didn't have an inkling that she was faking ninety percent of her frailness.

She liked to ignore the ten percent she wasn't. That darn TIA had only been good for giving her the excuse to play the invalid and get her family to come running. But frankly, she was over this. Tanner and Juliet needed to realize they should be together so she could go about living the rest of her life while waiting for those great-grandbabies to come along.

"*Silencio, Señora.*" Ermalinda closed the door to the sitting room behind her. "If Mr. Burt hears, he's going to wonder why you're laughing."

"And we'll tell him it's because I'm so happy."

"He will be happy to hear that. He worries about you." Ermalinda picked up the television remote from beside the recliner and handed it to her. "What movie do you want to watch today?"

Penelope nudged her guilt aside. Burt wouldn't appreciate her motives, but then, he was biased against Tanner. If her son weren't so blinded by what his ex-wife had done, he'd see that Juliet wasn't *quite* as perfect as he thought she was.

It took a woman to see that. One who loved Juliet very much. Which was why she was keeping up this pretense. Juliet had suffered enough. She deserved to be happy, and Tanner made her happy.

Juliet also made Tanner happy and if he could only remember that, he'd be able to forgive her for her desperate actions.

"No movie. I'm tired of movies. I want to jump for joy instead and take a jog through the rose garden."

Ermalinda shook her head. "And then you will have to explain to everyone why you are suddenly fully recovered."

"We can just say that the Lord works in mysterious ways."

"Not so mysterious." Ermalinda patted her on the shoulder and handed her the romance novel Ermalinda's mother-in-law had recommended.

The minute Penelope had read about the meddling grandmother who'd plotted to have her granddaughter share a house with the guy who'd been her first crush so they could get it ready to put it up for sale, which then allowed them the time and opportunity to fall in love and live happily ever after, was the day Penelope had known the perfect way to help Juliet get her man.

Not that she'd manufactured her little stroke, but it'd happened when she'd been trying to come up with some believable illness she could be cured from that would cause just enough worry to make everyone come running.

The Lord did, indeed, work in mysterious ways.

The pain and the fright had almost been worth it—and would be if she got some great-grandchildren out of this.

"*Mi suegra* was so happy you read the book and took her advice. But I hope neither of you ever plays a trick on me. You're both too good. Ladies your age are supposed to sit around and knit, not get into mischief."

"I'd be more than happy to knit up a slew of baby sweaters if those two could have worked this out on their own, but they're both too stubborn. Or scared. I haven't figured out which Tanner is, but I know Juliet was worried about making the first move because she thought it'd make Tanner end their marriage. She's been carrying her guilt all this time. But that can only go on for so long. She didn't mean to hurt him; that poor girl has been in love with him her entire life. It's time she gets over herself and starts working on her future."

Ermalinda sat on the ottoman and clutched a pillow to her stomach. "You are taking a risk with Tanner, though. He's been hurt badly."

"I know. And he's such a good boy—er, man. I keep forgetting they're all grown up." She set the book on her knee. "But just because they are grown up doesn't mean I can't help them along."

"I don't know *Señora*. You aren't acting very grown up with your play-acting."

Penelope sat back and intertwined her fingers, tapping the index fingers against each other. "Sometimes, Ermalinda, the ends justify the means."

"I'm not sure I want to understand that particular phrase. I just know that *mi suegra* is a matchmaker in my town, so she must know what she's doing."

"Well, it's gotten Tanner here, and he and Juliet are touching. I might be an old lady, but I still remember what sparks feel like and if those weren't sparks flying between my granddaughter and her husband, I'll… why, I'll stay in that godforsaken wheelchair for another month after their next wedding."

Ermalinda crossed herself. "Hush, *Señora*. Don't tempt fate."

"Tempt it?" Penelope fanned herself with the book. "I'm not tempting it, Ermalinda. I'm helping it along."

Chapter Twelve

Phew. He made it.

Tanner shut the guest bedroom door behind him, resisting the urge to slam it. He couldn't have gotten out of the kitchen fast enough, the visions of him and Juliet in the back seat of one of her father's Lincoln Towne Cars chasing him the entire way.

He yanked a pair of gym shorts and a t-shirt out of his bag and grabbed the blue towels Juliet had left on the dresser. He wished to God he had his own bathroom, but wishing didn't make things reality, so he was going to have to brave the memory-laden dining room to get to the bathroom and a cold shower. Between the memories, the scent of Juliet's lotion, and just being around her—not to mention his seven years of self-directed celibacy—temptation was not just rearing its seductive head, but roaring through this tiny house, gobbling up everything in its path.

He took a deep breath before opening the door, then strode across the living room, thankful she had her back to him. Though, of *course*, she turned when he was passing the table.

"You'll want to jiggle the shower nozzle if the water pressure's too low. I have to get someone in to look at it."

"Probably just a clogged shower head. I can take a look at it tomorrow."

"Oh, that'd be great. Thank you."

He smiled—thinly—not wanting to interact with her. He'd thought this would be easier; that his anger at her would be a sufficient buffer. That the time apart would be a sufficient buffer. But, apparently, memories were stronger than distance.

He shoved the bathroom door—and stopped cold.

Good God. The room couldn't be any more Juliet than if she were standing here.

He turned around to make sure she wasn't behind him, caught a glimpse of her hair as she rose from the table, and, this time, he did slam the door.

Besides the purple that was an essential part of her wardrobe and what he thought about when he thought about her, the room smelled like her. He should have figured it would since there were a couple tubes of that lotion she liked in a basket on the back of the toilet.

He pulled back the floral shower curtain. A bottle of bluebonnet bath gel was in the wire rack hanging from the showerhead. And he'd bet that loofa smelled like it, too. The loofa that she used on her body.

Damn. Shit. Hell. He couldn't say enough words to block out the images assaulting his brain. They'd gotten funky a few times in the shower back when they'd been teenagers and able to make those contortions. God, it'd been amazing.

He undid the button on his jeans and yanked the zipper down, peeling his clothes off as fast as he could, then turning the nozzle all the way to the right for the coldest water he could get. It'd be the only thing that would get him through a couple of minutes in an enclosure that smelled like her.

Or so the theory went. But from her lotion to the soap, to that damn loofa that was hanging right at nose-level, he couldn't get away from Juliet. And then his brain got in on the party, imagining her in here, naked, wet, soapy, gliding that loofa all over herself—

Shit. Damn. Hell. He was as hard as a rock and he had a feeling even if there were ice cubes falling out of the showerhead, he'll still want to storm into that dining room, throw her over his shoulder, and carry her back to his room where he'd make love to her for hours.

Tanner leaned his forehead against the cool tile, hoping—no, *praying*, and he wasn't a particularly religious guy—that this intense ache would go away. That his body would calm down, listen to the dictates of his brain, and get off its I-want-Juliet kick.

Lathering himself up didn't help. Neither did washing his hair because he wanted her fingers combing through it. In the end, he removed the showerhead from its holder and held a steady stream of ice water on a certain part of his anatomy so he could at least walk the few steps necessary to get out of the shower.

He used the blue towel she'd given him, among her sea of purple ones, scrubbing perhaps a tad too hard, but he needed to put an end to this insane testiness running below the surface of his skin. As if there were a living thing beneath it, trying to claw its way out.

How could he have forgotten this insane reaction he had to her? This intense desire to haul her up against him and forget the world existed?

He'd thought she'd killed that with her lies, but apparently, absence made the hormones grow fonder because this heart definitely wasn't involved.

Dude, you're still married to her... Why not take advantage of that fact?

Great. Just what he didn't need—permission from his libido to assert his husbandly rights. He was her husband in name only and he'd do well to remember that.

He tossed on his clothes, force-feeding himself the litany that she was his wife only on paper. That just because some Justice of the Peace had said mumbo-jumbo over their joined hands seven years ago didn't mean they had a happy marriage or he had the right to those husbandly rights in any way, shape or form.

How about those contorted shower forms?

He turned on the sink faucet and cupped his hands, slashing more cold water on his face.

Nope, still wanted her.

He dragged the towel over his face, sopping up the water. Hell, maybe this was that proverbial seven-year-itch. Since he hadn't been scratching in the last three-quarters of a decade, it was acting up. Demanding release.

Release would be nice...

Shit. Damn. Hell.

He scrubbed the towel through his hair, tugging it a litter harder than necessary, hoping to focus on the pain on *this* head instead of the one that was jumping for joy at his libido's argument. He did not need a party going on in his pants the next time he faced Juliet.

Which would be in about two minutes—just as soon as he got his junk under control and walked calmly out the door.

She was sitting in the living room, the kitten curled in her lap, her laptop open on a tray table in front of her, a book in her hand, and the news mumbling in the background.

"Since when did you start wearing glasses?" Dammit. He should have kept his mouth shut and gone into his room where he could've spent the rest of the night reading financial statements. Nothing killed a hard-on like spreadsheets. He knew; it'd been his main source of reading material for the past few months as he'd tried to figure out his future, and even though he didn't have a girlfriend he was pining after—because he had a wife, one he'd tried to block from his thoughts—sometimes his body demanded attention.

At least he hadn't caved and bought bluebonnet hand lotion to help take care of that issue. Mainly because it would've created a bigger problem. Both literally and figuratively.

Kind of like the one that started happening again in his shorts.

Damn it.

"Oh, I've, uh…" She slid the glasses into her hair, pulling the fall of gold off her face.

Damn, Juliet was pretty. Naturally so. Like most women, she wore makeup, but unlike most women, she didn't need to. She looked just as beautiful without it. Sure, her lips and cheeks were a bit paler, but that just made her blue eyes stand out more. He'd always loved losing himself in her eyes.

He tore his gaze away and glanced out the window.

Big mistake. It was dark. A cocoon of black that enveloped them here in this house together.

He swallowed. Hard.

"Eye strain from all the paperwork and computer work. I find they help me when I'm tired. Make my eyes less scratchy."

"Ah. Good. Makes sense." At least something did. "Speaking of tired…" He pointed to the door to his room. "Night."

He was pretty sure he heard a "Goodnight" as he reached his room, but his heart was pounding too heavily, the blood rushing through his veins too loudly for him to be sure. And that was a good thing. Because no matter what way he looked at it, being in the same house—especially if they were on opposite sides of it—did *not* constitute a good night in his book.

Juliet closed the book. She hadn't been reading the words anyway. She'd tried to, but the truth was, she'd been listening to him in her bathroom. Had heard the pull of the rings across the shower curtain bar. Heard the squeak of the faucet as he'd turned on the water. Heard him pull the shower curtain back into place, and heard the change in the fall of the water when he'd been under the spray.

And then her imagination had gone wild. And she'd let it.

While she remembered very well what Tanner looked like naked, that little show a week and a half ago had only sharpened the memories. Fine-tuned them. Honed them. Into the perfect projectile to spear her heart.

The kitten stretched against her thighs, her own little projectiles spearing into Juliet's flesh, doing a fabulous job of pulling her out of her hormone-induced stupor.

"What do you want, baby?" She picked the kitten up and nuzzled her nose with her own, then tucked her into the crook of her neck. She knew what that kitten wanted; the same thing she did: someone to curl up with tonight. To feel safe with. To feel loved.

Sighing, she nudged the tray table out of the way and then clicked off the TV. She usually had the television on for background noise, but the news was too depressing. Lord knew, she didn't need anymore depressing things in her life. Keegan's death, Nana's illness, and the end of her marriage were her triple play. Three strikes and she was out. Things could only go up from here.

But then her doorbell rang.

Chapter Thirteen

H ey, Juliet! Great to see you!" Delia, a former member of the cheerleading squad, second runner-up for homecoming queen, and the girl Tanner had called a Juliet-wannabe the entire twelve years they'd been in school together, waved at her from the front stoop, then walked up and gave her a hug as if the last time they'd seen each other was a few days ago instead of over a decade ago.

Why did Juliet think this impromptu visit right after Tanner got back to town wasn't an accident?

"Hello, Delia. What can I do for you?"

"Well, you know." Delia put the little bounce into her pose as she crossed her arms and cocked a hip to the side. "A bunch of us were out to dinner tonight, talking about school, and someone mentioned they heard Tanner was around, and I figured, since I was going by your neighborhood on my way home anyway, I ought to stop in and check on the two of you. For as visible as you two were in high school, you've been veritable hermits since we graduated. Surely you're ready to share him with the world after all this time?" She smiled and winked, pretending they were the best of friends and she had the right to say these things. But even if all of that was true, Delia was the last person Juliet would give the skinny on her marriage to.

"I'm running my father's company now, so that takes

the bulk of my time. And Tanner's busy, too. He's still traveling a lot."

"Well, that must be a bummer for you. Finally don't have to sneak around, and now he's in another part of the country. Ain't life a bitch?"

Delia sure was. The woman was fishing with a big ol' skimming net, looking for scandal. Juliet was not about to give her any. She'd worked hard to keep the story of their happy relationship going among those who knew her best, so she surely wasn't going to blow it with someone who wanted to gossip about her. One whiff of the truth reached Delia's nose and it'd all be over in an instant.

"It's a juggling act, but we've managed to make it work." If that's what one could call it.

"Well, where is your big strapping hunk of a husband? Gosh, I haven't laid eyes on him since the day you guys got hitched."

Delia had always wanted to lay a lot more on Tanner than her eyes. She was the chief barracuda among the sea of many that Juliet had had to worry about.

Or *not* had to worry about if she'd believed Tanner back then. But he didn't know what girls like Delia were like. And her cohorts-in-crime, Savannah and Jamison and Kiley. The four of them were like Medusa—minus the creepy hair. But they had tentacles out in all directions—slithering, slimy feelers of gossip that would never go away.

Yet now that *might* come in handy… "Tanner's in bed. Asleep."

"Aw, are you sure you don't want to wake him up?" Delia put an added emphasis on *wake him up* as if they were talking about someone's conquest and not Juliet's husband.

Husband.

It felt so odd thinking that word in relation to him when he was here. In her house. In her life.

But he was that. Her husband.

One Delia could keep her money-grubbing, social-climbing, leg-uncrossing paws off of.

"Not now, Delia. He just flew in this morning and is pretty tired."

The smile slipped just a fraction on Delia's face, but Juliet caught it. Another thing those beauty pageants had taught her: behind every beautiful smile were the eyes of a viper waiting to find a moment of weakness to strike. Juliet had no intention of being bit.

At least, not by Delia. Tanner on the other hand…

"Babe?"

Speak of the devil.

"Who's there?"

Juliet's head whipped around so fast, it was a good thing Delia wasn't standing as close as she had been or Juliet's hair would've done a number across her face. "Tanner?"

"Musta been waitin' for you, Juliet." Delia muttered, putting as much innuendo and suggestion into her sentence as was legally permissible in the state without being called lewd.

If only what Delia was thinking were true…

"It's, uh, Delia. Magellan. From high school. Remember her?" Juliet wanted to make some sort of sign to remind him of their cover story, but she could feel Delia's eyes on her like a hawk.

Yes, Delia had come fishing.

Tanner yawned as he walked over to her, his t-shirt hugging a mighty fine set of shoulders… and pecs… and abs, and his shorts riding very low on his hips.

He leaned against the doorframe and rested his hand on the other side, effectively having her back both literally and figuratively.

"Hello, Delia. Nice to see you again."

"Well it sure is good to see you, too, Tanner."

Juliet wanted to toss her cookies at the estrogen undulating off Delia in waves. This was exactly what she'd feared all those years ago and in two months he'd be up for grabs for the likes of women like Delia. And maybe *even* Delia.

She threw up a little in her mouth at that.

"What brings you here at this time of night?"

"*This* time? Why, Tanner Wentworth, I can remember when ten p.m. was your starting time. Right out of the gate like a racehorse at the Kentucky Derby."

Juliet had to unclog her ears. What was with the thick Southern accent? Since when did Delia sound like Scarlett O'Hara?

"Those were the days when I didn't have any responsibilities. Now Juliet and I are so busy with the businesses, we need to go to bed early. Get some sleep, you know?"

His arm slid around her waist, tossing the innuendo right back at Delia because *sleep* was not what he was talking about.

Damn if that didn't make the butterflies in Juliet's tummy go crazy. She wished they were going to do what he'd just intimated; she'd toss Delia off the front step so quickly, the girl would be glad she'd learned how to take a fall in cheerleading practice.

Delia was looking at them as if she didn't believe them. So Juliet slipped her arm around his waist too.

She had to stop herself from swooning, though. Seriously, her knees about buckled when she touched him. All that hard, sinewy muscle beneath her palm and against her forearm. And smashed up against the side of her breast. God, Tanner felt just as amazing as ever and it was killing her knowing she was going to have to let go once Delia walked away.

"Oh, well then, I guess I should be going. Wouldn't want you two lovebirds to miss out on all that, um, sleep. But I wanted to tell you that some of the football team and cheer squad are getting together tomorrow for a barbecue at three and we won't take no for an answer. You two have to come. No one's seen you in years and we want to catch up."

They wanted something all right…

Juliet kept her mouth shut. She actually wouldn't mind going with Tanner. Have them be there as a couple. Keep the image going. But that was because she wanted it to be reality. Tanner, who didn't, might have other ideas.

"We'll have to see, Delia. Juliet's grandmother is sick, so we don't make firm plans these days. Pretty much just fly by the seat of our pants."

Delia, damn it, checked out Tanner's pants. Well, his shorts. That showed off his thighs, and if he'd adhered to his old practices, was commando beneath.

The thought had Juliet's legs threatening to give out more so than his arm around her shoulders.

"Well, let me give you my card so you know where to find us. We're gathering at my place. The patio out back is delightful. My former husband was in landscaping."

Which former husband, Juliet wanted to ask. It was well known that Delia had a habit of marrying well. She'd gone to college for an MRS degree and had ended up with two.

Tanner was not going to be number three. If it was the last thing Juliet did, she'd make sure of that.

Tanner took Delia's card with the hand that wasn't plastered to her waist. Without glancing at the address, he handed it to her.

Juliet resisted the urge to crinkle the card into a ball. After all, she wanted to go to the party because if merely seeing Delia could get his arm around her, imagine what a group of former friends talking to them would get her.

Tanner's hand came off her waist the moment he shut the door on Delia. "So what do you say about going to that party?"

Hell yes and could they leave now? "I thought you wanted to see everyone."

"I do. Haven't thought about Sean or J.D. or Tank in years. But I asked how you felt about going."

"Oh. Well then, of course I'd like to." With some trepidation. "But what are we going to say, Tanner? About us?"

"Exactly what you've been saying all along. But we'll want to stick as close to the truth as possible. That losing Keegan was tough, and we had some things to work out. I can't imagine they're going to ask more pointed questions after that."

Probably not, since he'd be with her. Before? Everyone had wanted to know where he was and what he was up to. Why he hadn't come around.

"What have you told them that I'll need to know?"

Juliet searched her memory for the cover-ups. "You had a lot of business trips to Napa and Vegas."

"They didn't ask why I wasn't working for your father?"

"They did and I told them that you wanted to build your resume on your own and that other opportunities came up, so I stepped in to help Dad."

"Plausible, I guess. So what did you tell them I was doing?"

"Importing and exporting. It was the only thing I could think of that would have you traveling so much and that I wouldn't be expected to know the details of. And since I was in school and learning to run Dad's company, it seemed to appease them. I mean, how much could I be expected to know about two businesses, right?" It had come in handy for everyone to think she was a ditzy blonde. She wasn't— actually she wasn't *now*—but before, her biggest aspiration had been to be Tanner's wife and they'd all known it. She'd shocked them enough with the idea she was not only going to college but also going on to a master's degree that it'd stopped them from asking too many questions about Tanner.

"And now I'm in land deals." Tanner scrubbed his jaw. "Yeah, I can make that work. Say I found an opportunity and headed in that direction." He pushed off the wall and stretched his arms straight up over his head, raising the bottom of his t-shirt a few inches to reveal that washboard he called a stomach. "Well, hopefully, we won't have any more surprise drop-ins. I actually really do need some shut-eye." He dropped his arms. "Goodnight, Juliet."

She had to lick her lips before responding because that whole stretching thing... Wow. Just... wow. "Goodnight, Tanner."

Yes, she watched him walk back to his room. And, yes, she wished she were going with him.

Exhaling, she made sure the front door was locked, flicked off the porch light, scooped the kitten off the chair but then realized she should move the litter box to her room so the little Houdini wouldn't have to roam the house while she slept. The last thing she needed was to have to look for the kitten and run into Tanner in the middle of the night in the skimpy shorts and t-shirt that constituted her pajamas.

Which, of course, was exactly what happened.

Okay, so it wasn't the middle of the night and she wasn't yet in her pajamas, but when she came out of the laundry room, litter box under one arm, the kitten under the other, Tanner was coming around the corner from the kitchen with a glass of water in hand and, well...

The litter box hit the ground, scattering little crunchy pieces of litter that, thankfully, hadn't been used yet, followed closely by the glass of water, which shattered, and the kitten managed to leap out of her arms and dash into the living room without landing on the mess, preventing one disaster at least.

"Damn!" Juliet wanted to stamp her foot but didn't since she was barefoot and God only knew where the shards of glass were. All she'd wanted was to get into her room and away from Tanner, yet she'd literally run right into him.

"Don't move." Tanner held up his hands. "Let me get something to clean this up."

"Be careful where you're walking."

"I have slippers on. I'll be fine. Where's the broom?"

"In the pantry closet to the left of the fridge. Dustpan is hanging on the inside of the door." She leaned forward to flip the light switch on the corner of the wall. "Watch your eyes."

She ought to have watched hers. He'd taken off his t-shirt.

She'd seen it all before—most notably a week ago—but nothing could prepare her for a half-naked Tanner in her home, at night, standing three feet from her, his hair all disheveled as if he'd run his fingers through it a few too many times.

Or someone else had.

No. He'd said he'd been faithful to his vows, and if there was one thing she'd taken from the mess of their past, it was that she could trust Tanner.

"You okay?" Tanner came back around the corner, broom and dustpan in tow, looking way too good to be someone's maid. "No shards on your feet?"

"Can't feel any." Wasn't exactly thinking about them, either. Not with him sweeping up the mess, the muscles in his arms and shoulders flexing nicely.

"Okay, don't move. I'm going to run the broom over your feet."

"Wouldn't think of it." She propped her palm against the wall and giggled a little when the bristles brushed her skin.

"Still ticklish, huh?" He cocked his head to look at her, that grin of his doing not-so-funny things to her insides.

"I don't think you ever grow out of being ticklish."

He stared at her for a heartbeat or two, a couple of blinks happening before he looked away and she knew he was remembering the same thing she was. One night, after his parents had gone out, he'd invited her over, and they'd made a point of finding out just where each one's ticklish zones were—and had discovered quite a few erogenous ones along the way.

Thank God his parents had been gone for hours and her father had thought she was staying at Tricia's. Tricia had been her alibi on so many occasions.

She'd cried almost as hard when Tricia and her husband moved to North Dakota—of all places—as she had when Tanner had left her on that plane because it was one more person she loved leaving her.

She cleared her throat and pasted a smile on her face. She wasn't going to think about losing people. Tanner was here now and she didn't want to be an emotional mess in front of him or he'd be glad to get her out of his life. No, she had to be the sunny, sparkling, fun and happy Juliet he'd known back before she'd started making poor decisions. Well-intentioned ones, but definitely ill-advised. *That* Juliet was someone he could fall in love with again.

He cleared his throat, too, then hunkered down to sweep the mess into the dustpan. "Let me empty this and give it one more sweep before you move. Do you have a pair of slippers I can get for you?"

"In the closet in my bedroom. Right side. They're purple."

He smiled at her. "Of course they are."

She smiled back, the running joke putting them on the same page.

He strode into her kitchen to empty the pan into the trash, then returned, giving a quick sweep over the floor. He set the dustpan on the kitchen countertop. "Don't move. I'll be right back."

"Wouldn't think of it." Mainly because she got the going-away view.

Those shorts did some very nice things to his backside. Or maybe it was his backside that did some very nice things to those shorts. Whatever the case, she wouldn't mind removing the shorts and getting her hands on his backside.

Her palms actually got tingly at the thought, and Juliet shook her head. Seven years of celibacy and the guy of her dreams was half-naked in her house and—

"Found them." He held up her silly pair of slippers—the ones with the tiaras on the toes that Nana had made her buy when she saw them advertised on television. Since they'd made Nana happy, Juliet had bought them.

And with Tanner at her feet, slipping one on her foot like Prince Charming, they made her happy too.

"Don't need a bloody mess to clean up as well." He tapped her ankle and set her foot on the floor. "So now you can go in search of your kitten. I'll refill the litter box. I'm assuming you were taking this into your room?"

"Yes. I didn't want her running around at night bothering you."

"Yes, this bother was so much better." His smile took the sting out of his words as he pushed on his thighs to stand in front of her.

Right in front of her.

Time stopped. So did her breathing.

Her heart, however, thundered in her ears.

He was so close. Too close—no, not close enough. Not so close that she could wrap her arms around him and pull him up against her and kiss him until their knees gave out.

Which hers were threatening to do.

"Juliet…" His hand came up and for a second—a brief, hope-filled second—she thought he'd cup her head and draw her in for that kiss.

Instead, his hand dropped back to his side, his biceps tightening as if he'd clenched his fists, and he took a step back.

And another.

"Go to bed, Juliet. Now."

Go to bed. Not *come* to bed. That one word made all the difference.

She cleared her throat—again. "Goodnight, Tanner."

She sidestepped around him, careful not to brush up against even one hair on his forearm, then remembered she needed the litter box. "The litter—"

He muttered something beneath his breath. She was going with "shit" or "dammit."

"I'll bring it in. Go. Find the kitten."

She ran into her room and flicked on the light, looking around for—what? What was she supposed to find? Oh, the kitten. Right.

"Here, baby." She closed the door almost completely behind her, not wanting the kitten to escape. Bad enough she was going to have to face Tanner one more time over the litter; she didn't need to have to do it chasing the kitten around. With her luck, the kitten would find her way into *his* room, and that would start another round of fantasies she didn't want to have.

"Here, kitty." Juliet got down on her hands and knees to look under the bed.

Nope. Not there. Great, another disappearing act. The kitten had chosen her own name: Houdini.

Juliet opened the closet, moved her shoes around. The kitten was small enough she could have slipped into one of them.

Then she heard a rustling noise behind her and she turned around. There was the little disappearing act, walking along the headboard, her paws shifting the books and magazines around.

Juliet got to her feet then flopped onto her bed, reaching for her. "Come here, you cute little thing." She scooped her up and rubbed her cheek with hers as she rolled over—

Tanner stood in her doorway with a look on his face…

She scrambled off her bed—then chastised herself. She should have stayed. Tempted him.

"Here's the litter." He held up the box, his voice flat. Monotone. Tight. Unlike him.

Maybe she *did* tempt him…

"Um, thanks. Just put it down. I'll figure out someplace to put it."

He did. Then he stood again, staring at her, and if Juliet wasn't about to let hope get in the way of reality, she'd swear she saw a fire in his eyes.

How well she remembered that fire. Had thought of it every day for the past seven years.

"Goodnight."

That was three times he'd said it to her, but it didn't mean it would be a good one.

Because Tanner was going back to his room and she would be alone in hers.

Chapter Fourteen

Tanner's eyes flew open, the sunlight making him wince.

He rubbed them, making the spots disappear, then looked at his surroundings.

ThankyouJesus, he was still in his bed.

Well, his bed in Juliet's house.

Tanner ran his hands over the sheets. Gripped the edge of the mattress.

Ran his hand low on his abdomen.

He was still in his shorts.

Thank God. That dream he'd had had been just that: a dream.

His hand moved lower and found…

Okay, it'd been a wet dream, but still, a dream.

But, damn it, why'd he have to dream about making love to Juliet?

He shook his head, then looked around the room. How could he *not* have dreamed about Juliet? He was staying in her freaking house, for God's sake, and the room was imprinted with her. Hell, the damn sheets smelled like her. And he was only feet from her bedroom.

He'd been in her room last night and it'd taken every ounce of fortitude he'd had in him to walk out. She'd been sprawled across her bed, her hair all messy—just the way he liked it—her legs—dear God, her legs—spread enough that he'd had a instant and perfect flashback to so many times he'd taken her that way…

Damn it. He was getting hard again. He hadn't had a wet dream in years, and his first night under the same roof with her, he had one. This was going to be a lot tougher to do than he'd thought because it was easy to forget he was angry with her when she wasn't trying to play him.

What about playing with *you?*

He sat up. He needed to get out of bed now.

And he needed another damn shower. After he fixed the showerhead.

He grabbed his t-shirt that he should have kept on after going to bed, but he hadn't expected her to be standing in the hallway right outside his room when he'd gone for a glass of water. And then, well, she had been and he'd made that comment about being ticklish, and, well… Hell. There were so many memories tangled up in Juliet that it was inevitable he'd stumble across at least one of them with an innocent remark.

He grabbed his towel, draping it over his forearm and crossing that in front of him in case his little "nighttime emission" had left a telltale stain.

Turned out, he needn't have worried. Juliet had left him a note on the dining room table.

Tanner ~

Had to run into the office for a bit. The kitten is in the laundry room with the litter box. Help yourself to anything in the kitchen. Griddle is in the cabinet to the right of the stove. I remember how you liked pancakes. I should be home around two if you still want to go to Delia's.

~Juliet

He did like pancakes. Ermalinda had given them several cooking classes in preparation for their marriage— the first one—and pancakes had been his favorite. Her banana chocolate chip ones were his favorite. And Juliet had all the ingredients.

He slapped his abs when he sat down at the table after his shower and cooking his breakfast with a side of bacon and sliced peaches. Good thing he wasn't going to be dancing for a while, though getting back into shape was going to be a bitch.

He should probably do some exercises to keep in shape.

He opened the newspaper Juliet had left on the table and looked for a local gym. First order of business would be to get a membership.

Putting down roots, Wentworth?

He sat back. No, he wasn't putting them down, but he had to admit, this whole scenario was a little too perfect. His favorite food, the paper, Juliet's little note… Definitely too domesticated for his liking.

Or rather… not. He'd wanted domesticated back in the day. Truth be told, wouldn't mind it now. But not with her. He couldn't trust her and without trust, they had nothing.

Like all of this, for instance. Was she trying to play him? Set this up to show him that it could work between them?

He let go of the newspaper. He hated this. Hated not being able to trust her over even the simplest of things. This was the woman he'd once thought—hoped, had been excited about—spending his life with, and now he couldn't even trust her about breakfast.

It sucked. He'd loved her once. So incredibly much.

The thought squeezed his heart, a feeling he was all too well acquainted with and didn't want to be. Not anymore. He and Juliet were over and done. In the past.

Except he was going to have to pretend that they weren't at Delia's barbecue today.

That hold on his heart lessened. Which scared him more than he'd like.

***

Juliet worked her pageant smile so realistically that Tanner would have thought it was genuine if he didn't know her so well.

Though... *did* he know her? The Juliet he'd left behind had had zero intention or desire to go to college. All she'd wanted was to get married and have babies. To cook his dinner and warm his bed and raise his children. To be fair, he'd wanted her to do that, too. He'd never thought of her behind a desk or taking meetings or running her father's company.

Yet when she'd walked in at one-thirty, he'd been blown away by the executive in the form-fitting skirt and professional yet sexy-as-hell pale pink blouse.

She'd kicked her heels off as she'd walked into her room, giving him a flashback to the night she, a member of the student government, had dragged him along to help her scout venues for the senior prom. It'd been another night when his parents had gone out—gambling he now knew, but at the time couldn't have cared less so long as they weren't going to come home for a while—and he and Juliet had ended up in his place where she'd made a big production of stripping for him all the way to his room, tossing her dress onto his shoulder, draping her panties over the back of the sofa and her bra on his bedroom door knob. Her heels had been the first to come off.

"Sweetheart, would you like another beer?"

He shook off that memory and glanced around Delia's backyard before looking down at Juliet as she stood beside him, looking just as beautiful as she always had in her blue-and-white striped sundress.

The color set off her blue eyes that held not one whit of subterfuge. No one would suspect she didn't mean that *sweetheart* anymore than he meant what he said next.

"Sure, honey. I'd love another."

Well, okay, he actually would love another beer, but that *honey*...

The scary part was how easy it was to slip back into their old habits as if the past eleven years had never happened.

"Damn, man, I'd think you and Juliet would've cooled off a bit, but those sparks are still flyin' huh?" Tank, his teammate from their football glory days, nudged him with his shoulder as Juliet headed toward the outdoor stone kitchen set-up in Delia's pool house. "You are one lucky SOB. Wish I still felt about my wife the way you do about yours."

Tanner kept that damn smile on his face as he raised the last of his beer to his lips. He didn't have a clue how to respond to that.

"So." Tank cracked his neck, one side then the other, then rolled his shoulders while he checked out Candy Simpson's ass as she walked by. Some things never changed—especially the fact that Candy Simpson swished her ass now every bit as much as she used to. No surprise the woman was on the prowl for husband number four.

Tank cleared his throat, then looked back at Tanner. "I've got season tickets this year for the Cowboys. Maybe we can take in a couple of games. What do you say?"

Tanner had always loved the Cowboys, but he wasn't going to be here come football season. No one else needed to know that yet, though. "Yeah, let's do that."

"You plannin' to be in town more nowadays? Me and Sara would love to have you and Juliet over to the house."

Just hand him a shovel and let him dig his own grave. He could see what Juliet meant about having to keep up appearances. He couldn't come clean now with the truth. He didn't know what Juliet was going to do when he eventually did leave and she had to own up to what they'd done.

Maybe she'd just say they got a divorce and leave it at that. With the country's divorce rate, it shouldn't be hard to believe—except for the fact that Tank was seeing sparks where none existed.

Or, well… Scratch that. The sparks were still there, it was just that the rationale behind them didn't make sense anymore.

"Did I hear my name?" Tank's wife Sara, walked up beside her husband and slipped her arm around his waist, her pregnant belly making a bigger entrance.

God, he'd loved when Juliet had been pregnant. Had loved feeling Keegan kick inside her. Had loved what pregnancy had done to her breasts—

Shit. This was so not where he wanted to go with his thoughts.

"Hi. I'm Sara." Tank's wife held out her hand.

"Tanner Wentworth. Nice to meet you." He shook her hand, glad to hear his voice didn't shake. He'd gotten better at masking his emotions around pregnant women over the years.

Juliet, however, didn't seem to have. She walked up to them before Sara's pregnancy registered and Tanner knew the moment it did.

"Juliet, sweetheart." He had to cover for her. Nothing was worse than the pity. "This is Sara. Tank's wife."

"Ah, yes. I remember. We met last summer, I believe." Juliet handed him his beer and pasted that beauty queen smile onto her face so quick that the only reason he'd seen the anguish in her eyes was because he knew her so well.

"At Maryellen's bridal shower?"

"I think it was the Tim Jackson's graduation party. His MBA?"

"Oh, right. That's it. I forgot. Too many parties, and now with all these hormones rushing through me…" Sara rubbed her belly. "I'll be glad when this one is born and this whole placenta-brain syndrome goes away."

"Placenta brain?" Juliet cocked her head.

Tank sighed and put his arm around his wife's

shoulders. "Sara's convinced that her forgetfulness is due to the fact that she's pregnant. Says her ma told her once you get knocked up, your brain goes to mush."

Tanner would give anything to change the conversation, but he didn't know what to change it to. Or how. Sara and Tank were obviously very happy about the impending birth—and who could blame them—but it just hurt so damn much. And he could feel Juliet tense beneath his palm when he slipped an arm around her shoulders.

"Oh, hush, Tank. Don't go making me out to be some dingbat. Everyone knows pregnant women are a little forgetful. It's what happens when you're growing a person inside you. Do you have children?" she asked oh-so-innocently to Juliet.

He felt the breath Juliet took. Felt her shoulders stiffen.

And was proud as all get-out at the steadiness of her voice when she answered.

"Not yet, no. But we're looking forward to it."

It was the perfect thing to say. If she'd said *no*, as he often had, there were the "Oh, you don't know what you're missing" comments, and if he came clean about losing Keegan, well, it was uncomfortable for everyone. Saying they were looking forward to it one day was a common denominator and no one ever took offense to it.

But he could feel how much it cost Juliet to act so nonchalant. Her backbone was as stiff as he'd been this morning.

Probably not a good comparison for him to make.

Of course Delia would take that moment to show up. "Hi, y'all. Having fun?"

"Loads." Tanner guzzled half his beer.

"Now, Tanner Wentworth, is that sarcasm I hear? You always were the king of the one-liners, weren't you?"

"Was I?" He took another swig. They should have arrived late. Waited for everyone else to get here—actually they had planned to, but Delia had "accidentally" told them the wrong time since the party started at four-thirty. Thank God Tank and J.D. had been early, too, so they'd had people to talk to besides Gossip Hound Delia.

"You know, I forgot to ask if you two have had any more kids since high school?"

Tanner set his beer on the stone wall beside him. It was either that or bash the woman over the head with it.

They shouldn't have come. He'd let his desire to reconnect with old friends make him forget who and what Delia really was.

"Oh, but I thought you said you didn't have kids?" Poor Sara looked extremely confused. And poor Tank looked like he wanted to drink an entire keg.

"Let's go get something to eat, Sara." Tank clapped Tanner on the shoulder. "Sorry, man. Juliet." He nodded to her then ushered his wife away.

"Oh, dear, did I say something wrong?" Delia had been in beauty pageants, too, but she hadn't mastered the smile quite like Juliet.

"You know exactly what you said—"

"Tanner." Juliet put her hand on his arm and squeezed. Three times.

"Delia, since you haven't had children, I'm going to believe that you don't understand what a painful subject this is for Tanner and I. So please, let's not go into it, and if you'd not bring it up again, Tanner and I would greatly appreciate it."

He'd never been more proud of Juliet than he was at this moment. There was no reason to give Delia an out; the woman knew exactly what she was doing. She'd wanted to beat Juliet at so many things over the years and had always come in second that she'd seen her chance to hurt Juliet and had taken it.

Yet Juliet, who would be absolutely justified in lashing out at her, didn't. She didn't give Delia any more fuel for her fire, and she maintained her composure while giving the woman an extremely veiled—but extremely potent—put-down. Which was way more charitable than what he'd wanted to say.

Delia glanced at him and the first sign of remorse showed up in her botox-ed face. "I… I'm sorry. You're right; I wasn't thinking."

Oh she'd been thinking; she just hadn't been thinking of exactly what reaction she'd get. What emotions she'd unleash.

If it weren't so painful to think of not having Keegan in his life, he might let her comment go. Because for now, with this conversation, he and Juliet were together in the way they'd been pretending to be. But he couldn't let Delia get away with it; that'd just open the door to more insults and spitefulness.

"I think we should go." He slid his hand to the small of Juliet's waist, the fabric of her sundress thin enough that he could feel the heat of her skin. "Sweetheart? If you want—"

"No." Juliet's back got even straighter, though Tanner didn't know how that was possible. "I'm not going to let one unthoughtful comment make me leave. You wanted to see your friends, so we will." She picked up his beer bottle and handed it to him. "If you'll excuse us, Delia, I see the Markinsons have arrived."

Tanner bit back the words he wanted to say, following Juliet's lead. But if Delia—or anyone for that matter—tried to hurt Juliet by mentioning Keegan again, they'd answer to him.

Juliet let out the breath she'd been holding when she was on the other side of the pool deck. Delia was a straight-up bitch. She'd made plenty of snide comments couched as concerns after Juliet had gotten pregnant, but Juliet hadn't cared because the baby was Tanner's. Nothing could have touched her back then. Her life had been going along exactly as she'd wanted.

And now it wasn't, so of course, Delia would swoop in like the bottom-feeder she was. Thank God, though, that she'd revealed her true nature to Tanner. That was one woman Juliet could strike off the list of Tanner's possible next wives—

Oh, God. What if he did move back here and married someone else? He said he'd scout out a location for BeefCake, Inc. in town; would he stay to run it?

That thought hit her in the gut and she stumbled.

His arm shot around her. "You okay?"

The concern on his face was genuine and it gave her a modicum of hope that maybe he still cared about her.

"I'm fine. Now." She took a step back. Just one. But it could have been a thousand for the chasm it opened between them.

"Delia's a bitch."

"You're right."

"We shouldn't have come." He raked a hand through his hair then kneaded the back of his neck. He did that when he was pissed.

Many times, she'd removed his hand and massage his neck herself. But those were the good ol' days. "Nonsense, Tan. We never let her define us back in the day; we're not going to start now."

"*We* didn't?" He stopped kneading and looked at her. "That's not how I remember it."

"What are you talking about?"

"You can't honestly tell me you don't remember?"

"Remember what?" She remembered a lot of things.

"How you used to grill me about her. If she'd come to football practice, or had shown up at the pancake house after those late-night games."

"I…" She clamped her mouth shut. She had said those things to him. He, however, had laughed her off. Told her she was imagining things.

She hadn't been. Delia had wanted him back then and she wanted him now.

But the difference was… Tanner didn't want Delia. And hadn't wanted her back then, either. Juliet could see that with an eleven-year perspective. Delia had been the snake, and Tanner her non-willing prey.

"I owe you an apology, Tanner. Well, many. But I'm sorry I ever listened to her. *And* that I didn't listen to you about her."

"I told you she was bad news. That she wanted to *be* you. She still does."

That had Juliet chuckling and not in a good way. "Too bad she doesn't know the truth."

"The truth?"

"That my life isn't anywhere near what she thinks it is, and that you're here only for Nana. But, hey, she can set her sights on you once… well, once there's no longer any need for our subterfuge."

"If you think I'd have even the slightest interest in her, you really haven't changed at all." He downed the rest of the bottle. "I need another beer."

He didn't ask her if she wanted one when he left.

Damn it. Why couldn't she say or do the right thing around Tanner? Why'd she have to bring up the past?

A burst of laughter by the big built-in grill had her looking around at all their high school friends. Half the football team was here, lounging on the pool chairs or playing bocce on the almost-golf-course-perfect lawn or hanging at the no-expense-spared tiki bar attached to the pool house. Hell, being here with all of them, she and Tanner were *mired* in the past.

So much for moving forward.

"Hey, Juliet." Tamra, J.D.'s wife, walked up to her and gave her a hug. Tamra had figured out a while ago that things were not what the seemed, but she'd promised not to say a word—even to J.D.

Juliet wasn't sure how she felt about a husband and wife having secrets from each other, but what did she know? Tamra's marriage was going strong after ten years and Juliet's had never gotten off the ground.

That damn plane-trip-for-one. She'd never forget the

humiliation of being on a honeymoon by herself . Of having to get their luggage off the baggage claim carousel and into their villa. The pitying looks from the staff—and having to see Tanner's suitcases every day of the seven she'd been there. *And* schlep them home. Alone.

So if not telling J.D. was a good plan according to Tamra, Juliet couldn't argue with it. Maybe she ought to take pointers from Tamra.

"I see he's been attentive all evening. Does this mean you guys are going to try to work it out?"

Sandy was the only one who knew the whole truth, but Sandy was single and hadn't been around for all the backstory as it'd unfolded all those years ago. Tamra had been, so it'd been easy to confide in her, but it'd also been more humiliation piled on top of other humiliation. Juliet wasn't up for another round.

But when the eventual did happen, when word got around that she and Tanner had split, some truths would come out. It wasn't as if she was going to be able to hide from the gossip. Might as well enjoy the positivity and happiness now before it all went away. "We're talking."

"And he agreed to come here with you."

"Actually, he wanted to come more than I did." She fiddled with the top button on the bodice of her dress. "I couldn't say no."

"Of course not. That'd be taking five steps back. And if he wants to renew the relationships with his old friends, it could be that he's thinking long-term."

But long-term didn't mean long-term with her.

"We'll see. Taking it one day at a time." Juliet snagged a scallop wrapped in bacon from a passing server. "So how are things with you? What are the kids up to?"

Kids were always a painful subject for her, especially if the person she was talking to knew about Keegan, but to ignore other people's kids made the issue bigger. And she didn't want to pretend Keegan hadn't existed because he had.

Agony gripped her in the gut; it never failed to. And the shitty thing was, no matter what people promised her, the pain never lessened. Not that she really wanted it to. Because the pain—at the same level of intensity—kept Keegan alive for her. It kept him with her, as if it were yesterday. Those few precious moments when she'd held him and he'd been so beautiful and she could pretend he'd been asleep.

She grabbed a glass of champagne from the next waiter who walked by. She wasn't planning to get drunk, but a little alcohol could help with the pain.

Hmmm, maybe she ought to grab a couple of cases to keep around the house for the next few weeks. Lord knew, she was definitely going to need it.

"Geez, it's good to see you." Rick Stangler clasped Tanner on the shoulder and shook his hand. "You're the last one we'd thought would high-tail it out of town after graduation. Nice of you to show your face."

"Hey, been busy, you know. Lots to accomplish." Painful memories to run from.

Maybe he should have stayed. Looking around at most of the football team, he realized he'd isolated himself. Maybe it would have been better to hang out here among friends. Drown his sorrows with his buddies, the guys who understood him, instead of running off and trying to forget his past. Pretend it didn't exist.

But right here, this was proof that it did. Hell, Keegan and Juliet were proof that it did. He couldn't run from his past any more than he could run from the pain. He'd put it out of sight, sure, but it was always there, hovering below the surface.

"Can't believe you took a job that has you traveling so much. I mean, shit, Tan, you got Juliet. Finally. All yours, nice and legal. We thought for sure we hadn't seen you because you guys were you know…" He nudged him with his elbow.

"Yo, Rick. Enough. She's my wife." The words just

flew out of his mouth as if it was the most natural thing in the world to say.

Sadly, it was.

Talk about pain.

"No shit, Tan." Rick tilted his beer bottle at him. "Which is why I can't believe you've been travelling so much you couldn't even bother to get together once in the past, what? Seven years? I mean, it's not as if you guys moved to another state or something."

Yeah it was—"I, uh, had some… things to handle. Deal with. You know." He swigged his beer again.

Rick looked as if someone had nailed him in the nuts. "Aw, jeez, Tan, I'm sorry. I guess that was insensitive of me. Molly's always saying I talk before I think. I didn't think. I'm sorry, man."

Tanner kept the beer going in. "Yeah, thanks."

"Hey, Tan." Alcon James clapped him on the shoulder and grabbed a beer out of the cooler on the ledge beside him. "Didya hear about Mickelson? Got drafted in the tenth, then crashed the car he bought with the signing bonus. Was out before he ever played. Tough break, you know?"

Tanner knew all about tough breaks. Still, that was no reason to visit his misery on anyone else. "What's he doing now?"

The talk continued about them and their friends. Who was doing what, who was married to whom—who was divorcing whom—but Tanner felt removed from it all. As if he didn't belong here anymore.

Juliet wasn't having a picnic here either. He'd seen her drink at least three flutes of champagne. She'd never been a big drinker and he'd noticed there wasn't any wine at her place when he'd been looking for a glass for the water last night. That much about her hadn't changed, at least.

So her drinking now probably wasn't a good idea. Especially for keeping the secrets she'd want to keep.

He shouldn't have come. Should have left well enough alone, hung out at Juliet's or gone to the gym, and done his duty by her grandmother. Just bide his time until this was over and he could go home.

"Excuse me, guys." He placed his empty bottle on one of the platters set around the pool deck to collect used utensils and plates and glasses, then headed over to his wife.

His wife.

The words sounded strange to him. He used to practice them in the mirror—if any of the guys had found out they would have laughed him out of town. Juliet had written *Juliet Wentworth* all over her folders and notebooks in girlish, swirly cursive; if he'd done that his teammates would have taken away his Man Card, but he'd been just as nutso about her. So, yeah, he'd practiced calling her his wife in the privacy of his room, picturing what it'd be like when they were finally married.

Never in his wildest dreams had he conjured up this scenario.

"Hey, sweetheart." He swooped in with a kiss to her neck to distract her while he took the flute from her hand so she wouldn't complain.

That flush on her cheeks when he came up for air said there would be no complaining.

Or it could just be the effects of the champagne.

But what was *his* excuse?

"Nice to see you, too, Tanner." Tamra smirked at him. "Quite the greeting for the woman you've been married to for seven years."

He looked at her. Did she know something? "Tamra." He tucked Juliet's arm around his waist. "Mind if I steal Juliet away?"

"Be my guest." She raised her eyebrows as he steered Juliet toward a small café table in a grove of potted palms Delia had probably rented for the occasion.

Yeah, Tamra knew something.

"Tanner, that wasn't nice." Juliet's words were a bit slurred.

"Neither is getting drunk at Delia's party." He put his

hand in the small of her back to steady her. At least, that was his story.

"I'm not drunk."

"Let's keep it that way."

"Let go." She shoved him, but he had his arm locked around her.

"Juliet, don't create a scene."

"Why not?" She shoved some hair off her face with the palm of her hand, not the delicate, graceful Juliet he'd always known. "Delia would love it. And then no one will be surprised when you leave. I should put on a really good show. And maybe you could even leave now. I can tell Nana you got called away on business. She'd believe me. She always believes me."

"I'm not going to do that and you know it. Otherwise you wouldn't have asked me to come in the first place. You love your grandmother; you wouldn't do anything to hurt her. And neither would I."

Juliet's big blue eyes filled with tears and that full bottom lip that he'd loved to suck on pouted. "I don't ever want to hurt anyone. Never ever."

Oh boy. Those three glasses of champagne had gone straight to her head. She'd always been a lightweight; he didn't know why he thought time would have changed that.

Because time had changed other things about Juliet.

He wasn't going to think about that. "Come on, Jules. I think we should leave."

"I don't wanna." She hopped onto one of the stools.

Her dress hiked up her legs, revealing more tanned, toned thighs—

"Jules."

She draped her bare arms on his shoulders. "I like when you call me that, Tanner. No one else does."

That's because she hated the name. He'd only started calling her that when he hadn't known how to tell her he'd liked her back in fifth grade. So he'd annoyed her.

Stupid, really, but pre-pubescent boys weren't known for their logic and analytical thinking. It'd gotten her to pay attention to him, so he'd kept doing it.

Later, it had become a term of endearment that she liked. Something just between them. Like the three taps.

She'd tapped him earlier that way. He hadn't responded. Because those three taps had shot straight to his gut with a *thud*. Not so much her touch—because it was a "barely there" touch—but what those taps meant.

God, if only he could still trust in that sentiment.

"Let's go home, Jules. I've had enough."

"You? Had enough? Tanner, you never drink too much."

"I didn't mean alcohol."

She leveled her gaze with his, her perfect lips twisting sideways as she tried to figure out what he meant.

"Ohhhhh…" She tapped him on his lips. "Gotcha. Okay, then, we can go. We should say goodbye to Delia." She hopped down and would have taken off, but he caught her at the waist.

"Really? You want to give her a chance to comment on the amount of champagne you've had?"

Juliet shoved her fist to her hip. "I haven't had a lot of champagne."

"For other people, no, you haven't. But your limit is one and you've had three times that amount."

"You were counting?"

"I was watching. Alcohol tends to loosen tongues and we don't want to blow our cover story."

She licked her lips. "Is it going to loosen *your* tongue, Tanner?"

He didn't say anything. He couldn't.

It took her a few seconds before she realized what she'd said.

Her hand flew to her lip sand those gorgeous blue eyes opened wide. "Ooops. I didn't mean—"

"It's okay, Julies. Let's just get out of here."

For a second, the briefest possible second, he heard those words and imagined an entirely different meaning.

One that stuck with him the entire drive back to her place.

Chapter Fifteen

I wouldn't mind, you know. If the beer loosened your tongue." Juliet trailed her hand along the hood of her Mercedes as she headed toward her front door. "I mean, we *are* still married."

Not a safe topic. Best not to say anything. It was the champagne talking for Juliet, but if he spoke, it'd be all him. And with what he'd like to say…

Man, if only they *could* just have sex. Just jump into bed and scratch that itch, as it were.

"Tanner? Did you hear me?" She planted both hands on the hood of the car behind her and leaned back, trying to be provocative if her statement was anything to go by…

She was succeeding, dammit. But it wasn't a surprise. Juliet was sexy no matter what she did. She could be covered in mud and she'd be beautiful.

Dammit. He didn't need this. Bad enough he was still attracted to her, but to have her basically offering everything he wanted—

And everything he didn't. He couldn't trust her. Trust was huge. The biggest part of a relationship after attraction and respect.

So you're attracted to her and you respect who she's become. Trust can be rebuilt.

His damn libido again. If he listened to it, he'd never get out of bed.

And that would be a bad thing, why?

Because he didn't take advantage of people, and doing anything with Juliet right now would be taking advantage of her.

Do you hear yourself? Dude, she took advantage of you. Your feelings, your trust, your future. Turnabout is fair play.

He shut down the voice. Shut down the images. Shut down the temptation.

"Tanner?"

Shut down Juliet—by grabbing one of her arms and tugging her after him into her house, ignoring the top button that had come undone, threatening to give him more than a peek at what was beneath the bodice. "Coffee, Juliet. Now."

She stumbled after him. "I don't have coffee."

"Tea, then. I know you have tea."

"I don't want tea. It's already too hot out."

It was too hot *in*, but that didn't seem to register with her.

Or maybe it did…

"You've had too much champagne."

"Is there really such a thing as too much champagne?" She giggled after that, trailing her fingertips along the back of the railing up her front porch.

"Yes. There is. And you're the poster child for it." He held out his hand. "Inside."

She made a big production of exhaling as she tried to sweep past him in her best Southern belle flounce. He'd always loved watching her do that because she was so damn cute when she did it.

Things hadn't changed in that arena.

"You're pretty bossy. And it's not even your house." She leaned against the back of the chair that divided her living room from her foyer and crossed her arms.

That motion had been designed by the devil to tempt men more than any apple could have. And he was no saint.

"Juliet, please. You've had a little too much to drink. Let's get you some tea and you'll feel better."

"I feel just fine, thank you very much." She crossed her arms the other way and the bodice gaped dangerously. "And I don't need any tea."

"Yes, you do."

"Why? Whatcha gonna do about it if I don't drink it? You going to punish me, Tanner?"

The comment tossed images of her on her stomach, with that sweet ass in the air and—

No, he'd never be able to hurt Juliet. Not even if she begged him.

Jesus, man, you got it bad. Question is, what are you going to do about it? The woman is straight-out coming on to you. You gonna turn her down?

As much as it pained him—and he meant that literally—yes, he was going to turn her down. It'd be one thing if she were in full command of her faculties, but compromised?

No way in hell.

Tanner Wentworth didn't take advantage of drunk women.

He'd never had to and he wasn't going to start now. Especially with his wife.

Juliet heard herself say the words and wondered where her nerve came from.

Uh, the bottom of three glasses of champagne?

Actually, it might have been four.

Probably not the best idea to drink that much, but with Delia's comments and having to put up a front for their friends... man, did it feel good right about now.

Tanner felt good right about now.

She stood up and uncrossed her arms. Tanner liked her boobs. And she liked him liking them. And if he could focus on them instead of the past, if he could be in the moment now, maybe, just maybe, they could get beyond the mistakes she'd made and move forward. Together.

It was a shot she wanted desperately to take and if the champagne was giving her the balls to say what she wanted to say, what did she have to lose?

"So whatcha gonna do, Tan? Whatsamatter? Can't come up with anything? That's not like you." She walked toward him and ran her finger along his beltline. "It wouldn't be wrong, you know."

He squeezed his eyes shut and she made sure to brush her hair against his bicep. He'd always liked her to trail her hair over his skin. Mostly in other, um, more sensitive areas, but Tanner loved her hair. Loved bunching it up in his fist to keep her in one place...

"Juliet." His voice was tight. "Stop."

"Whatever you say." She stopped all right. Right beside him. Facing him. So her breasts were on either side of his arm.

A muscled in his jaw ticked. "Where's the tea?"

"In the kitchen. But I really don't want any."

"But *I* really want you to have some."

So he said, yet he didn't take a step away.

She tilted her head and her hair slid over her shoulder, the ends brushing his arm again.

She caught a quick shiver. "Why?"

"Why?"

"Yeah, why? Why do you want me to have tea?"

"To sober you up."

"Well maybe I don't want to be sobered up. Not yet anyway."

He looked down at her then, his brows arching and, if she wasn't mistaken, interest in his eyes.

She didn't want to be mistaken. She also didn't want to be imagining things. It was one thing if he was interested; it was entirely something else if he was humoring her.

He swallowed. Hard.

He wasn't humoring her.

He also wasn't avoiding her.

She wanted to make the first move. But even with all the champagne, she couldn't. It had to come from him. Otherwise he'd blame her for leading him on.

"Juliet…"

"I promise I won't tell if you won't." She tacked on a smile to make it easy for him. So he wouldn't see all her hopes and dreams tied up in this conversation.

One kiss. That was all she wanted. All she needed. All they needed. He'd take one kiss and he'd see—

"No." He shook his head and cleared his throat, and this time, he did step back. "No."

"Really?" Nothing like a buzz-kill to kill her buzz. And she couldn't believe it. He'd really turned away from her? Really didn't want to kiss her? Well thank God she'd had the four glasses of champagne. She might just want to go find a few more to drown the rest of her sorrows since the effect of those three had suddenly—and drastically—been reduced thanks to his lack of interest.

Tanner swallowed hard again. Clenched his fists. Rolled his head like he did back in the day to loosen it before a game to ease the tension.

Maybe he wasn't as disinterested as he was trying to be.

"Okay, Tanner, I guess I can't force you to want to kiss me." She flipped her hair back and let the strap of her dress slip over her shoulder, putting as much *blasé* into her little speech as she could muster. Let him think it was no big deal. He'd stew on that. And then he'd—

Kiss her.

By pulling her toward him with a hand on the back of her neck, his lips grinding down on hers, and his rock-hard chest pressed against her aching breasts, he ran his hand down her back and cupped her butt and pulled her against him where she felt—

Oh yeah. He wanted her.

Juliet sighed into his mouth, giving his tongue the entrance they both wanted. She slid her fingers thorough his hair, loving the way it curled over them, a bit longer than before. She stroked her thumb along his jaw, feeling his mouth open to devour hers, his tongue sweeping through hers, demanding hers dance with it.

God, she'd always loved kissing Tanner. The one time she'd played spin-the-bottle and had to kiss J.D. and Rick hadn't been anything like the first kiss with Tanner. Sparks had flown, colors had burst behind her eyelids, and goose bumps had set up camp all over her skin.

Just like now.

She tugged his hair, trying to get closer. She grabbed his butt, dragging him against her and—hell—she wanted to do a lot more with Tanner than this.

He backed her up against the chair, practically bending her over it with the force of his kiss.

She wanted his hands on her breasts. Wanted him to drag her shirt over her head and lick and tease and kiss and suck them until her legs gave out. She wanted to be naked and writhing with Tanner and she wanted to give him such pleasure he'd never think about leaving again.

He tried to drag his lips off hers. "We need to stop."

She wouldn't let him go, sucking his bottom lip into her mouth as she shook her head. "That's the one thing we shouldn't do."

He gripped her arms and Juliet had a feeling that, no matter what she said, she wouldn't get him to change his mind.

Then do something...

She pressed her breasts against his chest. Wrapped one leg around his calf. Groaned as she opened her own mouth beneath his, ready to beg for this. One night. That's all. Just one more night.

Tanner slid his hand around her back again as he took the kiss deeper.

But only for a few seconds.

Then he was pulling away, straightening, and running a hand across his mouth.

Erasing the taste of her?

Well, damn. Juliet let her foot drop to the floor.

"That was a very bad idea."

"I didn't think so." She wasn't going to pretend that flame didn't exist between them. His brain might have taken over at the end and put a stop to their kiss, but his body had recognized what it wanted and had been on its way to get it. And she would have let him.

She put her palm against his cheek. "You still turn me on, Tanner. And we're both adults. There are no illusions about what this is. You're divorcing me in a few weeks; this doesn't have to be anything more than tonight."

He opened his mouth to say something but then closed it.

He did it again.

"I…" The third time was the charm as he finally managed a full sentence. "I don't even know how to reply to that."

"Perhaps you don't have to. Maybe all you have to do is kiss me again and the answer will come to us."

"We can't get involved, Juliet."

"Oh, Tanner, don't try to fool yourself. We're already involved. We have been since we were kids and even if you divorce me, we always will be. We're a huge part of each other's life; that's never going to go away."

"Then we shouldn't complicate it."

"What's complicated about it? I want you; you want me. Not complicated at all."

"The emotions—"

"So leave emotion out of it." Brave words when this was *all* about emotion for her. And if she could just get the two of them into bed together, that could happen on its own.

Oh, God. What was she doing? Trying to manipulate

his feelings again? Use their lovemaking to keep him? That hadn't worked well before; it definitely wouldn't now.

"Tanner, I'm… I'm sorry." This time, *she* was the one who stepped away. She was the one who clenched her fists and straightened her shoulders. The one who took a long, deep look into his eyes and saw the fight going on inside of him, and she was the one who walked away.

If Tanner wanted her, it had to be of his own volition, not because she'd coerced or manipulated or forced him to want her.

"Juliet. Wait."

Chapter Sixteen

She froze. Didn't turn around, didn't take a breath. Didn't hope.

She heard him sigh. Heard him scratch his head in that rough way he did when he was thinking hard. Heard him walk up behind her.

"I want you."

Glory be and hallelujah! She wanted to shout it from the rooftops.

Instead, she took a deep breath of her own and slowly turned to face him. "And…?"

He arched an eyebrow. "And? I thought that statement was pretty self-explanatory."

"Well, Tanner, it really isn't a secret that you want me. Some things you've never been able to hide from me." She resisted glancing down at his pants, but only because she wanted to see what was in his eyes. Wanted to see if there was anger or derision or, God forbid, loathing, but what she saw…

It took her breath away.

"No strings." He took a step closer and raised a palm to her cheek. "It won't change anything between us. We're still getting a divorce when this is all over."

She didn't want to think about anything being over, but Nana's illness had brought home the fact that she couldn't take anything for granted. That there might not *be* a tomorrow so she shouldn't live with regrets. And if all she could have of Tanner was this one night, she was going to take it.

She couldn't *not* take it. "I understand."

"Don't go getting any ideas that this is going to be a happily-ever-after. I have a life elsewhere that I intend to go back to."

Except for the fact that he was talking about opening up a franchise here.

But she wasn't going to mention that. Not now.

"I understand, Tanner."

"Do you? Are you sure? Or is this the champagne talking?"

She mulled that around in her brain. Ran her tongue along her teeth and the inside of her cheeks. Not a trace of champagne to be found and her mind was as clear as day. Somewhere along the line, the haze of alcohol had given way to the haze of seduction and that was one she'd much prefer any day. "Not a lick of champagne to be had. Kissing me senseless has the added bonus of sobering me up, remember?"

It was as if she'd said some magic word or something because Tanner was on her so quickly, she couldn't catch a breath.

Not that it mattered; she would've lost it anyway.

God, she loved kissing him. Loved being held by him, caught up in his big, strong arms that had swept her off her feet more times than she could count.

She was adding one more to the list because sweep her he did.

And then he was moving. Across the living room and nudging the door to her bedroom open with his foot, then striding to the bed and standing her on it.

"On your knees, woman," he growled when his hands slid to her butt.

She wrapped her arms around his neck and lowered herself to her knees so their mouths were at the perfect height.

Tanner claimed them as if he were starving. She ought to know because she was.

He'd tasted amazing out there in the living room, but that had been a questioning kiss. One she wasn't sure would be repeated. This one, however… He was here, in her bedroom, and he'd stay for as long as it took them to fully enjoy each other.

For Juliet, that would be about eighty years.

"Touch me, Tanner." That *could* be the remnants of the champagne talking, but Juliet doubted it. She didn't need any false courage to want Tanner, and now that he was here, onboard with the plan, she *definitely* didn't. The chemistry between them would take care of the rest.

His hand slid over her collarbone, his fingers dancing along it delicately, but with enough fire to make her burn. And enough deliberateness to make her impatient.

"Lower."

"I'm getting there, babe. Don't be in such a hurry."

Seven years and he *wasn't* in a hurry? Either she didn't do to him what he did to her or the man had plans for her.

She shivered, praying it was the latter.

Then she shivered again because his lips moved to her throat, mouthing kisses down it, following the path his fingers had taken.

The fingers that were finally moving lower.

Her breasts ached, swelling for his touch, her nipples peaking even before he got to them, fire sizzling through her and spiraling down to her core. God, she wanted him.

"Jesus, Juliet, you still smell the same. Those damn bluebonnets."

She didn't know why they were damned; he'd always loved them before. Loved the memory of that field they'd made love in.

She shivered again when he slid the strap of her dress off her shoulder.

"I want you naked."

Well so did she.

Juliet let go of his shoulders—reluctantly, but it was for the greater good for both of them. The quicker she got naked, the quicker he would, too, and then they'd both be happy.

She undid the buttons up from her waistline, her fingers meeting his mouth between her breasts.

He nipped her fingers and she slid them in and out of his lips for a few seconds before the temptation to be naked won out, and she tugged her fingers away so she could shrug out of the sleeves of her dress

"Beautiful." His hot breath slid over her breasts, her nipples straining against the fabric of her bra.

She raised her hands to undo the front clasp, but Tanner waved them away. "Allow me."

Oh she'd allow him anything his heart desired.

One twist of his fingers and her bra was open and then, thankyoulord, his hands were on her breasts, stroking them, clutching them, tugging at her nipples.

She'd always had sensitive nipples, but it'd been seven long years—if he kept doing that any longer, it was going to be over before she was ready for it to be.

"I want to touch you." She ran her hands down his sides, bunching the golf shirt at the hem and shoving it up, running her hands up his abs. "You have great abs."

"Glad you approve."

There was a chuckle in his voice—they'd always been playful during sex, but she wasn't in a chuckling mood. She was in a growling mood. A nipping mood. An I-want-to-rip-your-clothes-off mood.

She didn't rip his shirt, exactly, but she did rip it off over his head and flung it around her room somewhere. She'd worry about that later.

"Oh, God, Tan. It's been so long." She hadn't meant to mention the time frame because she didn't want him thinking exactly how long it had been, but she couldn't help herself. She'd had her memories, but nothing—not even that show he'd put on for the couple dozen or so women in the nightclub—could compare to the actual experience of running her palms along those smooth, taut muscles and that dusting of blond hair that felt so good against her breasts.

And her lips.

Tanner groaned. Then sucked in a breath when she found his nipple. "Damn, woman."

"You like this." It wasn't a question because she knew exactly what he liked.

He groaned when she cupped him.

Moaned when she ran her hand along the length of him.

Hissed when she stroked him through his shorts.

"Let's get these off." She needed to touch him. Needed to be mashed up next to him and feel how much he wanted her.

Needed to take him inside her… and never let go.

Who was she kidding? She'd never let him go even when she should have and she probably never would. The divorce would be tough, but she'd have this memory to help her get through it.

She worked the button on his waistband, loving the way his stomach muscles contracted as her knuckles brushed against him.

"You're killing me, Jules."

"You are *not* dying on me, Tanner Wentworth. Don't even think about it."

His breathing got harsh as she slid the zipper down, being ever so careful because she knew he often went commando.

Today was no different.

"Oh, my," she breathed as she captured the weight of him in her palm.

Oh my indeed. This *was* hers. *He* was hers. And she had to make him see that. They were too good together for a divorce. And she didn't mean just physically. But this was her starting point, so she'd go with it.

"Shit."

Or not…

Juliet looked up at him. "What?" *Please don't ask me to stop. Please please please don't ask that. Anything but that.*

"Condom."

Condom. Dammit. She knew she should have bought them, but she didn't want it to look as if she'd been prepping for this. Manipulating him into it. "I don't have any."

"I do."

Her eyes shot to his. "You do?" Dare she hope? Had *he* been planning this?

He nodded and pulled back out of her grasp.

She had to let him go.

"Occupational hazard. If I have to fill in for someone and need to change costumes, I don't want my junk coming in contact with fabric someone else's junk has been in contact with. So I wear condoms."

"Well." She sat back on her thighs and shoved her dress down to her knees. "The unknown facts about exotic dancers. Most people would think you're all about wild sex and letting it all hang out. Interesting to know you, um, cover up, as it were."

"Is that what you think, Juliet? That I'm all about free love with anyone?"

"Tanner, if I thought that, we wouldn't be here right now. Can you please go get those condoms?"

"Con*doms*? Plural?"

She cocked her head, letting her hair fall over one breast. "When have you ever known us to need only one?"

"Good point."

She thought so. She also thought about *plural* condoms so she could make love to him until he couldn't see straight so he'd never be able to walk away again. She hoped he brought enough.

Maybe she ought to pick up a few boxes the next time she was out in case he hadn't.

As she shimmied out of her dress, her body was

humming at the thought of making love with him—not just now, but tomorrow. The day after. Every day until he decided to leave—

Or decided he *didn't* want to leave.

Don't go there, Juliet. Don't open your heart up to even more heartbreak. Bad enough you're going to be crying over this when he leaves, let's not add unrealistic expectations to the mix. You're an adult now. You know how this works. Enjoy the moment and let the future take care of itself. If you'd done that years ago, you wouldn't be in this mess.

Her conscience was seriously threatening to kill her buzz altogether—the sexual one, not the alcohol one because the champagne was long out of her system.

Thankfully, Tanner walked back into the room then. "Here we go." He held up a couple of foil packets. "Do you have a color preference?"

"No. Just grab one and get back here." She sat back up on her knees and held out her hand.

Tanner sucked in a harsh breath as he dropped the condoms in her palm. "God, Jules, you are beautiful."

"You make me feel beautiful." It was true. Yes, she knew what she looked like—she *did* look in the mirror after all, and after having gone through the pageant circuit, she couldn't *not* be aware of her looks—but Tanner made her feel beautiful in ways all the accolades and pretty words couldn't. He made her feel wanted—and not because of her looks, though she did like that he liked looking at her, that he found her pretty enough to stare at for hours on end. Which he'd done back in the day. She would call it the blush of first love, but that feeling had never gone away. No matter how many people told her she was pretty or beautiful, only Tanner's opinion mattered. She wanted to be pretty for him.

She set all but one condom on the nightstand then held out her hand to him. "Let me make you feel beautiful."

He shoved his shorts down his legs and reached for the condom.

"Let me." She tore the foil then unrolled the condom down the length of him, loving how he jerked under her hands. Loving the hard, pulsing strength of him in her grip. God, how she wanted him inside her.

He slid his hand beneath her neck and tugged her closer. "Damn it, woman, you drive me insane."

She was going to go with a good *insane* instead of the one he actually might mean, because she was going to enjoy this. Reality would come back soon enough.

She wrapped her arms around his back as he kissed her, his tongue making the motions she wanted that part that was pressed against her ribcage to make inside her.

She gripped his butt and pulled him closer, wanting to get him off balance and fall onto her, taking her down onto the bed, his weight covering her.

"Careful, babe," he said as he did fall over her, bracing himself with his palms planted on the mattress. "I don't want to hurt you."

She clamped both hands behind his neck and pulled him down onto her, not wanting to think about getting hurt. That was probably a given, but not now. Now was all about making each other feel good.

"I want you inside me, Tanner."

The words sparked a frenzy she hadn't expected. Oh, she appreciated it, but all of a sudden, Tanner was on top of her, his cock pressing against her abdomen so insistently, and he was kissing her as if he couldn't get enough of her.

Juliet kissed him back almost desperately, but then, maybe she was. This *had* to go well. It had to open some doors for them. To at least the possibility of… what? Staying married? Living together?

Juliet! Get your head back to this *moment. Now. Not the future. You can't count on the future, so enjoy what you have now.*

"Move back some." Tanner said it harshly while sliding a hand under her back and lifting her toward the head of the bed.

She scrambled as best she could to help him move her, the action bringing her into contact with most of his body. Every place he touched her lit up like a fireworks display. God, she wanted this man. This one. No other. There'd never been anyone else for her, not even those four years he'd been away at college. Oh, she'd dated a few guys, but she'd never done more than kiss them—because kissing them hadn't been better than kissing Tanner, and none of their kisses had led her to losing her mind with desire like one kiss from Tanner could.

And he was doing a whole lot more than kissing her now.

His hand raked down her arm to clasp her fingers. He brought their joined hands up between them and he kissed each finger, then flattened her palm against his chest. "Touch me, Juliet."

She needed no further urging. Palm flat against his pectoral, she circled his nipple, feeling it tighten. Tanner liked her to play with his nipples and she was more than happy to oblige.

She wiggled some more, opening her legs so he could lay between them, and she brought her other hand up to his other pec.

"God, yes, Jules. It feels so good."

He propped himself up on his palms, his back arched so his lower half was in direct contact with hers.

She circled his nipples again, flicking them when he groaned.

"God, yes, babe, that's it."

It *was* it; she could feel the growing evidence against her.

She wanted him inside her so badly. Had imagined it for years and now… Now… It might finally happen.

She opened her legs a little more, lifted one heel onto the back of his calf.

It did the trick. He slammed a kiss onto her mouth and thrust up inside her.

Juliet froze. The sensation… It was almost painful. Almost too tight. But the way he filled her… Maybe it wasn't so much a physical filling as an emotional one. He filled her. In every way. Her body, her mind… her heart.

She would never stop loving Tanner. Never. And as he thrust inside her—as he made love to her—she tried to show him that in every way she could without saying it. Because saying it would send him running.

She wrapped her legs around him to keep him in place and matched his rhythm.

"Ah, Juliet." He nuzzled her cheek. "You are so beautiful."

She smiled then because she couldn't *not* smile. "I l—"The words were almost too easy to say. "I like that you think so, Tanner." She blinked back some tears that were building behind her eyes. She couldn't cry in front of him. He knew her. Knew her too well. Had teased her about crying when they made love; said it was all the love she had inside her that came spilling out.

It was so very true.

She reached up to kiss him, needing to not speak because she couldn't trust herself not to say the words she so very much wanted to say.

He kissed her back, his body moving quicker against hers, his thrusts becoming deeper, his body trembling.

She locked her ankles and moved with him, feeling the tension build inside her.

She so loved this man. Wanted nothing more than to be here, like this, with him for the rest of their lives.

"God, Juliet, I can't…" His breath was harsh in her ear, sending shivers through her. "I need…"

"I know, Tanner, I know." She moved under him, using her heels for leverage, wanting—no needing—him to keep going.

He thrust into her faster, his skin slick against hers, the scent and sound of him loving her taking her higher, and she could feel desire spiraling low in her belly.

She arched up into him.

"That's it, babe. Come for me." He panted the words as a litany with every thrust and Juliet felt it rise within her.

She clutched his back, raked her nails across his skin, her breaths coming short and quick. Wanting to say the words, but wouldn't.

But she could think them.

I love you, Tanner. I love you, Tanner.

"God, yes, Juliet. Don't stop."

She'd never stop loving him. Ever.

She clenched him inside her, loving how he felt there. Loving how he made her feel everywhere.

"Oh, Tanner…" She bit back the words. But she couldn't stop the feeling inside her. Her heart swelled with the emotions she had for this man, and her body… dear God, her body was on fire, wanting to take him to heaven, wanting to give him so much pleasure.

He kissed her then and that was it. She could no more hold back her orgasm then she could the love she felt for him, and she came, pouring every bit of love into the kiss she gave him as she did.

Tanner's world was rocked.

Utterly and completely turned upside down, inside out, backwards, forwards, sideways and any other way he couldn't think about.

Jesus God, Juliet.

He jerked against her, the need to move inside her urging him on long after he'd come. But he couldn't stop. He needed to feel her around him. Needed to know he was inside her.

Where you belong.

That damn voice. It wasn't his libido talking this time; his libido was over on the floor twitching, humming to itself in satisfaction.

No, this was his conscience. His right-from-wrong, His

morality. His sense of self. And it was telling him he belonged here?

Had the world just gone nuts?

He *didn't* belong here—but he was dammed if he could move away.

He exhaled and let his weight fall onto Juliet. She wouldn't mind. He knew from past experience.

Another argument in his conscience's artillery.

You know her. You've loved her forever. She's changed. Grown up. Gone through the same loss you did. Put both of you out of your collective misery and tell her you still love her.

No.

That was where he put his metaphorical foot down. He wasn't in love with Juliet. He *couldn't* love someone who'd done what she'd done. No. There were no arguments to the contrary. Juliet had lied; he could never trust her. It was that simple.

And that painful.

Fine. Suit yourself. And lose the best thing that ever happened to you.

If Juliet's lies were the best thing that had ever happened to him, Tanner might just think of giving up and becoming a bum. What was the point of moving forward if he kept going backward?

"I can hear the wheels spinning in your head." She turned her messy bed-head toward him, her eyes sated and languid, her smile satisfied.

It was a look he'd always loved on her and now was no different. Some things were just hard-wired into his psyche.

Which could be the only explanation for having done this with her.

"Tanner? Please tell me you don't regret this."

He'd love to tell her he did. Give her the same kind of pain she'd given him, but he couldn't. It wasn't who he was. He prided himself on being honest. "No, Juliet, I don't. I am wondering, however, how we go on from here. What happens next. I'm still leaving, you know. The divorce will still happen. I can't live in the same vacuum I've been living in these past seven years. I want my life to start. I want to move forward. Have a future. There's too much past between us for that to happen."

She blinked. A few times. Rapidly. But to her credit, she didn't cry.

Maybe Juliet was growing up after all.

So what does that mean for you, buddy boy?

Nothing. Not a damn thing. Too much hurt. Too much pain. They couldn't go back and they couldn't go forward. Not together. They had to move on.

"Don't overanalyze it, Tanner. Let's just appreciate it for what it is. We've always been attracted to each other— that obviously hasn't changed. You have your life; I have mine. We're here together because of Nana. Let's let it be just that. Why analyze it? Why put more pressure on ourselves? Why worry it's something it's not? Let's just enjoy it." She raised an arm over her head and stretched. "I certainly did."

He looked at her. Studied her eyes. There was no guile there. No calculating going on. Just honest and open and— her pupils were dilated. Juliet's pupils always dilated when she was aroused.

He felt himself stir and had to smile. Some things obviously didn't change in seven years.

"You're smiling."

Including the fact that she could read him like a book.

"Does that mean you enjoyed it?"

He grabbed her hand and dragged it down to his groin. "What do you think?"

He shuddered when her fingers closed around him.

"I think the jury needs some more convincing."

God help him, he let her "convince the jury." Let her take him in her mouth, and then, when he was just about ready to pull her head away and roll her over, she pulled another condom off the nightstand, sheathed him, and climbed on top, and it was a long time before he was thinking about anything.

And if her father hadn't shown up at Juliet's front door, it might have been a lot longer.

Chapter Seventeen

"D ad?"

That one word, in that tone, had Tanner jumping out of Juliet's bed and yanking on his clothes in two seconds. Her father showing up wasn't a good thing.

Thank God Juliet had thrown a pair of shorts and a t-shirt on instead of answering the door in her bathrobe, but that wouldn't help Tanner get the hell out of her bedroom without her father knowing exactly what they'd been doing.

Though… that might be a good thing. It'd bolster their story.

Great. Now *he* was figuring out how to lie.

"What's wrong? Is it Nana?"

"Your grandmother is fine. It's me. I'm here to find out what the hell you and Wentworth are trying to pull."

"Pull? What are you talking about?"

Tanner walked to the bedroom door, his ear at the opening.

"May I come in?" Mr. Chambers was nothing if not a stickler for propriety and rules. It made him a good businessman but a pain in the ass as a girlfriend's father.

Tanner wasn't sure what that made him as a father-in-law since he hadn't really experienced that part. But if showing up late at their home—okay, his daughter's home, but the guy thought they were back together, so it should be considered *their* home and Tanner would worry how he felt about that later—was any indication, Tanner wasn't a fan. Especially when the guy had interrupted him making love to his wife.

Wife.

Damn. That word rolled way too easily off his tongue.

"Oh. Um. Sure." Juliet stepped back with a rake of her hand through her hair already messy hair. Jeez, her bed-head couldn't scream *sex* any louder. "But please be quiet. Tanner's sleeping."

"Where?"

Well that got right to the point.

Juliet looked away and Tanner could see the blush on her cheek.

That got to the point too.

"You're *sleeping* with him, Juliet? You haven't learned your lesson already?"

"Dad, Tanner is my husband."

"Are you sure about that?"

The question made Tanner's blood boil. How dare her father question *his* integrity. He was about to open the bedroom door when Juliet responded.

"Yes, I'm sure about that, Dad. Tanner and I are still married. And he's honored his vows, just like I have." She closed the front door. "I know he's not your favorite person, but our relationship is none of your business."

If she were saying that as part of their cover story, she couldn't be more convincing. If she actually believed it, she'd finally learned to take him at his word.

He felt a little flutter in his chest at that thought.

"You've made it my business by lying to your grandmother. I will not have it, Juliet. She gave up her life to help me raise you. This is how you repay her?"

"That's enough, Burt." Tanner couldn't stay in Juliet's room any longer. "Juliet would never hurt her grandmother and you know it. I know you're worried, but you shouldn't take it out on your daughter."

"Should I take it out on you?" Mr. Chambers wasn't a small man, but he wasn't in Tanner's league. Not that Tanner would ever hit him, but Juliet's father clenched his fists, looking as if he wanted to take more than a few swings at him as they met in the middle of Juliet's living room.

"Juliet is trying to make her grandmother happy. So am I."

He father rubbed the side of his neck. "By lying to her? You can't tell me the two of you have suddenly discovered you can't live without each other. Not after all these years apart."

"We're… working on it."

"And then what?" He arched an eyebrow. "My mother gets well and you walk out again?"

"Daddy—"

"No, Juliet. I want to hear what he has to say. He's left you twice already. Why are you opening yourself up to a third time? Do you like getting hurt? Do you like having to pick up the pieces? Why on earth would you let yourself be roped into this?"

"I wasn't roped into anything. If we were trying to 'pull something' as you said, don't you think I would've had him come back when she went into the hospital?"

"Why didn't you?"

"Because I didn't want Tanner to *have* to come back; I wanted him to *want* to."

Tanner had seriously undervalued Juliet's acting ability. She almost had him convinced.

Her father's fists landed on his hips. "You expect me to believe this is just a coincidence? I didn't get to where I am today by burying my head in the sand, Juliet. I know a snow job when I see one."

Tanner wanted to come clean; he'd told Juliet they couldn't pull this off. But he'd seen Nana. She'd been happy to see him, but there was frailty under her smile. If keeping the pretense a little longer would help her get well, he was doing it. In for a penny, in for a mortgage…

"Of course I came back when Juliet told me what

happened—but it was because I wanted to. Because it was time to." There. That was as close to the truth without being a lie that he could go.

"And what do you think will happen, Juliet, when he leaves? Do you think your grandmother will be happy with that?"

"Who says I'm going to?" Tanner couldn't believe he said the words.

Juliet's father obviously couldn't either. His eyes narrowed and he pointed at Tanner. "You." He pulled himself to his full height which was a good five inches below Tanner's, but the guy was still as intimidating as he'd been when Tanner had been eighteen. "For some God-only-knows-why reason you make Juliet happy and my mother knows it. I won't have her hurt again. She's done too much for this family to have her emotions played with. I don't know what you and Juliet have concocted, but you will not hurt my mother, is that clear? I still have that mortgage."

"Dad—"

"Juliet." Tanner stepped forward. As much as he'd like to set the guy straight, he wasn't going to and risk what he and Juliet had already worked out.

He took a deep breath and did something he'd never thought he'd be able to do.

He lied to Juliet's father.

"Juliet and I have had some issues but we owe it to ourselves, to what we've meant to each other, to try to work them out. Yes, I'm here because Juliet told me about her grandmother, but that's not the only reason I came back. I'm here for the right reasons. I have no intention of hurting your mother or your daughter, Burt." That part was at least true. They'd already laid out the ground rules; if Juliet got hurt, it was because she'd built this into something more than it was. It wouldn't be his doing; he'd been honest with her.

"But you never do, do you? You just up and leave, and the rest of us get to help her pick up the pieces."

"Daddy, that's not fair."

"Haven't you heard, Juliet? Nothing's fair in love and war. I just haven't figured out which one this relationship between the two of you is."

Tanner didn't want to try to classify it. "Juliet and I are adults. We've discussed the situation from every angle. You don't have to worry about your daughter. She's fine."

Fine? Juliet wasn't sure about that. She actually wasn't sure about anything because hearing what Tanner was saying…

She wanted it to be true. And if they hadn't had that talk before going to bed together, she might actually think it was, he was that convincing.

And he looked so right talking to her father here in her living room in his t-shirt and shorts and bare feet. As if this was where he belonged.

Her tummy fluttered, imagining it. What it'd be like to go to bed with him each night, to wake up with him each morning, to make him breakfast in bed—or he'd make it for her; they'd liked doing that for each other those few short months they'd moved in together before they'd lost Keegan. She could picture him sitting on the back patio, reading the paper. This house had seemed so tiny before and should, by rights, feel even smaller with Tanner in it, but it didn't. It felt…

Like home.

"He's right, Daddy. Tanner and I have talked all about this. You don't need to worry."

He glared at Tanner. "I'd like to have a word with my daughter."

"Daddy, anything you have to say, you can say it in front of Tanner."

"No, Juliet, that's okay." Tanner touched her shoulder and it felt… genuine. "I'll leave you two alone." He walked toward the guest bedroom.

So much for genuine. If he really meant what he'd said—what they'd just done together—he would have gone back to her room.

She had to get her head on straight. That wasn't what they'd agreed on before going into her room. She couldn't let what they'd done color what they were trying to do: convince her family they were back together.

Her father took a seat when Tanner closed his bedroom door. Juliet had to take a deep breath before she could face him. "Dad, it will be fine."

"Will it?" He rubbed his temples. "Look, sweet-heart. I know you think you're doing a good thing for your grandmother, but she's going to be upset when he leaves. You should have seen her after you left today. I haven't seen her smile that much in well, long before the stroke. And she ate tonight. I didn't have to coax her."

"See? All good reasons to be glad he's back."

Her father leaned forward and rested his elbows on his thighs, his hands hanging between his legs. "This is exactly what I was worried about, Juliet. You're too vulnerable when it comes to Tanner Wentworth. You always get your hopes up and then you get let down. He hasn't been around for any reasonable amount of time for seven years, honey. If he'd wanted to come back, he could have. I could have had grandchildren by now. But you're wasting your life waiting for something that won't happen. He's not the man for you. Whether it's because you have too much history or some other reason you're holding onto, the truth is, you have to let him go. You have to move on. You can't spend your life pining over a guy who doesn't realize how special you are."

Juliet bit her lip. She loved her father for saying this. He'd always told her how wonderful and special she was—especially in those early years after Mom had decided her boyfriend was more important than her daughter. But hearing the words from her father didn't undo her mother's abandonment.

The truth was, she'd never felt worthy enough. After all, if her own mother left her, why should anyone else not genetically related to her stick around?

Rationally, she knew Tanner couldn't be held accountable for her mother's actions, but emotionally, psychologically, she'd been terrified he'd leave her.

And then he had. And the sucky thing was, it'd been her actions to *prevent* it that had led to the very thing she'd feared most happening.

"Dad, you're just going to have to trust that I know what I'm doing."

"You don't have perspective, sweetheart. He left you when you needed him most. And not once, but twice. And now you've brought him back for a third time? I'd hoped you weren't carrying a torch for him all these years, but I see I was wrong." He held her chin. "You're going to get hurt again and there's nothing I can do to prevent it."

"Daddy, I'm a big girl and I've done just fine these last few years without him." *Few*, not *seven*, because she hadn't been fine the first couple.

"You've dealt with it, but you haven't moved on." He dropped his hand into his lap. "You haven't dated and you should. Get out and meet another man. One you can build a life with. A future. Have a family."

"I'm still married, Dad."

His eyebrows arched and he let go of her hand. "You think he cares about that? If he did, he would have been here. He could be dating and you wouldn't know."

"I would. I know Tanner. He's a man of his word. He spoke his vows and he meant them."

Of that she was sure. Now.

But she wanted to remind him of the most important one: *'Til death us do part.*

Her father's words were burning a hole in his heart.

Tanner stepped away from his door, the old adage about eavesdroppers never hearing anything good about themselves ringing true.

Mr. Chambers was actually encouraging her to cheat on

him. Tanner shook his head. He couldn't believe it. The opinion the guy had of him…

Yet Juliet had jumped right to his defense. Or was she saying that for her father's benefit?

He hated that he even had to *have* that thought.

"Let it go, Daddy, okay? Let's just be here for Nana. Everything else will work out as it's supposed to after she's better."

After.

It seemed to Tanner as if he'd been living his life with a big helping of *after*. *After* he turned thirty. *After* he got his trust fund. *After* he paid off the mortgage. *After* his divorce. Now he had to wait until *after* Nana got better.

When would he ever be able to live in the moment? To not have to wait for some big, all-important date to define his life?

He snorted. *After*, that's when.

"I don't want him running out again, Juliet. Not while it could hurt your grandmother. Do you trust him enough not to?"

"I do."

She said those two words more surely and firmly than she'd said them the day they'd gotten married. And this time, they slid through his veins and swirled around his heart in a way they hadn't when he'd thought she'd been saying them to trap him. But now, she was saying them as if she trusted him. Finally.

But when will you trust her?

That was the million-dollar question, wasn't it? Almost literally. But he wasn't here to trust her. He was here to honor their agreement and get the mortgage to the ranch. Then he could move on.

You sure that's what you want to do?

Of course it was. It was what he'd been planning for *after*.

But what about now?

Now?

He looked through the door and saw her sitting there, her knees pressed together, her hands intertwined in her lap, resolution etched across her face.

The Juliet he'd known had been clingy. Worshipful.

This Juliet was confident. Secure.

Different.

And still so beautiful she made his heart ache.

Why did her father have to show up? Why couldn't they have had tonight? Was it so much to ask?

Just one night. With his wife.

Juliet closed her front door after her father left, leaned her forehead against it, and took a deep breath. That had not been pleasant.

Dad had said everything she was worried about and she'd given him true responses. She did trust Tanner to not walk away—at least until he'd fulfilled his part of their bargain. Then he'd leave and she'd already sanctioned it.

She rolled her back onto the door and plastered her palms to it, giving herself a head-on view of Tanner's bedroom door. He had to have heard. She'd half expected him to come out to defend himself. But he hadn't.

Why?

She wanted to go to him. Wanted to invite him back to her room so they could continue where they'd left off. But she had a feeling that moment was over.

Sighing, she turned off the light by the sofa and headed to her corner of the house.

"Juliet."

His voice slid over her in the darkness just like his hands had. And with the same effect.

She took a deep breath. She didn't want to have to say goodnight to him like this.

But she'd agreed to his stipulations so she turned around.

He stood in his doorway, bigger than life. Just as he'd always been. "Thank you."

"For… what?" That was one she hadn't expected.

"For defending me."

"He shouldn't've said those things, but he's upset."

Tanner grabbed the doorframe over his head and leaned forward. "You don't have to make excuses. He was within his right to say them. I mean, after all, I *did* leave."

"With good reason."

He let go of the woodwork and took two steps out of his room.

Juliet's heart sped up.

"Look." He raked a hand through his hair. "Tonight, before your dad showed up… It was good. Right?"

She nodded, holding her breath, not wanting to say the wrong thing.

"So… What do you say about, you know, going back to where we were before he arrived?"

Say? She didn't want to *say* anything. She wanted to scream it for everyone to hear.

But she did show some restraint.

"I'd like that very much, Tanner. I don't want to go to bed alone tonight."

"Then don't." He held out his hand.

To Juliet, it felt like a lifeline.

Chapter Eighteen

anner placed the carton of eggs on the counter in Juliet's tiny galley kitchen the next morning and set the pan down gently so the metal wouldn't make any noise on the burner. Juliet needed her sleep.

Which was the only reason he was out here making breakfast and not in there making love to her.

Making love… There had to be a better term.

Images from last night flashed through his mind. What they'd done together was so much more than *having sex*, but it wasn't making love. Sure, he cared for her. He always would; she had that right. But he wasn't in love with her. He couldn't love someone who couldn't be honest.

But he could still care about her. He could care about the memories.

He cracked the eggs for her breakfast. Scrambled; that was the only way she liked eggs. Not hard-boiled, not poached, not over-easy… Just scrambled. She didn't even like omelets, though he put in enough cheese and ketchup and thyme that it might constitute one if she didn't insist on having the eggs chopped up.

Funny how he remembered it after all these years.

He tossed a couple of slices of bread into the toaster oven, poured two glasses of OJ, and looked through her fridge for some breakfast meat while the eggs were cooking.

He smiled. He could give her some breakfast meat…

While it was funny, it was also sad. If this were real, if they were really married and this was any other normal weekend, he might actually turn off the stove and go do that. He could always make more eggs.

For a few moments, the idea was tempting. Which showed just how *not* a good idea it was. He was staying put.

But then he heard the kitten meowing.

He closed the fridge door. Breakfast meat wasn't all that healthy anyway.

He turned the flame off then headed to the laundry room where they'd put the little thing when she'd tried to join them in the bed last night.

"Hey, baby. What's the matter? You missing your buddies at the store?" He held the kitten to his chest, then she clawed her way to his shoulder and licked his ear.

He scratched the top of her head then headed back into the kitchen. "Have I got a surprise for you, kiddo."

He turned the burner back on, flipped the eggs, then cut off a tiny piece for the kitten. He stuck it on his shoulder, ignoring her claws piercing his skin as she balanced herself there. Good thing he had broad shoulders.

"You are *not* feeding her people food."

He spun around at Juliet's indignant voice. "Um... yeah?"

"Tanner, you can't do that. She needs to eat her kitten chow."

"You're telling me that you think hard pieces of hard, crunchy whatever-they-are are better for her than a natural egg?"

"Kittens aren't supposed to eat eggs."

"Think about that statement, Jules." He tossed the eggs one more time then turned off the heat before he flipped the bread over in the toaster oven to brown on the other side. He opened the fridge door—slowly because the kitten was still trying to get comfortable on his shoulder and those claws were sharp—and grabbed the butter from the tray on the door.

"If she didn't know any better, then she wouldn't know any better." Juliet picked up the glasses and set them on the table.

"It's too early in the morning for word puzzles."

"I'm just saying, she can't miss something she never had. Now that you've given it to her, she's going to miss it when she can't have it again."

He shut the fridge door but didn't turn around, sucking in a breath. "Is that commentary about last night?"

"What—? Oh."

He heard her chair scrape against the tile floor but didn't turn around to see if she was sitting in it. He couldn't. He didn't want to see regret on her face. Didn't want to feel it when looking at her. He didn't regret last night—unless she did. Or, unless she was thinking of making it more than it was.

Maybe it *was* more than he thought it was. After all, something had compelled him to make that invitation after her father left.

Damn it, he should have listened to his conscience last night and just walked away.

But then he would have missed out on holding her. Which had been great.

Until he'd woken up with his usual morning wood. Hence the reason he'd come into the kitchen.

He shifted his legs, hoping to hide any evidence of it. "Any word about your grandmother this morning?" As a change of subject, it probably wasn't the best choice, but it was the first one he could think of to get off the topic of last night.

"No. But I want to go over there. You don't have to if you don't want to. She's seen you, knows you're here, has perked up some. That should be good enough."

He plated their eggs and toast, and carried them over to the table. "So one and done? You really think she's going to go for that? Your grandmother might be weak, but she's still as sharp as ever. I'm here, might as well use me." That didn't come out right. "I mean, I might as well put in some face time with her. Make it believable."

"Thank you, Tanner. I really appreciate the offer."

"You're welcome." He shrugged, then grabbed the kitten before she slid down his back, taking a few layers of skin with her.

He set her on the floor with another piece of egg.

Juliet raised an eyebrow when he faced her again.

"What? I can't help it. I have a soft spot for kittens. Sue me." He dug into his own eggs. "And speaking of the kitten, do we have a name yet or do I have to keep calling her *baby*?"

"I was thinking of Houdini, but she's a girl and he wasn't."

"As Mrs. Houdini was very happy to find out, I'm sure." Tanner swallowed another forkful of egg. "Why *not* name her that? Lots of people use gender-neutral names. Houdini was his last name, so it can be any gender you want."

She smiled and it was as if the sun rose in her kitchen.

Tanner shook his head. For God's sake, one night of sex in seven years and he turned into a poet.

His cue to get out of here while he still could.

He shoveled in his eggs. "How about you shower while I clean up? Then it'll be my turn and then we'll be on our way."

"What? You don't think I should show up at Nana's looking like this?" She patted her hair.

Instantly, he was thrust back to last night when he'd had his hands in that hair—

He bent down to pet Houdini who was clawing at his leg, probably looking for more eggs. Juliet had been right. If he'd never had a taste of her last night, he wouldn't be wanting more today.

He sat back up and shoveled the rest of his eggs in. Looked like it was another cold shower for him.

***

"Gin. I win again." Nana dragged the poker chip to the stack in front of her. "You aren't letting me win, now, are you, Tanner?"

"No, ma'am." Tanner tilted his hat back and leaned back in his chair, resting it on the two back legs. "I know better than to let you do anything."

"That's right. It's not worth anything if you don't do it yourself." Nana shuffled the cards.

Juliet was amazed at the change in her. A week ago, Nana had barely been able to get out of bed, so to see her now, sitting here, playing cards for—Juliet checked her cell phone—over an hour... She'd made the right choice in bringing Tanner back.

The downside to Nana's great improvement, however, was that Tanner wouldn't have to stay for very long. Once Nana was back to her normal self, they could come clean and he could go, taking the mortgage and her heart with him.

"Cheer up, Juliet." Nana dealt the new round. "My winning streak can't go on forever. You'll win a game, I'm sure."

Juliet fanned her cards—not a pair in sight. Sigh. "Maybe if we keep playing for another hour, but you need your rest."

"Balderdash." Nana shifted the cards in her hand. "I've had so much rest in that darn hospital, I didn't think I was ever going to wake up again. It feels so good to be home and among my familiar surroundings. Don't you agree, Tanner?"

Tanner tapped his hand on the table. "I think it's good for you to be home. I hear people recover better when they're out of the hospital."

"I meant you. It must feel good to finally be able to settle in and relax at home. Juliet picked a nice cozy place for the two of you, didn't she? I really wanted you both to move in here at the ranch, but she said she wanted her own place. Something for just the two of you. Can't say that I blame her. I remember when William and I first got married... We definitely needed our alone time."

Juliet felt her face flame in light of last night.

It burned hotter when Tanner glanced at her. "But Juliet and I didn't *just* get married."

Nana waved her hand then reached for a card from the draw pile. "That's just semantics. You've spent enough time apart that it must seem like a second honeymoon now that you're together again." She tossed a card onto the table.

Tanner picked up the discard and slid it into his hand. "Something like that."

"Oh, lord. There goes me and my big mouth. I guess some things are private after all, but I'm just so darn tickled pink that you're here and we can be a real family that I guess I forget myself. Don't mind me. I'm just happy you're home."

Juliet took her turn, drawing a three to go with all the other unrelated cards in her hand, content to let her grandmother do the talking for her since she was saying everything Juliet wished she could.

"Well, I'm glad you're happy Nana. It's good to see you up and around."

"It's good to be up and around. I have a whole new lease on life. Things like strokes and whatnot, they make you examine your priorities. What you want out of life."

Juliet knew what she wanted and he was sitting across from her.

Nana played her hand. "I've decided to volunteer at the hospital when I'm well enough. Do you know how lonely and depressing it can be when you don't have any visitors?" She discarded the card she drew from the deck. "I was lucky that I had a slew of visitors, but some of those folks didn't have anyone. Half of the flowers Burt's clients sent me went to those patients. The scent was just too overpowering in my room and what did I need all of those for anyway? Though I did keep the bouquet you and Juliet sent."

Oh crud. Juliet forgot to mention that.

"I always did love bluebonnets, my dear boy." Nana patted his hand. "Now, play your hand. I have a feeling I'm going to be winning this round."

Penelope *knew* she was going to be winning this round.

And a whole lot more. Poor Tanner looked thunderstruck at the mention of the flowers.

And Juliet thought she could pull one over on her? Ha. She hadn't been born yesterday and that girl needed a lot more years under her belt to come anywhere close to it, especially if these two thought they were fooling her. She knew just what they were doing and why they were doing it.

They thought she'd had this big, nasty stroke and they were worried. She let them think that even though she'd had a less-severe TIA and was milking it for all it was worth so she could plant the ideas in Juliet's head. Or should she say, bringing out the ideas that were already in Juliet's head so her granddaughter could act on them?

Penelope knew just what she was doing. Just like with the bluebonnets. Why, anyone had been able smell Juliet a mile away when that boy had been around. She'd poured the bluebonnet lotion on like it was water, and Penelope had known why.

How did those kids think those flowers had gotten there anyway? William had trucked in an 18-wheeler's worth to give her that instant field. She, too, had smelled like bluebonnets for years. Still kept a dried sprig of the first one he'd given her in the book beside her bed. And she'd been known to dab on some lotion every so often.

These kids thought they had the market cornered on romance. Ha. What they didn't know wouldn't even fill her teacup. And as long as she could keep Tanner around, they weren't going to stand a chance against her.

"Gin." *Lucky in cards, unlucky in love* her patootie. She'd had a wonderful marriage and her matchmaking efforts were going to work out just as well for her grand-daughter.

"Again?" Juliet sighed and tossed her cards onto the table. "Maybe I should call *you* Houdini instead of the kitten since you seem to be able to whip up cards out of thin air like magic."

"Ah, but everyone has their own kind of magic, Juliet." Penelope took the winning poker chip and stacked it on her pile. "Want to take a break?"

"Why? Do you need one?" Juliet jumped out of her chair and was around to Penelope's side in a flash.

She did so love her granddaughter.

"No, I'm fine. But you two might need a breather from the trouncing I'm giving you. Besides, there's something else I want to do while I have you both here."

"What is it?" Tanner, bless his heart, gathered the cards and stacked them neatly in the center of the table.

He was going to have to move them for what she had in mind.

"I'd like you to get that box over there." She pointed to the box she'd had Burt gather for her. He'd grumbled the entire time, but when she'd pointed out that this was to help solidify Juliet's marriage, he'd stopped complaining.

Her son loved his daughter and only wanted to see her happy. No man would ever be good enough for Juliet in Burt's eyes, but he did acknowledge that there'd been a time when Tanner had truly loved her. Penelope had tried to convince her son that Tanner still did love Juliet, that he'd left because he'd been so hurt by what she'd done. If anyone should understand, it should be Burt. But he wasn't about to admit that.

That was why her lil ol' TIA had come into play. She shrugged off the niggle of guilt at worrying her son and lying to everyone. This was for the greater good. She needed to get these two together so they could live happily ever after and give her and Burt some babies to enjoy.

Which was why she was about to put the next phase of her plan into action.

Chapter Nineteen

Maybe lying to her grandmother hadn't been such a great idea. Juliet came to this great realization as Nana had Tanner unload photo albums onto the table.

She didn't want to relive where they'd been. That wasn't why she'd brought him here; she wanted to think about the future. Move forward. How could they do that by wallowing in the past?

Tanner wouldn't look at her. He had to be as uncomfortable about this as she was, so she was thankful he hadn't gotten up and left. She couldn't have explained that to Nana. After all, if they were reconciled, why would pictures of their past upset him?

Thankfully, the albums held good memories—a lot of she and Tanner together since their families had been close before his father had gotten too deep with his gambling debts.

"Who's this, Nana, with Dad?"

"Her? Oh, that's Nancy. Nancy Hillson. She was a lovely lady, but your father didn't quite see it."

"Dad? You mean he dated her?"

"Only once or twice I believe."

Juliet studied the picture. The woman wasn't ringing any bells. "Did he date any other women?" Because that wasn't ringing any bells either.

Nana took the picture and looked at it. "Not really. I

think there were one or two others. I'd had hopes for Nancy, but…" Nana sighed and put the picture down. "He said he wasn't ready. Didn't think it was a good idea to introduce someone new in your life."

Juliet had asked her father for a baby sister at one point and the look on his face had ended that discussion then and there. Now, knowing what she knew about her mother, she could see why he'd been hesitant to bring women into her life if they weren't going to stay, but it was a shame that he was alone now.

Juliet didn't want to end up alone. But she didn't want just anyone either. No, she wanted Tanner and she had a feeling no one else would ever measure up. Which didn't bode well for her future.

"Was he really so much in love with… Elaine?" She'd never been able to refer to her as her mother when talking about her; it made the woman's defection too personal.

Nana's lips twisted as if she'd sucked on one of those lemon sticks she'd bought Juliet at the town fair every year when she'd been younger. "I think it was that he was so disillusioned with her. It wasn't easy when she left him. He had a business to run, a child to raise and help cope, and then, to top it off, the gossip to deal with."

Gossip was just one reason Juliet hadn't wanted anyone to know Tanner had left her. The other was the irrepressible hope that he hadn't. Not for good.

She looked at him, willing him to understand why she'd done what she'd done. Why they could still make this work.

He was looking through another album.

"Oh my goodness, will you look at this?" Nana held up a photo from one of the countless company barbeques her father had held here at the ranch. "I have that hideous pouf on the top of my head. Someone should have told me I looked ridiculous."

The change in subject was definitely called for. "I think you look beautiful, Nana."

"Yes, well, you're biased, dear." Nana slid the picture

to Tanner. "Now tell me, Tanner. Do you find this hairstyle attractive on a woman?"

"Depends on the woman." He winked at Nana and the two of them laughed.

It was so good to hear Tanner laugh. Juliet hadn't forgotten that deep belly laugh he had, but it hadn't been forefront in her mind because she'd so rarely heard it over the last decade.

Though he'd laughed last night when she'd found one of his ticklish erogenous zones.

It'd been a pure, honest moment of happiness that had turned heated in the next second. She hadn't minded, obviously, but she would have liked to have heard his laugh a little longer, knowing she'd caused it.

"Look at this." Nana held up another photo. "Isn't that that cheerleader who thought she was your best friend? What *is* she doing here?"

Tanner took the photo. "Yes, it's Delia. I think she's trying to figure out how to dive into the pool without getting her hair wet."

"That girl doesn't have two brain cells to rub together. Though I've heard she's good at finding rich husbands."

"Plural being the operative part of that statement." Tanner flicked the picture onto the table.

"Yes, well, not everyone can have Juliet's intelligence. Beautiful *and* smart. Tanner, you are a lucky man."

Thankfully, Nana looked down at the next photograph so she didn't see Tanner raise his eyebrows, but Juliet did.

Her back got a little straighter. Okay, so she'd done some ill-advised things in the past, but not maliciously. And she was so much more than those two bad decisions and he ought to remember that because he had loved her for a reason back then, and she, fundamentally, was that same person. Especially after last night.

Tanner might not be in love with her now, but he'd definitely been in lust with her last night.

Thankfully, Nana kept pulling out non-controversial photos. The town's Community Day celebrations, football games, vacations, barbeques, block parties... All good memories.

Tanner pulled another album out of the box and set it on the table.

His smile got tight when he opened the cover.

"Oh, look at how happy you two are here." Nana pointed to one of the photos.

Juliet leaned over. It was an un-posed shot someone took while they'd been waiting for the photographer to set up the lighting for their official engagement photo—the first engagement—under the magnolia tree in the front yard.

Tanner was looking at her with undisguised happiness. His smile was as big as she'd ever seen it and he'd put a hand on the back of her neck, drawing her in so their foreheads touched. She remembered what he'd whispered to her at that moment: "I will love you forever, Jules. I couldn't be happier."

And then he hadn't been.

"And this one." Nana pointed to the next one. Their engagement party when their friends had decorated the chairs like thrones and made a crown of the gift bows for each of them. God, the laughter.

And her belly.

Keegan had been there. He'd been kicking inside her all afternoon. They'd joked that he wanted to come out and party—a chip off the old block. But they couldn't agree on which block, hers or Tanner's.

"Uh, I just remembered I wanted to ask Burt something." Tanner shoved his chair back and headed toward her father's office.

She couldn't blame him.

That picture... She slipped it from the jacket in the album. It was both heartbreaking and unbelievably happy at the same time. This was how they should be.

How they could be.

"There will be more babies, Juliet." Nana's hand covered hers with surprising strength.

"I hope so." But they wouldn't be Tanner's.

"Have faith. You and Tanner, you've gone through so much and have come out stronger for it. I have to believe that you will live a long and happy life together."

That's right; Nana had to believe it. At least for a little while.

Juliet bit her lip as she put the photo back in the album. This was the hard part, pretending it was all true when she so very much wanted it to be and it wasn't.

She shouldn't have slept with him last night. She was going to have to watch him walk out of her life for a third time, and she had a feeling this would be the worst. Because then there'd be nothing to bring him back.

Tanner headed through the first open door he found, then bent over, hands braced on his knees and tried to catch his breath. Those photos… God, those photos had sucked the air right out of him. His life had been right where he'd wanted it and then… It'd been gone.

"If you're looking for my daughter, she's not here."

Tanner shot up. Shit. This *was* her father's office and her dad was sitting with his feet propped on that massive desk that had always made Tanner feel as if he were being called to the principal's office.

Now was no different.

"My, uh, back. It was giving me some trouble." He planted his hands on his lower back and stretched for good measure.

"I imagine all that dancing you do can give you some sore muscles."

"Danc—" He stopped stretching. "You know?"

Mr. Chambers—Burt—planted his feet on the floor and pressed on his desk to stand up. "Tanner, there's not much about you I don't know. Except maybe why you're here.

Though I have a pretty good guess about that as well. You might have Juliet fooled, but I'm not blinded by love for you."

The guy had liked him at one point. The one right before he'd found out Juliet was pregnant.

Probably wouldn't endear him to him to point out that it'd taken two to get her in that state, though to be honest, it'd only taken one: Juliet. With a pin-pricked condom.

Yeah, not something a father needed to hear. "I'm here because your daughter asked me to come. Because she loves you and her grandmother, and wants everyone to be happy."

"And you? Why'd you come? Do you want everyone to be happy, too? Is that why you waited seven years to come home? A big celebration?" He rapped the desk twice with his knuckles. "Absence making the heart grow fonder?"

Tanner reined in his anger at the mocking tone in his voice. The guy was still Juliet's father and wanted what was best for his daughter. If his own father had had a thought like that, he wouldn't have *had* to marry Juliet because there would have been no mortgage to hold over his head. "Look, Burt, I don't want to fight with you. We both care about Juliet—"

"You have a shitty way of showing it."

"Hey—" Tanner bit back the harsh words he wanted to say and scraped his hand over his mouth. "Look, this situation isn't optimal for any of us, but we're doing our best. It'd help if you'd—"he wanted to say *back off*, but that would only make their relationship more tense—"give us the privacy and time to deal with this. Juliet doesn't need you encouraging her to go out with other guys."

Her father shoved his hands in his pants pockets and raised an eyebrow. "Seriously? That's what's got you all pissed off?" He walked around from behind the desk and leaned against the front, resting one ankle over the other and crossing his arms. "It's been seven years, Tanner. Seven. Do you really expect me to believe that you've remained celibate all that time? You might have Juliet fooled, but a guy who does what you do for a living? Please. I'm not that naïve."

"I haven't slept with anyone since Juliet."

"I don't care, frankly. I don't care if you've been a monk. The problem is, you haven't been a monk *here*. You haven't been here at all. My daughter deserves better. I know you have your nose bent out of joint about the whole wedding thing, but if you'd learned your lesson from the first go-round and kept it in your pants, it wouldn't have played out the way it did. All you had to do was respect my daughter by putting an engagement ring on her finger before taking her to bed. But you couldn't do that, could you? Even had the gall to do it in my own home. Were you planning for me to find out?"

Oh hell. The guy didn't know. Juliet's father didn't know that she'd set him—them—up.

It was on the tip of Tanner's tongue to tell him, but… What would that prove? It was in the past. Did he really want to destroy the guy's illusions of his daughter just to be vindicated? In five and a half weeks, it wouldn't matter. And given Nana's improvement since he'd arrived, it might not even be half that time. Tanner had nothing to gain by telling her father the truth, and for all Juliet that had put him through, he didn't want to destroy her relationship with her father. He didn't hate her.

Maybe he should, but he'd loved her for so long that he just couldn't.

"You know…" Burt unfolded his arms and legs and walked over to the mini bar in the corner. "This could have been so different if you'd stuck around." He took a tumbler from the glass-fronted cabinet and poured two fingers. He offered it to Tanner.

Tanner waved it away. The last thing he needed was a fuzzy head when dealing with her dad.

"I would have given you Juliet the mortgage, you know. Can't have my grandchildren's grandparents indebted to me. It would've gone away. But instead, *you* did. I know all about your trust fund, Tanner. Your father told me about it years ago. I want it. I'm calling in the mortgage on your thirtieth birthday. If your dad can't come up with the funds—which he can't—you're going to. And it's going straight into a trust for Juliet that you can't touch. Because if you think you can come here and pretend to want to be married to her so that you can get half of it in a divorce settlement, you have another thought coming."

Tanner was shaking he was so angry and had half a mind to tell the guy all about Juliet's promise, but if he did, Burt would find some way to prevent it.

He wanted his parents' mortgage; Juliet owed him that. And he wanted his trust fund so he could go into business with Gage and Bryan. He had to keep his cool and let Burt think he'd won.

Instead, he gripped the arms rests, and, for the second time in his life—and both within the space of twenty-four hours—he lied to her father. "You go right ahead, Burt, and call it in. What do you think I was going to do with the trust fund anyway? Once I pay it off, you have no hold over me."

"Good. I'm glad we agree on something. Finally. You'll pay it off, and then you can let my little girl have her life back. Let her move on and find someone who appreciates her." He tossed back the whiskey, slammed the tumbler on the bar, then strode out through the French doors to the back yard, leaving Tanner to process what he'd just said.

Juliet with another guy.

He shouldn't find that strange. What did he think she'd do when he divorced her? Join a convent? Did people still do that?

Tanner shook his head. Seriously. What had he thought? That Juliet would live the rest of her life alone?

She wanted children. Thirty was a good age. She could still have the family she'd wanted.

But she'd wanted it with him. And he'd wanted one with her.

You could still have it.

He wanted to listen to that little voice. Wanted to believe that it was possible. But how could he ever trust her again? Trust, once broken, was so hard to regain.

Especially since she was out there lying away to her grandmother.

And you're in here doing it to her father… what's the difference?

Tanner stood up. He was doing it because Juliet had asked him to. Because she'd bribed him to.

So you're doing it to benefit yourself. And you're different from Juliet, how? Pot, I'd like you to meet Kettle.

Well… shit. Tanner leaned against the edge of her father's desk. He didn't like the parallel. But he wasn't going to ignore it.

She had something he wanted, so he was doing what he needed to to get it.

Juliet had wanted him; she'd done what she'd needed to to get him.

It sounded similar, but there was a difference between a mortgage and a life.

Really? That's your justification?

He shook his head, pushed off the edge of the desk and headed toward the door. It wasn't a pretty truth he was facing, but it was one nonetheless.

How could he be mad at her when he was doing the exact same thing?

***

"Juliet? Can I see you for a minute?" Tanner poked his head around the corner from her father's office.

She wanted him to see her for a lot longer than a minute, but she'd take the opportunities when she got them.

"Go, dear." Nana patted her hand. "I'll put all the pictures back. Good therapy. Beats digging for clothespins in a bucket of rice like the therapist had me do. Go see what your husband wants."

180

Husband.

Juliet pushed herself up from the table with shaky hands at that thought. This just kept getting more and more difficult.

"What's up?" She followed him into her father's office and tugged the door closed behind her. "Where's my dad?"

"He walked out back." Tanner headed toward her father's desk.

She followed him. "Why? What'd you say to him?"

He turned around. "More like what he said to me."

That didn't sound promising. "What'd he say?"

Tanner raked his fingers through his hair. "It's not important now. We just had a meeting of the minds. Set the record straight."

"You're scaring me."

"No need to be scared. Your father wanted to make sure I knew where he stood. And I do. It'll be fine."

She planted herself in front of him and stuck her hands on her hips. "That's not making me feel any better."

He sighed and raked his hand over his mouth. "It will be. I mean, look at your grandmother. She's better today than when I first got here. She's improving by leaps and bounds. I think she'll be strong enough to handle the truth. But I didn't tell your father about the plan. I didn't want to give him any more reasons to be upset." He brought his hands to her shoulders. "I wouldn't make his life—or yours—any tougher right now. I just told him that we need time and he needs to respect that."

Time was the one thing they didn't have because Tanner was right; Nana *was* getting better—and quicker than Juliet had thought she would. Not that she was complaining, obviously, but she'd thought she'd have more time with him. "Doesn't seem like he did much respecting since he walked out on you."

"That's not a bad thing, actually. It's not like we're best friends."

"I wish you were."

He sighed and removed his hand. Juliet felt the loss immediately.

"I wish a lot of things, Jules, but I'm dealing with the cards I've been dealt. As are all of us. Let's focus on that."

She wanted to just lean into him. Wrap her arms around him and tell him she loved him.

Instead, she cleared her throat and linked her hands in front of her. "So, why did you call me in here? What did you need?"

In a perfect world, he'd say he needed her.

But her world had been far from perfect since she'd made the decision that had changed everything.

Her. He needed her.

Tanner took a step back. Was he out of his mind? He shouldn't need her.

Damn, last night shouldn't have happened; it was putting crazy thoughts into his head. Like the ones he'd almost shared with her father. "I just wanted to make sure you're okay. You looked like you could use a break. You know, from those pictures."

He'd seen both stricken looks and haunted looks, and one glimpse of laughter in the ten minutes he'd been watching her after her father walked out, leaving him alone with his thoughts.

His thoughts weren't such a good place to be right now. They ran the gamut of wanting to get the hell out of here to wanting Juliet in here with him.

Choosing the latter should have surprised the hell out of him, but hadn't.

Just like last night hadn't really shocked him either. Going to bed with Juliet had seemed like the most natural thing in the world, even with the seven years of silence between them.

That ought to have him running for the first plane out

of town, but his integrity wouldn't allow him to renege on their deal.

"I…" Juliet tucked some hair behind her left ear. She always chose the left; never the right. Just one more random thing he remembered about her. "I'm okay. The pictures of… You know—"

"I know. It's why I had to leave the table."

"She didn't pull out the other pictures."

The other pictures. Tanner swallowed hard. Juliet knew him so well, she'd known what he'd been worried about seeing. First the engagement photos, then…

"I couldn't risk it." To this day, Tanner hadn't seen the photos of Keegan's birth. Her grandmother had taken them; said she'd wanted to have pictures of their child.

Tanner had hardly been able to look at Keegan; pictures of him? No way in hell. He didn't need to relive the pain. Not with pictures anyway. He relived it every time he thought about his son.

"She wouldn't have done that. Not to us. She might look at them, but she knows how we feel."

"Have you ever…" He turned his head, blinking the tears he refused to shed.

"Yes."

Her voice was soft. Emotional.

He looked at her then. "You did?"

"I needed to. I needed to see him. See *us*. Him and I. My memories are so hazy from the pain and the meds and the emotions… It was later. After…"

After he'd left. She didn't need to say the words; he understood. But he didn't understand looking at the pictures. "Didn't it…" He swallowed. "Didn't it bring back the pain?"

"The pain's always with me, Tanner. It just gets put aside for a while when I deal with life. But it's always there, ready for me to feel it if I choose."

"Why would you choose to?"

"To remember him. To make him real. If I run from it

or pretend I'm not feeling it, it's as if I'm pretending he didn't exist. I can't do that. He was too important. Too real to me."

"Me, too."

"I know." When she touched him this time, he didn't pull away.

"And with what happened to Nana… It just makes life more precious. So I remember him. Memories are all I have."

Tanner slipped his arms around her and pulled her close. It was the most natural thing in the world and he couldn't *not* do it.

She gripped his back and squeezed.

He lowered his chin to the top of her head, feeling her warm breath against his throat. "I loved him so much, Juliet."

He ground the words out through a clogged throat, trying not to cry. He'd done that once and it'd been hard as hell to recover from.

As was this. Holding her.

He should stop. He should unclasp his hands and walk away from her. She was still the woman who'd tricked him into marriage not once but twice. He couldn't go through a third time.

No matter how much he'd wanted her—and still did— if there'd been one thing Tanner had had driven into him in the past eleven years, it was that you didn't always get what you wanted.

Once he'd believe that life was fair. That if you lived your life in a good and honest way, treating others as you wanted to be treated, good things would happen.

So much for that.

"I'm sorry I called you in here." He sighed then removed his arms. And his chin. And every other body part that had been mashed up against her. This wasn't doing either of them any good.

I beg to differ—

He shut that thought down the second he felt a stirring

in his shorts. Now was not the time nor the place. Nor the woman, if truth be told. Last night might have been great, but it didn't negate all the years before. It couldn't.

"Why?" Juliet blinked up at him.

There were tears in her eyes.

God, he'd thought he'd become inured to her tears. After all, she'd shed so many and they'd only caused him more heartache. But, no. Seeing Juliet ready to cry ripped open several scars he'd thought had been welded shut.

"Because." Tanner took another step of self-preservation back again. "Because you should be out there with her making her happy. Thought I was helping, but I guess not."

He willed her to walk away. To turn around and head back to her grandmother and not give him a backward glance.

Juliet, being Juliet, did neither. Instead, she cupped his cheek with one hand. "We are making her happy. Just by being here."

"But that's only temporary. And she's going to be hurt more when I do leave. I don't know that this was such a good idea."

She brought her other hand to his face. "If there's one thing I've learned, Tanner Wentworth, is that recriminations don't change how things stand. We just have to keep moving forward and learn from our mistakes. For what it's worth, I don't think this is a mistake." She ran her thumb across his lips. "And I definitely don't think last night was one either."

She didn't give him a chance to reply, taking a step back then striding out of the office.

Tanner sagged against the edge of her father's desk again.

He wasn't sure last night was a mistake either.

Chapter Twenty

Y ou seriously want fried chicken over Ermalinda's food?" Tanner turned right into the local strip mall the next night, enjoying the power of Juliet's Mercedes. The fleet cars had been reserved for a corporate event so he'd been driving Juliet to work, then going to the gym and doing odds and ends around her house until it'd been time to pick her up. A little more domesticated than he'd planned, but she needed the things done and he didn't want to risk being alone with Nana. Lord only knew what *she'd* say.

At least with Juliet, they were on the same page. Knew what was going on and what subjects to avoid.

Kind of like that sleeping-together thing. They had yet to discuss it and it was starting to grow roots and plant itself in the middle of her living room.

"Nana's having some of her friends over and I'm not really in the mood to deal with all their questions as well. Everyone will understand that we want a night to ourselves." Juliet pointed to a spot at the curb. "Pull over there and I'll run in."

Tanner turned into a parking space instead and put the car in park at their favorite high school hangout. "I want to come in. Been a long time since I've been to Pappy's."

But apparently not for Juliet because there was a loud, "Jules!" from behind the counter when they walked in.

Connor Crayton. The guy who'd wanted Juliet since first grade.

But even then, she'd been his.

Tanner got no small amount of satisfaction from that—until he realized that once Juliet signed the divorce papers, it'd be open season. Crayton would be after her in a heartbeat.

"Great to see you again, honey."

Maybe he already was.

That thought didn't sit well with Tanner either. What was with the *honey*? And the *again*? Had Crayton been using *his* absence to get up close and personal with Juliet? With his wife?

Dude? You're divorcing her; you get no say in the matter.

He didn't care. Right now she was still his wife and if Crayton was coming on to her, Tanner would shut that shit down real quick.

"Crayton." Tanner put every bit of testosterone in his body into that one word.

Crayton straightened. Oh yeah, he'd gotten it in one. "Wentworth. Hadn't heard you were back."

"Must not have gotten the invite to Delia's. We were there a few days ago." Yes, he put a slight inflection on the *we*—to clear up any doubts.

"Yeah, well, Delia and I... Can't say we're the best of friends."

Couldn't say that about Delia and anyone, but Crayton must not have done well enough in life to be considered husband-material in Delia's book. And for once, Tanner would take a page out of that book. Crayton would not be marrying Juliet when he was gone. He wasn't sure how he was going to ensure that, but that was *not* going to happen.

"Well, it's good to have you back, man. You staying this time?"

The guy could take the hopeful, shit-eating grin off his face.

He slid his arm around Juliet's waist and ignored the

question. "Sweetheart, go ahead and order." Man, even his Texas drawl came back for that manly show of possession.

The raised eyebrows Juliet turned his way said she'd noticed. "Uh, sure."

Tanner got immense satisfaction at watching Crayton's gaze shift between the register and him while Juliet rattled off her order. Not once did the guy look at her.

Good. Message conveyed.

"And what would you like, Tanner?" She turned those big blue eyes his way and Tanner's breath lodged in his throat.

She was even more beautiful than when they'd been in high school.

"Tan?" She nudged him with her shoulder.

"Oh. Right." He shifted his stance. Should have been paying attention and not mooning over her as if he were still sixteen.

Then he caught a glimpse of Crayton's face: crestfallen. Crushed. Good. He'd let him think the pause was because he'd been swept off his feet by his wife.

Actually, dude, that is *why you went radio silent there. Shut. Up.*

He rambled off his favorite menu items, wondering if Crayton would do something as sophomorish as spit in his drink.

He'd like to think not, but then, he also would've bet he'd never go Caveman about a woman.

Luckily, Crayton wasn't working the kitchen, so all he had to do was bag up the food and fries, and a teenage girl poured their drinks. Still, Tanner watched him like a hawk.

And he didn't take his arm off Juliet's waist.

Juliet wasn't quite sure what was going on, but the fact that Tanner called her *sweetheart* and put his arm around her waist had her thinking that he thought Connor was interested in her. He'd be right—Connor had asked her out a few times since Tanner had left, but she'd always told him the same thing: that she was married and her husband was out of town on business. She hadn't lied and it was the perfect excuse to keep him at arms' length. What was going to happen once she signed those divorce papers was something she'd deal with when the time came.

God, she didn't want to think about that. Why couldn't this be real? Why couldn't Tanner's arm around her mean he wanted it there and not because of some stupid *machismo* parade?

"Don't forget the extra cookie," she said when Connor set the bags on the counter.

"I thought you had the best cook in the state working for you? Why do you want some mass-produced cookie instead?"

"Connor, don't let Ermalinda hear you say that; she's the best cook in the *country*, not the state."

"You got that right. Last time I had one of her desserts, I wanted to steal her away. But your father pays her too well, or she loves your family too much because she just laughed in my face."

"It's the family." Tanner all but yanked the bags off the counter. "She's fiercely loyal. But then, the Chambers make it easy to be." He nudged her with his shoulder. "Ready to go home, sweetheart?"

She was if he kept talking like this. And the fact that he almost sounded jealous...

"Um, sure." She used the opportunity to tuck her arm around one of his and waved at Connor. "Thanks, Con." For more than he knew. "See you around."

"I'd like that, Juliet." Connor gave her a genuine smile—much more real than the one he wore when he looked at Tanner and said, "Good to see you, Wentworth."

"Yes. Yes, it was." Tanner gave him that guy head-flip/chin-up thing and nudged the door open with his hip. "After you, Jules."

She literally almost tripped over the threshold. Tanner had always treated her well, but she couldn't remember the last time he'd held a door for her. Definitely not leaving the courthouse when they'd gotten married.

Hmmm, she was liking this jealousy thing. Now how could she use it to her advantage—

No. She wasn't going to manipulate him. Shame on her for even thinking it. If Tanner was going to come back to her it would be because he wanted to. She didn't want to spend the rest of her life wondering if he was going to leave again. No, however hard it would be to watch him walk out of her life, it was better to have an answer than always be wondering if he was going to.

"So you see Crayton often?" Tanner set the bags on the floor behind the passenger seat.

Good; she liked having him drive. Just like when they'd been in high school. He'd had a clunker of a truck while she'd had the Jetta her parents had given her for her sixteenth birthday. Tanner had called it a girly car and said that if she wanted to be with him they were going in his truck. She hadn't minded; the truck had a bench seat and lots more room.

She smiled at the memory.

"That's quite a reaction." Tanner didn't sound happy.

Oh, he thought she was smiling about Connor.

Just because she wasn't going to manipulate him didn't mean she had to correct his wrong assumptions. "Not really. I only stop by there occasionally." As in, once every three years.

Tanner didn't respond, but he did slam the back door hard enough to make her wince. Thank God for German engineering; her car could take his jealousy.

She could too. She liked it. It meant he felt something other than disdain for her.

She tried to keep the smile off her face when she got in the car. Didn't want to make him think too much was going on with Connor or he'd wonder what the other night was about.

She was wondering what the other night was about. Oh, she knew why she'd let it happen; she wanted to know—desperately—why *he* had.

She also wanted it to happen again. Sadly, last night, he'd made dinner while she'd showered after work, then he'd pulled out his laptop while she flicked through the channels and played with the kitten until he called it a night and gone to bed. Alone. They'd been together, but not.

"Nana wants me to take her to get her hair done tomorrow," she said when they stopped at a traffic light. "She won't let Dad come, says he's hovered enough over her. But I'm worried about transporting her and I was wondering—"

"If I'd go with you." They'd finished each other's sentences back in the day. "Of course. I'll get her situated in the salon then go hang out with Rick or someone."

"Did anyone ask any awkward questions at when you saw them at Delia's?"

He glanced in the side view mirror then changed lanes. "No. Which I guess makes sense if we really are together. They still see us as a couple."

Because they should be one.

"They do want to get together Thursday night. Guys' night out. I told them I'd check with you. See what the plans were."

"It's okay, Tanner. You're allowed to have a life here. It's normal for married people to have different interests and go out with their friends. We don't have to be joined at the hip."

There was silence between them. They'd been joined at more than the hip the other night.

God, she wanted to go there with him. It was this big white elephant in the car and they weren't addressing it. Part

191

of her wanted to push the issue, the other part wasn't ready to. Didn't want to hear the, "We can't do that again" speech. And anyway, actions—or lack thereof—spoke louder than words.

Change of subject was definitely called for.

She pulled out her phone. "I have to go into the office tomorrow first, though." She punched in a number and counted the rings until Steve picked up. "Hey, Steve, it's Juliet. Can you do me a favor?"

"Of course, Ms. Wentworth. What can I do for you?"

The deference in his voice was still difficult to get used to. For so many years she'd shown up in Dad's office as merely his daughter. Half the staff had known her when she was in diapers and had seen her in her cheerleading uniform. It'd been a bit intimidating to go in her first day as Dad's replacement in a suit, but everyone had been more than willing to give her a chance. Then, as she'd had some success, and the friendships she'd built with the staff while being her father's daughter had helped ease the transition to being their boss.

"Can you check to see if any of the fleet cars are available yet? I thought the team was supposed to be back tonight. If so, can you have one delivered to my house, please? Put it under my husband's name for insurance purposes."

"Your… husband." There wasn't a question mark on the end of that, but there could be.

"Yes. Tanner Wentworth." Steve had only been with the company for five years. She would have assumed he'd heard about her past, but she couldn't really blame him for not retaining that information.

"Will do, Ms. Wentworth. I'll have Dispatch get one out as soon as it's been detailed if there's one available."

"Thanks. And please have them leave the keys in the planter on the left of my front porch." She didn't want a knock interrupting whatever she and Tanner had going on. *If* they had anything going on…

"Certainly. Have a nice evening, Ms. Wentworth."

"Thank you, Steve. You, too."

Tanner glanced at her when she hung up and it made her self-conscious. "What?"

"You. You sounded so… I don't know, professional."

"I am a professional."

"I know but it's just…" He cocked his head. "It's different. You're different. From what I remember."

"I've grown up, Tanner. We all do."

Chapter Twenty-One

Juliet didn't get much sleep after they'd eaten the fried chicken in a, well, if not comfortable silence, at least it hadn't been silent. Seeing Connor had brought up memories of high school and they'd actually had a couple of good laughs as they'd tripped down Memory Lane, though studiously avoiding any mention of Keegan.

But it wasn't that or the white elephant that had tiptoed through her dreams that accounted for the lack of sleep, surprisingly. No, that she could blame solely on Houdini.

That kitten was going to be spending a lot of nights in the laundry room. The little high-octane curiosity-seeker had decided the dresser was a skating rink, the chair in the corner was a jungle gym, and Juliet's belly was a trampoline. Juliet got maybe a total of three hours of sleep before dragging herself out of bed at five thirty and sneaking into the bathroom to grab her shower and get ready for work. She fed the kitten then locked her into the laundry room, and was on her way to the office before Tanner woke up.

She didn't want to think about him waking up. How he looked with sleep-hooded eyes, and his hair all mussed, and his chest… Tanner had slept naked for as long as she'd been sleeping with him. Which wasn't nearly as much as she wanted it to be.

The head of accounting poked his head out of his office. "Juliet, got a minute?"

Not really. She wanted to get to the executive washroom and run cool water over her wrists because memories of Tanner heated her in a way she didn't need in this weather.

"Sure, Jim, what's up?"

He walked out of his office and flipped open a file. "There are some capital expenditures that your father wanted us to make next quarter and I'm not sure we'll want to do that cash outlay now that… well, we're not sure if the focus of the transportation arm is going to be as aggressive as it had been projected to be."

Her father had been all about growing the company but he'd known the business from the ground up. Juliet was still learning the ropes, and while she wanted to adhere to her father's vision, she didn't want to do so blindly. Slowing the pace might be best so she could evaluate the future of the company. Even with Dad's guidance, she was the one calling the shots so she wanted to understand every nuance before making a decision.

"Can you set up a meeting this afternoon—oh, darn. I forgot. I have to take my grandmother out." Juliet pinched the bridge of her nose. Work days following sleepless nights weren't the best of times any way you sliced it; toss in an appointment and a sudden meeting, and her day got thrown more off-kilter than it'd started.

She was kidding herself; that'd happened the day Tanner had arrived.

"Check with Maggie and see if she can move my morning appointments to tomorrow, then set up a meeting with Scott, Bill, and Madison as soon as possible. I want everyone weighing in on this issue."

"Will do." Jim nodded and headed toward Juliet's assistant, Maggie's, desk.

First wrinkle in her day.

Well at least it kept her from thinking about Tanner.

Tanner couldn't stop thinking about Juliet.

He climbed out of bed, grimacing at the morning wood that was way too interested in wondering if Juliet was still in the house.

He stepped into a pair of shorts. Probably should have slept in them last night, but part of him had wanted to *not* need them.

Except he'd done nothing about it.

That was because, while hanging out in her living room the past couple of nights with her sitting there, looking so darn cute as she played with the kitten—and then so damn hot as she headed into her bedroom—had been torture, rational thought had kept him rooted in his chair with his focus on the laptop screen. Once was allowed; curiosity, old times' sake, whatever he wanted to call it, they were allowed that one night. But to continue… That'd be setting up something he wasn't prepared for.

Something he didn't want.

Sure about that? Your not-so-little friend this morning says otherwise.

He swiped a hand over his face. Yeah, sure, he wanted *her*. That was never in question. It was all the stuff that came with her: relationship, trust, family… They'd tried that not once, but twice, and well, their track record pretty much sucked.

Third time could be the charm, buddy.

Or it could be the one that did him in.

No thank you. He had has life planned and it didn't include Juliet.

Thankfully, she wasn't in the house when he left his room. He checked the garage. The Mercedes was gone, but the Towne Car was on the left side of the driveway where Steve had left it. Or whoever had dropped it off.

He opened the front door and dug around in the planter for the key, then called Rick to set up getting together when he dropped Juliet and her grandmother off at the salon later.

He grabbed a quick shower and was making himself breakfast when he heard the kitten mewing in the laundry room. Poor thing must be lonely.

Tanner opened the door and she darted out, rolling over herself in her dash for freedom. "Hey, you. Come here."

Nope, she kept running, straight into Juliet's room.

Of course.

Tanner sighed and followed her. Weren't cats believed to be instruments of the devil in the old days? He could understand why.

He paused at Juliet's bedroom door. The last time he'd been here for more than a few seconds, she'd invited him. Now it almost seemed wrong.

Until he saw the kitten hanging from the curtain rod. Upside down.

"Come here, you little heathen." He reached for her, but she scrambled onto the top of the rod, Juliet's curtains gaining a couple of slices in the process.

"Houdini, get down here." He reached for her again, but she ran along the thick wooden rod like a gymnast on the balance beam—and executed an, um, interesting dismount off the end onto Juliet's bed.

He should have suggested Beezlebub for her name.

She looked like she'd either gotten the wind knocked out of her or the surprise of her life, but at least she was sitting still.

Until he went to pick her up. Then she streaked across the bed, leaping like a BMX-er and shoving off his thighs—cat claws included—and ricocheted onto the footstool by the rocking chair, then landed on the floor, and ran under the dresser.

Of course.

Tanner sighed. He ought to just let the thing go. If she got lonely, she'd come find him.

Or she'd shred Juliet's curtains.

He walked over to the dresser and was about to hunker down when something on top caught his eye.

It was a side-by-side frame. On the left was a picture of him and Juliet at the prom and on the right—

A deep, burning gasp of air filled his lungs.

Keegan.

Juliet had kept one of her grandmother's photos.

He hadn't seen the pictures. Hadn't wanted to. He had his memories. But now…

Now he couldn't look away.

He picked up the frame. Even now, all these years later, his throat closed and he had trouble seeing through the mist of tears in his eyes, but he made himself look.

Keegan had his nose and his chin. He couldn't tell about the eyes because they were closed, but the curve of the cheek… That was Juliet's. He hadn't had any hair yet and his fingernails were practically transparent and, Jesus, so tiny. So freaking tiny.

He set the frame down. It wasn't fair. Look at the two of them, him and Juliet. So happy, the world at their feet. Even the pregnancy hadn't been the end of the world— rather, the beginning of it. But then it had all come crashing down when they'd lost their son.

Tanner set the frame onto the dresser and sank onto Juliet's bed, dropping his forehead onto his palm. Dear God, it still hurt so incredibly much after all this time.

And she looked at that picture every day.

Punishing herself? Making herself remember?

It wasn't as if he could ever forget.

He reached for the frame again, but then let his hand fall to his thigh. He couldn't do this. He couldn't stay here and pretend that they could be friends or move forward. Not with that picture right there. Glaring at him. Daring him to say that his life *could* be the same.

A knot tightened in his belly and Tanner had the urge to just roll over onto his side and curl into himself and cry. Just cry for everything he—no, *they*—had lost. If Keegan had lived, they might have had a chance.

He sucked in a ragged breath. Much as the idea of shutting out the world and giving in to his grief sounded good, he'd done that before and knew the headache and nauseous feeling that would follow. He had things to do today, people to see. Juliet, her grandmother, Rick. The last thing he wanted to do was show up puffy-eyed with a splitting headache.

He cleared his throat and pressed his thumb and forefinger against his eyes. He'd been down this road before; he didn't need to do it again. He loved his son and always would. But life did go on, as awful as that sounded, and he had to get moving.

Of *course* that was when the kitten decided to peek out from under the dresser, her "meow" sounding like a question.

Well, it was said that animals could sense a person's mood, and his was probably blaringly obvious to her.

He held out his hand and damn if the cute little thing didn't climb right into his palm and lick his wrist, looking up at him as if she were the most innocent thing in the world, full of trust and love.

He sighed and shook his head as he stood, then placed her onto his shoulder. She licked his earlobe and curled into a ball in the curve of his neck, purring contentedly.

"Come on, you. Let's get some breakfast."

His phone rang as he was walking into the kitchen. He ran to his room, grabbed it off his dresser, anticipation taking a hit when he saw that the call was from Gage and not Juliet.

He'd worry about that feeling later. "Hey, Gage."

"Tan. I mentioned to my real estate broker where you are and our expansion discussion, and he just called about a warehouse that's for rent about a half hour from you. Any chance you'd want to go check it out?"

"Yeah, sure. Hang on while I find a pen." He walked out of his room and headed for the kitchen.

Juliet had tons of take-out menus, but not one blasted thing to write with.

He looked around her living room but was out of luck. No way was he heading back into her bedroom, so that left her office.

"Give me another sec."

He didn't particularly relish the idea of going into her private sanctuary, but then again, he couldn't imagine anything more personal than the photo on her dresser, so he'd brave it.

She had a coffee mug filled with pens on her desk, and a pad of sticky notes beside it.

"Okay, what's the address?" He wrote it down, juggling Houdini as she moved from one side of his neck to the other "Is anyone going to be there to show me around or am I just doing a drive-by?"

"He said to let him know what time works for you. Here's his number. He'll meet you there."

"Okay, sounds like a plan. I have to run Juliet and her grandmother somewhere, but then I should be able to swing by."

"Sounds good. Let me know. And if you need more time down there—"

"I'll let you know that, too." Didn't want to discuss that with him. "Thanks, Gage."

"No problem."

He hated getting this personal with Gage, but Gage had a nephew with health issues, so the guy was no stranger to this situation. Sucked that they both were dealing with this, but it solidified his desire to want to work with them. The guys had their priorities straight.

He turned around to leave and caught sight of Juliet's degrees mounted on the wall beside the door. He hadn't seen them on his rush in to find the pen, but now he that did, he went over to examine them.

Juliet Chambers-Wentworth.

It was only fitting, he guessed, that they were made out in her married name, but he couldn't believe she was using his name. He would've thought for sure she would've stayed with her maiden name. After seven years apart—and a honeymoon by herself—he wouldn't have thought she'd want any remembrance of him, let alone attach his name to hers.

He ran his fingers over the glass protecting the parchment. It felt both weird and right seeing it there. Something he'd planned for for so long, that he'd wanted, and now…

And now what?

He didn't know what. He didn't know a lot of what he was doing here or what he was feeling here; but all he knew was that he had a job to do for his future and wallowing in their past wasn't going to be productive.

He reached for the kitten and cradled her to his chest. "Come on, little lady. Let's get something to eat and then I need to get going."

To Juliet's other office. Where he'd find her. And her grandmother. The two women responsible for that image of Keegan. The one that wouldn't leave his brain.

This day was just getting better.

Chapter Twenty-Two

Thank you for picking me up, Tanner." Juliet's grandmother put her hand on his arm when he settled her into the front seat of the Towne Car. The house was on the way to Juliet's office and it made more sense to do so instead of backtracking, and backtracking was a habit with Juliet, one he wanted to break.

"My pleasure, Nana."

"And it's my pleasure to see you and Juliet have worked out your differences. Love is worth it. It's not always easy, I know, but then, nothing good ever is. If it were, we wouldn't value it. In the end, it's all about the love you leave behind, not things. Not business, but family. That's what's important."

"I know. It's why I'm here." Which wasn't a lie.

"So Juliet tells me you're looking to expand your business in town?"

He certainly hoped Juliet hadn't told her *what* business. "It's a thought. As a matter of fact, once I take you and Juliet to the salon, I'm going to take a look at a location."

"Wonderful. Just make sure it has a large parking lot. From what I've heard about BeefCake, Inc. you're going to be wildly successful here."

Tanner almost drove off the road. "You know about the club?" He never would have thought Juliet would mention the strip club to her grandmother, but then, what did he know of their relationship over these past seven years?

"Of course I do. I might be a different generation, but I do know how to use the Internet. Your friends have quite the successful business going."

"You looked us up?"'

"I had to do something while I was recovering. My body might not be up and dancing, but my mind is still active. I'm quite handy with a search engine, you know."

Nana looked quite pleased with herself.

"I…"

"You might want to suggest to the owners that they offer some sort of pay-per-view online streaming. It's not pornography if you're not naked, and just look at that Channing Tatum movie trailer. You could do something like that to make extra money."

He couldn't believe he was having this discussion with Juliet's grandmother. "I'll, uh, mention it and see what they say."

"You should. There has to be a way to monetize your shows for more than just drinks and tips."

He'd never felt uncomfortable with what he did for a living, but this discussion was doing the job.

"Tanner Wentworth, are you blushing?"

"No, ma'am." Okay, he'd just broken his rule about not lying to her.

"Yes, you are. And I must say, I find it endearing. But then, I always have found you endearing. You used to look at Juliet with such puppy love in your eyes when you were in elementary school. I knew it'd only be a matter of time before the two of you figured it out. Gemma and I were so happy when you asked Juliet out that first time."

He had a vague recollection of the night his mom had driven him and Juliet to the movies. He'd been all sorts of embarrassed at having his mom take them, but of the three parents and Nana, she'd been the one he'd thought would embarrass him the least.

Now, to find out she and Nana had been discussing them…

"You *are* blushing." She patted his hand.

"I can't deny it." He managed a smile and prayed it wasn't a sickly looking one.

She chuckled and put her hand back in her lap. "Love is funny, isn't it? The greatest feeling in the world, but it also makes us our most vulnerable. To put your complete trust in someone and hand over the essence of who you are… That's quite a big step. It can be scary. Especially when you've been hurt once already."

Twice, but who was counting?

"I have every confidence you and Juliet will make it work this time. You two were meant to be together. We knew it from the first time you saw her."

"Nana…" He cocked his head. It was one thing to show up here and say they were working on things; it was another to lie outright and say that they'd all live happily ever after. "We were babies. Whatever chemistry you thought you saw, that was probably gas."

It was good to hear her laugh. "Oh, Tanner, you'll see. Someday, you'll see what I'm talking about. There's an… I don't know, an aura maybe around the two of you when you're together that most couples, even those who truly love each other, don't have. Almost makes me jealous. But I had a wonderful relationship. Not unlike yours, I like to think. So I know that if you two can get to where you stop blaming yourselves, you'll do just fine."

Blaming himself? What was she talking about? He didn't blame himself. He'd gone into the marriages with Juliet—the one that didn't happen and the one that did—with an open mind and a heart filled with love for her. She was the one who'd messed things up.

Yes, he blamed her. Because that was where the blame should be. He'd done nothing wrong.

But, as with her father, he wasn't going to destroy her grandmother's illusions. His time here was supposed to give her hope for Juliet's future, not tear down their past.

"So how long will this hair appointment take, do you think? I'm headed toward the other side of town, about twenty minutes or so from Juliet's office."

"About two hours. I'm getting it colored." She patted her hair that had a streak of white among the rest that was as blonde as Juliet's. "I guess it seems pretty silly to do this considering that it really doesn't matter, but a woman does like to have some vanity and mine is my hair. Did you know, it used to be as pretty as Juliet's back when William and I were dating?"

"I seem to remember it being pretty when I used to live here."

"Oh my, Tanner, you are smooth. No wonder you are the most popular dancer at that club."

His face flamed. How on earth had she heard about that? "Uh—"

She laughed again and patted his arm. "You are just too much fun to tease, Tanner. Just because I'm a grandmother doesn't mean I'm not a woman. I have been known to frequent establishments such as yours on occasion. Maybe I'll even come see you and your friends once you set up shop around here."

He wanted to crawl under the seat and block out the images she was putting in his head. "Uh, Nana?"

"Yes?"

"Could we, uh, maybe change the subject? I don't know how appropriate this conversation is given that I'm married to your granddaughter."

"That's right, you are. And don't you forget it."

With the grip she had on his arm, Tanner wasn't going to for a very long time.

If ever.

***

He'd never been so glad to see an empty building in his life.

Tanner was still trying to put Nana's conversation behind him. From the fact that she knew what he did for a

205

living, to the fact that she actually *knew* what he did, to the whole married-to-her-granddaughter comment that had just slipped out… The woman might be ailing but she could still pack a wallop.

"Doesn't look like much."

He glanced at Juliet in the passenger seat. Her grandmother had insisted that Juliet come with him, that she didn't need Juliet staring at her while she got her hair done so she might as well learn something about Tanner's business since that was what married people did.

Neither of them could argue with that logic and keep their cover story going, so Juliet had come with him.

He'd called the agent to arrange the meeting, but after that, it'd been a silent ride—for which he was thankful. The other night just got bigger and bigger the longer they didn't talk about it, but what could he say? *Thanks for the lay?*

He wasn't about to propose his undying love and suggest they get back together, so, really, there was no point. It was what it was.

And it'd been pretty spectacular.

He shook his head. Time to get his mind off sex and onto business. "It's not the outside of the building I'm concerned with." Well, aside from the access, which was off a main thoroughfare so that was good, and the parking, which was plentiful—he smiled as he remembered Nana's comment—so that worked as well. The locale wasn't bad either; the area hadn't become too rundown, and with the development of this site, it could be revitalized. "I have to see inside to see if the space can support the staging and the bar and seating areas."

The real estate broker was waiting for them when they pulled up.

"Wentworth? James Pfeiffer." The guy held out his hand. "Nice to meet you."

"Thanks for meeting me—us—on such short notice."

Pfeiffer shook Juliet's hand next, then nodded at the

building. "This place has been empty too long. It's becoming an eyesore. The city is giving me good money to find a tenant, so I'm more than happy to. Shall we?" He swept his hand toward the plate glass door.

The façade needed work, and the corrugated tin awning would have to go, but the exterior seemed large enough to house the facility Tanner was thinking of.

Pfeiffer gave them the tour, showed them the electrical hookups and water lines, walking them through the utility section that could be incorporated into a kitchen. Now that Bryan and Gage had included dancers of both genders in the shows, the club was becoming an evening destination, and the demand for more than bar food had made them add a make-shift kitchen in their flagship location. Subsequent sites would have the kitchens built in.

Pfeiffer left him and Jules to walk the space themselves, pulling out his phone and saying he'd be outside making calls if they had any questions.

Tanner pulled out a laser tape measure he'd bought on the way here and took some measurements. The staging would work if they ended it where he was standing.

He looked around. "Jules, can you hand me that bucket over there?"

"This?" She picked up the empty drywall compound bucket.

"Yes, put it there." He pointed to where the corner of the stage would be. "And that crate. Grab that for me, but be careful of splinters."

He took it from her and put it at his feet.

"This is the stage?"

"Yeah. We'll put tables there." He circled his hand in front of the stage. "That ought to leave enough space for dressing rooms backstage."

"Don't you mean *un*dressing rooms?" Juliet muttered beneath her breath.

Tanner bit back a smile. What he did for a living *did*

bother her. And if he were honest with himself, he'd admit that he liked that it did.

But that was all he'd admit. Because it didn't matter. He was going to go home and do what he'd planned before he'd come here, great night of sex notwithstanding. "The bar will go along that wall. Probably twenty stools, so that's a decent amount."

"I can't imagine too many people are looking at the bar when they're here."

"You'd be surprised." He dragged a broken two-by-four to where the bar would be. "BeefCake, Inc. isn't a strip joint, Jules; it's a night out. Couples come, bring their friends. The menu is growing. It's becoming a hot spot and not just for the show. I'd like to work in a dance floor if I can, so we can make it a nightclub once the show's over."

She crossed her arms and tilted her head. "You've really given this some thought."

"Like I said, there's a shelf life to this body. I don't want to be dancing long after I should have put the Velcro pants away."

Her eyes slid down his torso.

Lower.

Just like that, it was the other night again and he wanted her every bit as much as he had then. The difference was, this time he had a recently updated memory of how amazing sex with Jules was to add fuel to the fire.

And, yeah, he was burning.

He cleared his throat and spun around, striding away from her. He'd take pictures. Send them to Gage and Bryan. Get his mind off how hot Jules was in her straight red skirt that hugged those hips he'd gripped, and her gorgeous legs that looked even sexier in tan heels that were perfect for the office but whose little bows on the heels begged a man to untie them, and the tailored white blouse that curved in at her waist and opened just above her cleavage and shouldn't be sexy, but given that he knew what was beneath it… was.

"It's okay. I know this isn't easy." He should step away from her. He knew that. Instead, he brushed a few strands that she'd missed.

Her lips moved—tightening, then being nibbled on, then tightening again, but she finally managed to get some words out. "Thank you, Tanner. For that. The hug. And… for saying that." She cleared her throat. "Well. I guess we ought to get going. Let Mr. Pfeiffer off the hook. Poor guy must be so embarrassed."

Tanner took a longer look at her. The Jules he remembered would have clung to him, begging him to stay. He wasn't used to this new, independent, grown-up Juliet.

But he liked her.

Which was a dangerous enough thought to get him moving. Liking Juliet always got him in trouble.

He took two steps to the front door and pushed it open. "After you."

He smelled that scent of hers for the rest of the afternoon.

Chapter Twenty-Three

S o….” Sandy sashayed around the edge of her sofa with a bottle of wine and two hand-painted wine glasses. One said *Therapy* and the other said *Excuse*. “Which one will you choose?” She waggled them at Juliet.

Juliet rolled her eyes and grabbed the *Excuse* one. “This one. Because it’s closest.”

“Uh huh.” Sandy curled her leg under her and sat on her floral sofa. “So now you can go ahead and do naughty things with that hunk you’re still married to and claim it’s the wine’s fault.”

Too bad she hadn’t had this glass the other night.

“Oh my God.” Sandy’s eyes got big. “You already did naughty things with him, didn’t you?”

“What? Sandy, you’re delusional.” Juliet took a hurried sip of wine.

“And you’re horny. Or sated. Or horny wanting to be sated.” Sandy used her wine glass to point at Juliet. “You did the nasty, didn’t you?”

“The *nasty*? Seriously, how old are we?”

“Don’t deflect me, Juliet. You slept with your husband.”

Juliet leaned forward to set her wine glass on the tray on the large ottoman in front of them—and to have a few seconds to get her blush under control. “Will you listen to that sentence? There’s absolutely nothing wrong with it.”

"Unless you've been separated from said husband for seven years and wish like hell you can stay married to him forever."

Sandy, unfortunately, knew more details than Tamra.

But she didn't know all of them and if Juliet could just keep the smile off her face from the memory of the other night, Sandy wouldn't have any confirmation.

She sat back and nibbled her lip to contain her smile, confident that she wasn't giving anything away.

Sandy cocked her head. "I know you, Juliet. You aren't fooling me with your lip-gnawing. You slept with Tanner and you're not sorry about it."

"Would you be?" Dammit, she shouldn't have answered her.

"Aha! I knew it!" Sandy raised her glass. "'Bout time you got some sense in you. Letting that hunk of burnin' love live nine states away all these years… You must have rocks in your head, girl."

"You know why—"

"I know why you *said* you wouldn't go to him, but any fool can see that you two belong together. I might only have known you since I started working for your father, but it's always been plain to see. Someone mentions Tanner Wentworth and you light up like a Christmas tree. And if what I saw when we went to his club was any indication, the man feels just as much for you. You two need to work out some sort of forgiveness pact and just make it work already. Hell, I'm three feet from you on the sofa and the man's not even in the room, and I can feel the heat rolling off you. I have no idea why you're sitting here with me when you have *that* waiting at home for you. If I were you, I'd be there."

"He's out tonight." Juliet adjusted the pillow behind her back. "With his high school friends."

"You're telling me that his drunken buddies are more of a draw than his gorgeous wife? I don't think so." She nudged Juliet's knee. "If you both stayed in that cozy little house together, you might find you don't really want to go anywhere else."

Juliet sat back with a sigh. "It's complicated."

"Oh, I know. You told me. And it sucks at what you've gone through. But if you love each other—and you can't tell me that you don't—then it can work out." Sandy sipped her wine.

"We're too far apart." Juliet raked a hand through her hair. "Maybe if he'd stayed after our wedding, or if I'd gone after him, but… He has a right to be mad at me. He has a right not to trust me or forgive me."

Sandy took her wine glass from her lips. "I think *you* need to forgive you, Juliet. You've been carrying this around for all these years. Yes, you made some questionable decisions, but you were young. We all make questionable decisions when we're young. Hence the divorce rate in this country."

"I made two questionable decisions that affected his life."

"You didn't drag him to the altar."

"My father did."

Sandy rested her arm along the back of the sofa and touched Juliet's shoulder. "But that wasn't you."

"It might as well have been."

"And he still could have walked. But he didn't. Why?"

"Because of the mortgage."

"Really?" Sandy cocked her head. And her wine glass. Which spilled some on her t-shirt. "Oh, shit. Red wine stains and this is my favorite t-shirt." Sandy jumped up from the sofa and headed into her kitchen. "You're telling me that Tanner was going to sacrifice the rest of his life for his father's gambling debts? Think about that, Juliet. Your parents weren't going to kick his parents to the curb. They've been friends for years." She opened the refrigerator. "Tanner's father could have sold his part of the business to him instead. He had choices. Maybe Tanner *wanted* a reason to marry you—to ease his guilt of having walked out on you after you lost Keegan. Maybe he felt guilty about that, did you ever think about that?"

"Tanner had nothing to feel guilty about. It was all me. If I hadn't gotten pregnant on purpose, we wouldn't have lost Keegan." To this day, she still thought it was karmic payback for what she'd done and no one was going to tell her different. She just hated that Tanner and Keegan had had to pay the price. "And if I hadn't set up that night—"

Sandy poked her head out of the kitchen. "Bullshit."

Juliet shook her head. "I'm sorry?"

"I said, *bullshit*. You keep coming up with excuses, but what you're not seeing is that Tanner has always come back. Even now. There's a reason, Juliet, and it's not because he's a nice guy." She ducked back into the kitchen. "I guarantee he wouldn't do this if one of the strippers he's friendly with asked him to. The man is into you and you need to make him realize it."

Sandy had gotten her hopes up until she added that last sentence. Juliet grabbed her wine again. "No way. All I've done all along is manipulate him. I can't do it again. He deserves better. Hell, *I* deserve better. Tanner has to want to be with me because he loves me, not because he's stuck with me or feels obligated or guilty or sorry for me. If I can't have all of Tanner, I don't want any of him."

"Now that's the first grown-up thing you've said since we started this conversation. You know what the next needs to be?'

"What?"

"That you're going to go out and get your man."

Juliet looked at the kitchen door way. "There's a lot more to Tanner and I than hormones."

"Honey, don't discount the power of the hormones. Things have been known to cause wars."

"Exactly. And I don't need anymore in my life. Helping Nana get better is enough of one these days."

Sandy came back into the living room, dabbing at her shirt with a paper towel. "I know. It's scary. And hard. But I know your grandma and the one thing she is *not* going to want you to do is let Tanner get away. Why, whenever his name comes up, she gets a smile on her face almost as big as yours. She wants some great-grandbabies. And she wants 'em named Wentworth. And you do, too. Y'all just have to work through your past to get to your future. And having him here is too big of an opportunity to waste. So get that cute little backside of yours home and figure out some way to get him there with you."

Juliet took another sip of her wine. Just a small one because, if she and Tanner were going to talk—and Sandy had given her compelling enough reasons to bring that white elephant out into the open—she wanted a clear head when Tanner came home tonight.

Unfortunately for Juliet, he never did.

Chapter Twenty-Four

Tanner had a headache bigger than the state he was in. Jagermeister shots. What the hell had he been thinking?

He'd been thinking that he better not go home last night. He'd been thinking that if he did, the same thing that'd happened the other night would happen again and he didn't want to complicate matters any more than they already were.

But, Jesus. His freaking head.

"Yo, Tan. Doin' okay, bro?" Rick's voice sounded as if it echoed off the walls of his man-cave.

Tanner peeled one eye open. A decidedly girly man-cave. The curtain on the windows might be Cowboys blue, but the bows at the top of the valance killed the masculinity in one fell swoop. And the silver sequins on the bar stools…

Rick had taken the ribbing with a good-natured shrug of his shoulders. "Sometimes, guys, it ain't worth fightin' for. And sometimes, the reward's worth it."

No need for him to go any further. They all got it.

And they were all getting it. Everyone but him.

You got it the other night.

Yeah, an aberration that shouldn't have happened.

He winced. Calling what he and Juliet had done an aberration was… well, an abomination.

"Here you go." Rick held a double shot glass under his nose. "Hair of the dog."

One whiff and Tanner was rearing back. "No thanks. Get that shit away from me." He grabbed his head. Should never have had that sixth one. But he had wanted a reason not to go back to Juliet's.

He'd gotten one.

Hell, he probably shouldn't go now.

He checked his cell phone.

No text. No call.

He wasn't sure how he felt about that.

"Seriously, Tan, drink. It'll help with the hangover."

"I deserve the hangover. Hell, we all do. Do we think we're still teenagers?'

"Yeah, because thirty is so old." Rick, the bastard, punched him in the shoulder. "I thought you were looking forward to the big three-oh. Gonna be a rich man, right?"

Tanner rubbed the back of his neck. He'd told the guys about the trust fund years ago and they'd been ribbing him about it last night. Luckily, no one knew about his father's gambling problem, so they all thought he was planning some grandiose purchases the day he turned thirty.

They'd been more than a bit bummed to learn he was investing it in a business venture. He'd gone with *nightclub* and left it at that. If they knew he was dancing…

"So, you seen your folks?" Rick set the glass on the table then grabbed a few empty beer bottles from it, the clinking grinding through Tanner's skull.

Or maybe that was Rick's question.

"Not yet."

"You gonna?"

Tanner opened one eye. "Why?" There was something… odd in Rick's voice. And his question. Tanner couldn't remember the last time Rick had even mentioned his parents let alone was interested when Tanner had talked to them.

"No reason. Just that I see your old man around town and he's … well, he's not lookin' so good."

"Is something wrong with him?"

Rick spun around, the plastic trash bag banging against the coffee table in another nerve-destroying crash of glass. "The fact that you're asking me is a problem."

"It's… complicated."

"Guy's your dad, Tan. Might want to check him out."

One more thing he hadn't wanted to face by coming back here.

Tanner grabbed the shot glass from where Rick had set it on the table and tossed the contents back. The liquid scorched the back of his throat all the way down.

Well, *that* was a wake-up call.

He shook his head, then scrubbed his fingers through his hair and stood up. He needed a shower before he could deal with Rick's question and the associated reality. Not to mention Juliet. He didn't want to face her either.

Luckily, at this hour, she was probably on her way to the office so going back to her place ought to be safe.

***

Wrong.

He knew it the moment he opened the front door. He could smell her. Those bluebonnets…

"Tanner? Is that you?"

"You expecting someone one else?" He headed into the kitchen. She didn't have coffee, but tea had more caffeine. He needed that. And some OJ.

What he didn't need was Juliet showing up in a dress that hugged her chest and flowed over the flare of her hips to fall to right above her knees, leaving nothing to his imagination. Because he knew what was beneath it.

"Where were—Oh. Are you okay?"

"Look that bad, do I?"

"It's… well, you have looked better."

"Felt better, too." He shook his head and even that hurt. "I don't know what we were thinking."

She grabbed a glass from the cabinet and handed it to him. "Just like high school. You guys get together and have the collective brain cells of an amoeba."

He grabbed the OJ from the fridge. "Do amoebas even *have* brain cells?"

"You get my point."

"Ouch, Jules. Don't have to be so harsh." He took the glass from her, giving him a second look at that dress. "Is that what you're wearing to the office?" Damn it, why'd he ask her that? It was none of his business what she wore to the office. He splashed the OJ into the glass.

"Why? What's wrong with it?"

He shrugged and dragged the glass to his mouth. Better to have juice going in instead of his foot.

"Seriously. What's wrong with it?" Juliet looked down the front of it, then over her shoulder, which stretched it across her chest.

"Nothing." Everything. Tanner gulped his juice.

She looked back at him and smoothed the dress over her hips. "I've worn this before."

"I said it's fine, Jules. Don't mind me." He grabbed a mug out of her cabinet and filled it with water, then stuck it into the microwave. He needed caffeine. Now.

Though, actually, the sight of Juliet in that dress jump-started his blood faster than caffeine could. "Aren't you going to be late?"

"I handled my email from home this morning. I wanted… I wanted to talk to you."

Warning signs went off in his head—which didn't help the hangover. He didn't turn around. "Talk about what?"

"About…" She exhaled. "The other night."

There was only one other night and he didn't want to talk about it. "I think it's better left as it is."

"And how is it?"

He spun around—damn it. His brain was a few seconds behind his body so it rattled around in his skull. "What do you mean, *how is it*? It is what it is and we should just leave it in the past."

"Why?"

"Why? Because it doesn't change anything, remember? That's what we agreed on." The blood was throbbing through his brain and he wanted to attribute it to the stress of her question and the volume with which he'd answered her… but he didn't think so.

"I remember, Tanner. I remember a lot of things. Like how it always was between us."

"That's what this is all about, isn't it? That's why you came to my club to find me. You want me—us—back. Is your grandmother even sick or did you make that up?"

Juliet gasped and reached for the counter. "How can you even ask that? Of course she is. I wouldn't do that. You saw for yourself. "

Shit. He felt worse for that question than he did because of the hangover. He raked a hand through his hair then braced himself with his palms on the counter behind him. "You're right. I'm sorry. That was uncalled for. Of course she is. I know you wouldn't make that up." He scrubbed his five-am shadow. "Look, Jules. There can't be anything between us. There's too much baggage. Too much mistrust. We can't go back."

"I don't want to go back."

He couldn't have heard that right. He wiggled a finger in his ear. "Huh?"

"I don't want to go back. You're right; there *is* too much baggage. Too much hurt and bad decisions and lies to wade through. But we can move forward, Tanner. We could if we wanted to."

That was the thing; he didn't want to.

Really? That's not what you were saying the other night, and you can try to blame it on hormones or distance or whatever, but the reality is, you wanted Juliet then. And you went back for seconds. There's something between you; there always has been. You owe it to yourself to deal with it instead of running from it. You've been running ever since Keegan died. Time to stop and smell the bluebonnets, buddy.

Right. And visit his parents, too. Gee, this trip was just a ball of laughs.

Tanner flexed his fingers against the edge of the counter. "I can't do this, Jules. Not now."

She opened her mouth to say something, then closed it. But he felt those slate blue eyes of hers trying to dig into his psyche. His soul.

Once upon a time, they'd been able to. Because they'd *been* his soul.

"Okay, Tanner. You're right. Now's not the time. I have to get to work and you have to… Whatever it is you have to do today."

"I'm going to see my parents."

The words shocked him as much as they did her.

"Do they know?"

He winced when he shook his head. "I didn't know 'til just now, so no, they don't."

"Are you going to call them?"

He shrugged and pushed himself off the counter then opened the microwave. "I don't know. Probably not. In case I change my mind."

"Are you sure that's wise?"

"No. But then, neither was the other night and I survived that."

Sort of.

***

He'd *survived that*.

Survived.

So much for Sandy's great insight into Tanner Wentworth.

He really didn't want to try to make things work with her.

And you're surprised why?

Because… she wanted to. Because she'd thought the other night meant something. He still wanted her physically. He'd held her after her father had left. He had to feel something for her to do that, right?

Except he didn't want to talk about it. Didn't want to revisit it. Didn't want to hear her out.

Juliet moved the sticky note from one side of her desk to the other—as she'd been doing for the past five minutes. She had to get her mind on work. Back to the day-to-day. The future was too tough to think about.

"Juliet?" Maggie, her assistant, buzzed her from her desk.

Juliet moved the sticky note back to her calendar and punched the mic button. "What's up, Maggie?"

"Mr. Wentworth is here to see you."

"Tanner?" Juliet tried not to squeak his name out, but she wasn't very successful.

"Uh, no. A Mr. Palston Wentworth."

Tanner's father? What could he possibly want with her?

Juliet took a couple seconds to gather her wits, then pushed the mic again. "Send him in, Maggie."

"Will do."

Juliet's office was only five feet from Maggie's desk so it didn't give her a lot of time to steel herself for her father-in-law's arrival.

Father-in-law. Funny that that was her first thought of the man. She hadn't seen Tanner's parents since his mother had stopped by to ask for a picture of Keegan. They'd been at the hospital that night when Nana had taken the pictures. Mr. Wentworth hadn't come anywhere near her since the hospital and she hadn't seen him since. He hadn't even shown up at the courthouse for their wedding.

Of course, with the mortgage issue, she hadn't really blamed him. But Tanner had.

The man didn't look anything like she remembered.

Gaunt, his shoulders bent and his hair that had once been thick and blond like Tanner's now gray and thin… Mr. Wentworth had aged more than the years that had passed.

"Mr. Wentworth." Juliet rounded her desk and held out her hand. Her grandmother had made sure she knew her manners. "What can I do for you?"

Tanner's father looked at her outstretched hand as if he wasn't quite sure what it was. But then he grabbed it with his gnarled one. "More like what I can do for you."

He gave her one last shake, then reached out to the back of the chair in front of her desk and lowered himself into it gingerly, setting a small pouch on his lap.

"What you can do for me?" She walked back behind her desk, foregoing the chair beside him. This wasn't a social visit and he'd never acknowledged her as his daughter-in-law. Then again, he'd never really acknowledged her at all when she'd been to Tanner's house. More often than not, he'd pull Tanner aside and discuss football with him. Juliet had been relieved to spend the time with Mrs. Wentworth as Tanner's father had always been gruff and stand-off-ish.

"I know you know about the issue with your dad and I." Mr. Wentworth shifted in his seat. "About the mortgage."

"Yes, I do."

He drummed his fingers on the pouch and looked at her while he gnawed on the inside of his cheek.

Then he set the pouch on the end of her desk and rested his hands in his lap again. "I'm here to pay you back."

Juliet didn't respond. Didn't know what to say. She knew why her father had bought the mortgage from the bank; knew why Mr. Wentworth owed it to them in the first place. If she told him she was forgiving the note and he had all that money, there was no telling what he'd do with it. And if she told Tanner… Well, then there'd be no reason for him to stay.

She needed time to think. "All right. I'll have to let our lawyers know so they can draw up the paperwork. Do you want to hang onto that, um, pouch, until then?"

"No." He scratched his jaw. "No, you hang onto it. Give me a receipt; I trust ya."

He'd never been a man of many words, but she could hear the tightness in the ones he'd said. This wasn't easy for him.

Truth be told, it wasn't easy for her either. She didn't want to have to hide this from Tanner, but she also didn't want to make it easy for him to walk away. He had to stay. For Nana's sake.

And hers.

Chapter Twenty-Five

Tanner?" His mother's mouth fell open—ushering a ton of guilt into Tanner's heart. He shouldn't have lost touch with them. No matter what they'd done, they were still his parents.

"Hi, Mom." He swept her up in a hug.

She still felt like his mom. Still wrapped her arms around him the same way she'd done since he'd been little. He'd forgotten what it felt like. He hadn't exactly been in a wanting-hugs mood when he'd been forced to the courthouse, which was the last time he'd seen her.

He should've come back. If only for a visit.

"My, look at you. It's been so long."

"I know, Mom. I'm sorry."

There were tears in her eyes. "Well, now, you're here. That's what's important." She stepped aside. "Come in. I'm just sorry your father's not home to see you. You'll come back, won't you?"

"Dad's not here? Where is he?" Tanner didn't want to ask, but something compelled him though he was half afraid of the excuse his mother would come up with. His father had a gambling problem and she'd enabled it.

Tanner had hated them both for it when he'd last been here, but now… Now he felt sorry for them.

He wanted to get the mortgage back for them. Give them a chance to start over. But he'd insist on counseling for both of them. Dad couldn't lose the ranch again because Tanner wasn't going to be able to bail him out a second time. He had his own life to worry about.

"He said he had some errands to run."

"What kind of errands? I thought he was working the ranch?"

"Oh he is. But a load of cattle just left and he came in with a big smile on his face, kissed me on the cheek, and told me, 'Gemma, I'm goin' out. Don't wait up.'"

Shit. Shit. And triple shit. That didn't sound good.

"But you can visit with me a while, right? It's not just your father you came to see."

His guilt doubled. Ah, well, it wasn't as if his father couldn't have gotten in trouble the past seven years. One afternoon couldn't do much more damage.

"Of course I can, Mom." He closed the door behind him. "You don't happen to have any of your cookies around here, do you?"

"Now Tanner Nathan Wentworth. What would the Wentworth Ranch be without my homemade chocolate chip cookies? The hands still come in on their breaks for them, same as they did when you were haulin' hay." She shooed him back toward the kitchen. "Come on, I'll get them for you. If I'd known you were coming, I would've made a batch for you to take back with you."

Another knife to his heart. For the too-short time he'd been a parent, he knew what it meant to love a child and he'd denied his mother that.

"I'm, ah, here for a while, Mom."

The smile on her face when she turned around both warmed him and filled him with more regret for causing her pain. "Oh, sweetheart, I'm so glad to hear that. Where are you staying?"

And now for the hard part…

He followed her into the kitchen. "With Juliet."

Mom's steps faltered. "Ju… Juliet? Chambers?"

"Wentworth, Mom. We're still married."

His mother got *very* busy searching for those cookies in the cupboard. "You are? I would've thought you'd taken care of that years ago."

"No, I didn't." He didn't want to broach this subject with his mother but it needed to be said. He'd held his tongue for too many years and he knew how worried his mother had been when Burt had bought the mortgage.

He walked to the cupboard and took the cookie jar from her. "Let's sit."

She blinked at him but didn't say anything. She didn't have to. He could see that same fear in her eyes.

"It's okay, Mom. Everything's going to be okay." He held out a chair for her.

She sank into it. "What do you mean, Tanner?"

"I mean, I'm taking care of the mortgage for you." The hope that leapt into her eyes was his reward and confirmed that he should be here, live the lie Juliet concocted, for more than just her grandmother.

"But how—?" She covered her mouth. "Your trust fund." Now his mother's eyes grew hard. Determined. "No, Tanner. I won't allow it. That money is yours and it's not meant to bail your father and I out. I will not hear of it."

"Mom—"

"No. You can't do it." She stood and twisted the dish towel that was hanging from her apron pocket. "You have lost out on so much already in your life. All the things that should have been—" She didn't need to recite the list; they knew it by heart. "I won't have you losing your future, too. That money is for you. To buy a home, pay student loans, get a car. Whatever you want to do. My father set it up for just that reason and I won't have you handing it over to us. We won't take it."

"Mom, hang on. You misunderstand."

"No, I don't. You can't work up some scheme to tell me that you're not really doing it when that's the only way you possibly could. I won't allow it, Tanner, do you hear me? I won't. I'd rather live in the poor house than see you give up that financial cushion because of your father's… well, his troubles."

"Mom, Dad has a gambling addiction. It's not just a trouble."

"Be that as it may, Tanner, you are not to concern yourself with it. We will get the ranch back. Your father, he's working harder than he ever has and we're able to see daylight again. It'll be all right. I promise you."

He grabbed her hands. "No, Mom, what you don't understand is that I'm not going to use my trust fund to get it. Juliet's giving it to me. Free and clear."

Now her mouth fell open and for once, she didn't have a thing to say.

But he could see the question in her eyes. "Because I'm helping her with something, and for that, she's willing to forgive the debt."

Tears slipped from the corner of her eyes. "Why? What could you possibly be doing?"

He exhaled and released her hands, and leaned back in the knot of hard wood on the chair back. "I'm pretending to be her husband."

"But I thought you were. Didn't you just say you weren't divorced?"

"Yes, but we will be. We're pretending that that's not going to be the case, though, for her grandmother."

"Her grandmother? "

"Nana had a stroke and she wasn't recovering well. Juliet thought if her grandmother had something happy to focus on, that she'd want to get better. And it worked. She got well enough to be discharged from the hospital before I came. And now she's doing a lot better. Still tired and has some coordination issue with her one hand, but she's up and about. Even went to get her hair done the other day."

"All because you've come back to town?"

"Well, because she's seeing Juliet's happy and that's making her happy."

"But what's going to happen when Juliet's sad?"

"What do you mean?"

"Come on, Tanner. You know Juliet. Heck, everyone knows how Juliet feels about you. Do you think for one minute that she's just going to be able to watch you walk out of her life again and be happy about it?"

"She has to be. It's our agreement. She just wants her grandmother to get better."

His mother drummed her fingers on the table. "Well, it's already done, I guess, so there's nothing we can do about it now but see it through, but let me be the first one to tell you that I don't ever want you pretending to be something you're not for me. And I can guarantee you Penelope doesn't want that, so you and Juliet need to come to a decision. This limbo you're both floating in isn't good for anybody."

"It's just for a little while. My birthday at the latest, ironically, though her grandmother is doing so well that it might be over sooner so we can end this."

"The lie or the marriage?"

"They're one and the same."

His mother cocked her head. "Are they?"

"What do you mean'?"

She leaned forward and cupped his cheek. "I see the way you look when you say her name. The same way you always have. You still care for Juliet and you have a history together."

"A not-so-great history if you remember."

"I remember. But I also remember how in love you two were. She was young. You were young. She was scared that you'd leave her."

"Mom, she planned to get pregnant."

"I know, sweetheart. But you weren't exactly making sure it didn't happen."

"I wore a condom." He couldn't believe he was having

this discussion with his mother. His father had read him the riot act at the time—not for the fact that there was a baby involved but because he couldn't play ball.

His mother opened the cookie jar and pulled out three. She set two on a napkin in front of him on the table and used the other one as a pointer. "But condoms aren't one hundred percent effective, Tanner. Everyone knows that. So it was always a possibility. You were taking a risk with Juliet every time." She took a bite of the cookie, wiping stray crumbs with the back of her hand. "Who's to say, if she hadn't done what she did, that she wouldn't have gotten pregnant anyway? Who would you blame then? It's the nature of the beast, Tanner. If you play with fire, you could get burned. And the more you play with it, the bigger the risk. You got burned. But it wasn't so bad, was it? I remember how thrilled you were with Keegan. How you and Juliet decorated the nursery and how you kept rubbing her belly. It was sweet. Just like love is."

Tanner tapped the edge of the cookie on his napkin. "So what are you saying? That I should forgive her for ruining the life I'd planned and just let bygones be bygones and stay married to her as if nothing had happened?"

His mother took her time taking another bite and chewing it thoroughly, making him squirm under her scrutiny.

Finally, she finished. "In a word, yes. Sure, she's made some decisions that weren't the best, but at the core, it was because she loved you. She was afraid of losing you."

"Yet she did."

"Exactly. Do you think that girl hasn't paid enough all these years? Self-recrimination is a horrible thing to have to live with." His mother blinked and looked away. "I should know."

Tanner took a bite of the cookie. Or rather, a chomp. "Yet you're still married to him, Mom. Why?"

She sucked in a breath and blinked, then cleared her

throat. "Because I love him. Because there is good in him. Oh, I know you thought I enabled him, and maybe I did, but I like to think that I'd stopped him from being worse. That without me, he would have lost everything."

"But you could have lost the ranch, Mom, if Mr. Chambers hadn't stepped in."

"But he did and we didn't. And we still won't, even without your help. Because your father, with my love and support, got help."

"What sort of help?"

"He's going to counseling. Has been for a while. He let someone else handle the books. We now have an accountant. Becky is so meticulous in making sure everything is done the right way that we finally have some extra. And your father doesn't gamble it away. He's taken me to a couple of nice dinners. Gave me the money to buy a new dress. Is talking about taking a vacation next year. Imagine that. A vacation. I can't remember the last one we took."

Tanner did. It was to the state fair the summer he made Varsity. After that, the betting on his games had begun. Or, if it'd started before, it'd escalated to a point where his father couldn't sustain it.

"So it's working, then? The therapy?"

"Something is. I haven't seen him this happy in years."

"That's not what my buddy Rick said. He said Dad doesn't look the same."

"Oh he's not. He lost weight. I tell him he's working too hard, but he just shrugs it off and goes about his business. But he gets up every morning and is right there with all the hands. And then… then, at night, he goes to the fishing shop downtown. He's started putting in some time there. Says it relaxes him. Soothes his mind. And the pay isn't bad. Gives us our little extra."

His father had a part-time job on top of running the ranch? He'd hired someone to do his bills? Tanner couldn't imagine they were talking about the same man who was so controlling over his business that he kept the books locked up in the safe in his office.

Something didn't compute.

"But a little extra isn't going to pay off the mortgage, Mom. Let me do this. Hell, let Juliet do this. She owes me. She owes all of us."

Mom slid her hand across the table to grab his. "Forgive her, Tanner. It's not good to have that much anger inside of you. It colors your thinking. Your perception. She made a mistake. Lord knows, none of us is perfect."

"She made two."

"Okay, so she made two. But how many other right decisions did she make? Surely there was something good you saw in her or you wouldn't have been with her to begin with. Focus on the good, not the bad. Life's too short for the bad."

So she wanted him to, what? Enable Juliet to run his life? No thank you.

That had happened before and everything had been out of his control. He'd been powerless to stop losing everything he'd wanted in life, from the pregnancy to the miscarriage to his scholarship and even to marrying Juliet—it'd all been decided for him, the ability to choose his own way taken from him. That's why he'd left; he'd needed to regain control of his life.

And now he had.

Some control. You're hiding a couple hundred miles from your friends, your family, everything you grew up with. Is resentment toward Juliet worth this? Did it get you anywhere other than sitting in your mother's kitchen eating cookies? What kind of life it this? Limbo is the right word. Jesus, dude, live a little.

He *was* living, dammit. Or, he had been before he'd been forced back here by Juliet.

She didn't force you; she asked you. Big difference. This time, you had your eyes wide open to come back here.

You came back because you decided to, not any other reason. Think about exactly why that is.

He didn't need to. He knew exactly why he was doing what he was doing, and why he'd done what he'd done.

And it wasn't about the mortgage, was it?

Damn that little voice of reason.

He shoved his chair back from the table. "I gotta go, Mom."

"Oh, but your father—"

'I'll see him another time. Right now, I just need to think."

"You've had seven years to think, sweetheart. Don't you think it's time you started acting instead?"

Her words had him spinning around. "Acting? I've been moving non-stop since I left here."

"I know. Too busy to come home. Making your way in the world. It's why I didn't insist that you come back. I knew you needed time on your own. Remember, Tanner, Keegan was our grandson. We loved him every bit as much as you did. As much as we love you."

Those words were like a blow to his heart. He hadn't thought… Hadn't realized…

Now he really needed to think.

"Mom, I have to… I have to go."

"Just don't go far this time, Tanner. You can't outrun your memories."

Chapter Twenty-Six

He tried to. Lord, did he try to. But it seemed, as he went for a jog to clear his head, as if he was running *toward* them.

Tanner slowed his pace as Juliet pulled into her driveway when he was half a block from her house. He slid in behind an overgrown bush someone seriously needed to trim off the sidewalk. But right now, he was enjoying the hiding space it provided him.

Hiding space? Really? From his own wife? A girl he'd known his entire life?

Or so he'd thought.

But this Juliet… He watched her climb out of her car, the leg she was showing making his mouth go dry in a way his run hadn't. He didn't know this Juliet. That dress should only be for nights on the town. With him. No one else should see her in it and he was suddenly very angry that that Steve guy probably had. That any number of guys probably had.

He watched her round the back of her car, the dress clinging to her backside. And those heels she wore… son of a bitch, they had straps that wrapped around her ankles.

He ought to just keep running.

But his mother was right. That was the realization he'd come to during his run. He and Juliet needed to talk. To clear the air. To say things that needed to be said. They weren't kids anymore and if this was the end of it, the end of their relationship and their marriage and everything that'd gone on between them for the past almost thirty years, there needed to be some closure.

And if it wasn't…

Which did he want?

That was the ultimate question: what *did* he want? A lifetime of painful memories of a woman he'd once loved? Or a life with the woman he still loved?

He stumbled. He still loved her? How? Why? Just because she'd, what? Grown up? Gone to college? Was running her father's company? Had swallowed her pride and her hurt enough to come find him not for herself but for her grandmother?

Yes. Those. They were reasons to look at the Juliet he'd known before and see she was so much more now.

Maybe there *was* a chance for them.

His mother's words ringing in his ears, Tanner jogged to the front door. They needed to talk.

Unfortunately, when he walked inside, he heard her in the shower. That would *not* be the place to hold the conversation he wanted to have.

And then he heard her singing.

He had to laugh. Juliet had a beautiful voice—it'd been her talent in her pageants—but the woman could not sing a country song to save her life. Since he didn't like country music, it wasn't an issue, but Juliet did. So she sang. Tried to put the twang in there, but it came out sounding like she'd garbled the words. It'd irked her no end while it'd made him smile.

Like he was doing now.

Juliet made him smile. She made him laugh. She made him feel things.

Feel alive.

That was it, this feeling coursing through him. It wasn't the high from his run—that paled in comparison. Juliet made the world seem brighter, the days longer, the nights better, the highs higher, the lows lower…

He looked around her home. It said so much about her.

She'd worked and studied to be able to make it on her own. Make her way. The house wasn't grandiose or overdone, but with just enough rooms and decorated comfortably... The perfect home for her.

And she was home for him.

He exhaled. This could all be his if he just forgave her. "Meow."

The kitten wound against his ankles, her green eyes blinking up at him.

He picked her up. She, too, reminded him of what a home should be. Buddy had given his apartment life. Had filled the emptiness of being alone in it. Since the cat had died, he'd been there as little as possible because it just wasn't the same. Yet he hadn't gotten another cat.

He knew why. He'd been protecting himself from caring. From loving someone or something so that he wouldn't have to lose someone again. But that wasn't living.

This, having a home, someone to come home to, sharing the highs and lows of life, the cares and the triumphs... That was living. That was what life was about. His mother was right. Juliet's grandmother was right.

He did still love her and he wanted to make that life together happen.

He set the kitten on the sofa then stripped off his shirt and flung it down the hallway toward the laundry room, stepping out of his running shoes and shorts on the way to the bathroom.

His wife was in there and it was time he started living again.

Juliet washed the shampoo out of her eyes as she finished the Rascal Flats song, wishing she could wash the image of that pouch out of her mind just as easily.

Why couldn't Tanner's father have waited to give it to her? Why'd it have to be now? Why not next month when it'd be a moot point? But now she had the responsibility of telling Tanner, giving him the perfect reason to leave. The mortgage hold would be gone, he'd have his trust fund, and Nana was definitely on the road to recovery. He'd have no reason to stay.

Unless she gave him one.

She brushed the water out of her eyes. What other reason could she give him? They'd slept together but that hadn't changed things. They needed time to be together for him to forgive her. And hopefully fall in love with her again.

That was the thing; there was no guarantee he would. And that was what scared her the most. The idea of her life without Tanner in it…

Now she brushed some tears out of her eyes.

She didn't want to lose him, but if he found out about his dad's money, she would.

She straightened her spine. She wasn't a teenager anymore; she was an adult. One who had to own up to the truth and deal with the chips as they fell. She had to come clean. No more playing games.

She'd tell him when he got home.

She picked up the soap and was about to launch into her favorite Carrie Underwood song when the door to the bathroom opened.

"Tanner?"

He shoved back the shower curtain over the tub and there he stood in all his naked glory.

And it *was* glorious.

"You were expecting someone else?" He stepped into the tub.

"I wasn't expecting even you."

He yanked the curtain closed. "You said you wanted to talk."

Not exactly the place to have a coherent conversation because her brain was fast losing its sharpness the longer he stood there. "I wasn't exactly thinking we'd talk in the shower."

"Good."

And that was the last word he said for a very long time.

Oh, lord. It'd been so long since they'd made love in the shower. Juliet wanted to know why now, but with his tongue in her mouth, she wasn't about to ask him.

She certainly wasn't about to bring up the money either because his hands felt so good sliding over her body that was still slick with soap, pulling her against him as the water cascaded over them. She had to close her eyes, but that was just a precursor for when the feelings got too intense. In the past, they'd tried to look at each other to the end at times, but there always was that moment when Tanner would take her out of herself and she had no control over her actions; she was just responding to what he was doing to her.

This was one of those times.

His hands cupped her bottom and he turned to the side, wrapping her legs around his waist as he pressed her up against the wall.

"I want you, Juliet, " he growled into her neck.

"Okay," was all she managed to pant out. The water was hitting her on the forehead, making it hard to talk and breathe, but she wasn't going to ask him to stop.

She turned her head to the side, resting it against his forehead as he licked his way up her neck to her lips while his cock twitched against her.

God, she wanted him inside her.

And then he was.

It was as natural and right as it'd ever been between them. As if seven years hadn't passed. As if the other night hadn't been the first in so long. They still knew each other. Still knew where to touch and where to kiss and lick and nip. How to breathe with their tongues making love to each other, how and when to grasp and tighten, when to release only to build the tension again.

She and Tanner worked in tandem. They always had in everything—well, everything but what she'd screwed up.

Her breath hitched and she missed a movement in their rhythm.

"Juliet?" Tanner pulled back to look at her, the concern in his eyes wanting to make her cry.

Thank God for the shower; he'd never know that a few tears leaked out.

"Don't stop, Tanner." She pulled his lips back to hers, not saying the rest of that sentence. *Don't stop loving me.*

He hiked her up a little more against the wall, spreading his legs beneath him, and he rocked into her.

Juliet moaned. God, he felt so good.

He dug his fingers into her hair, turning her head to just the right angle. Juliet clenched her thighs around him, smiling when he hissed.

"Like that?" she managed to murmur between tongues.

He growled and thrust deeper inside her.

Juliet couldn't hold back the tears then. This was no after-party, hyped-up hormonal thing. This wasn't haven't-see-you-in-so-long sex. This was Tanner opening her door, coming into her shower with the express purpose of doing this with her. He'd made that decision and she was so very hopeful to find out why.

Bur first…

She wiggled against him. He needed to keep thrust-ing. She didn't have much opportunity to do more than wiggle being caught between his glorious warm chest and the cold wall tile with soap slicking their bodies.

"More, Tanner." She groaned. "I want more."

With a toe-tingling kiss, he gave her more.

Tanner clenched her butt as he moved in and out of her, and he made love to her mouth with his tongue, holding her head so that she couldn't go anywhere—not that she would. All she wanted—all she'd *ever* wanted—was right here in this shower with her.

His thrusts quickened. She slid one hand down to his backside. Tanner had an amazing backside. She grasped it, pulling him into her with this rhythm.

"Yes, Juliet. That's it. Touch me, sweetheart."

She ran her other hand up his side and over his nipple. He gasped when she did that… So she did it gain.

He pulled back—not too far, but enough for her to know she didn't want him to go even that far.

"You're not playing fair," he said harshly.

"Did you want fair? Or did you want great sex?"

The heated look in his eyes answered that question. "You, Juliet. I want you."

He didn't give her the chance to answer as he thrust into her again, taking her to that place where she could only feel. She'd think later.

Juliet felt like heaven. Wrapped around him, clenching him internally… It was impossible to feel where his body ended and hers began.

It'd always been like this between them. There'd never been a time when he hadn't felt this all-encompassing togetherness when they'd made love.

If only they'd both held onto it.

Her heels banged into his ass, keeping his pace. This too, had always been good between them; they picked up the other's rhythm perfectly.

He angled his hips, remembering how that'd sent her skyrocketing into the stratosphere and now was no different. Her eyes flew open and she looked at him—really looked at him, there in the moment with him, seeing into his soul and showing him all of hers.

Juliet was love. For him, by him, in him… He'd been so wrong not to give them another try.

He wasn't going to make that mistake again.

Her muscles spasmed around him, and that was all it took. He followed her so powerfully, it was as if fireworks were going off in the air around them.

Jesus God, she felt so good.

So right.

Shivers raced over them, aftershocks. They'd always

laughed about them before, but now… he couldn't laugh. Hell, he could barely form a coherent sentence and all he wanted to do was stay like this forever.

But of course, he couldn't. The water grew cold, her legs lost their grip, and he had to ease himself out of her to let her down.

He reached over to turn off the faucet. "Cold?"

She caught her bottom lip between her teeth. "Not in the least."

God, he loved her.

He cupped her face. Brushed his thumb over that bottom lip so she'd give it to him. Then slid his thumb between her lips.

She licked it and his dick sprang to life as if it hadn't just had one of the most shattering orgasms he'd ever had.

"Don't." He shook his head, not quite sure what he was asking her not to do.

She nipped his thumb instead. It had the same reaction.

Tanner sighed, shuddering, unsure of what to say. He'd stormed in here all purposeful and full of testos-terone, with the need to claim her as his wife. And now…

Now, he had to tell her what he wanted. Her. Her life. Their life.

And maybe even a child

A chil—Shit. He hadn't used a condom.

"What's wrong?" Juliet gripped his arms.

"We didn't use a condom."

"Oh." She nibbled her bottom lip again, but this time he was too worried about what they'd just done to think about it being sexy.

Well, almost too worried.

"What are we going to do, Juliet?"

"There's that morning after pill. I'll just go get that. No worries, Tanner. I'm not trying to make you stay."

He deserved that. But she did, too. It was a valid reaction on his part if he'd thought that.

If.

But he hadn't. She hadn't expected him to show up in her shower and when he had, he hadn't given her the chance to even remind him about birth control. And since *he* hadn't been thinking along those lines, there was no rule that said *she* should be.

There was a reason a lot of the population could call themselves "oops" babies.

He wouldn't mind an "oops" baby.

He sucked in a deep breath. "Don't."

"Don't what?"

"Don't take that pill."

"But—"

"Let's do this, Juliet."

She cocked her head, her beautiful eyes narrowed. "Define *this*. Because we just did *this* and now we're having a discussion about morning after pills and condoms. Things we should've discussed beforehand."

He grabbed her hands and brought them to his lips, kissing her knuckles. "Us. Let's do us again."

Her fingers flexed and she sucked in a breath. "Tanner, what are you saying?"

He kissed her hands again. "Not here. This is not the place I want to have this discussion. Can you be dressed in about ten minutes? I'd like to go someplace special for this conversation."

"I can do it in five."

He laughed at her then. "The Juliet I knew ten years ago couldn't have done it in a half hour, let alone five minutes."

"I'm not that Juliet."

"I know."

He swatted her on the butt playfully when she walked out of the room ahead of him, laughing when she squealed and shoved her hands behind her to cover herself.

"Too late. I've already seen every part of you, Jules. I know how perfect your butt is."

She looked back over her shoulder, a blush blazing in her cheeks. Juliet was like that; could be a tiger in the bedroom but would blush about it when he teased her outside of it.

He'd missed the teasing.

He ran into his room and threw on a t-shirt and shorts. He was going to take her to the field. The one filled with bluebonnets. They'd talk and they'd work things out and then… then he'd make love to her there. Again. A new beginning.

He looked at the nightstand. He'd put the condoms in there—and that was where they'd stay.

Maybe today could be a whole slew of new beginnings.

Juliet didn't quite make it in five minutes. It was closer to eight, but Tanner was willing to give her all the time she'd need as long as she showed up.

And she did, in a sexy little sundress and her wet hair pulled back in a bun. "Will this do?"

"God, yes, Jules. That'll do." All he could imagine was getting his hands under that dress and shimmying it over her head.

Maybe they'd talk later. Maybe right now, he could take her back to bed and they could talk there.

No. He wanted to do this right. Wanted it not to be about making love—at least until after they ironed out their past and talked about their future.

He very much wanted one for them. Together.

"Ready to go?"

"Can't wait."

Tanner opened the door for her and—

His father stood there, hand raised to knock.

Rick had been right; his father looked different. Too thin, his hair gray and thinning, his clothes hanging off him. Mom thought this was better? "Dad."

"Son."

Tanner winced. He was rarely "Tanner" when his father spoke to him. "Son" was a more important status it seemed than who he actually was. "What are you doing here?"

"I need to talk to you. Your mother told me I'd find you here."

Juliet gripped his arm. "Um, Tanner? I think—"

Tanner held up his hand. Juliet didn't need to worry; she was more important than his father. What they had to discuss was far more important. "It's going to have to wait. Juliet and I were just going out."

"It can't. I need to talk to you. It's important."

He was torn. He wanted to hear his father out, but he wanted to start his life together with Jules.

His father stepped over the threshold. "I just need a few minutes. It won't take long."

Tanner looked at Juliet. She stood there, her fingers tight on his arm, nibbling on her bottom lip again. He wasn't sure why.

"Sweetheart? Are you okay? I don't have to do this now."

"I think you do, Son."

He didn't even look at his father. The day the man called him by his name would be the day he'd start to feel as if he mattered to the guy. Until then, as far as Tanner was concerned, Palston Wentworth was just the guy responsible for almost losing his mother's home.

"Go, Tanner.' Juliet pulled a shaky smile onto her face and wrapped her arms around her waist. "But remember, I love you. I always have. And I always will."

The words were what he wanted to hear, but her tone…

His instincts rose. Something was up. It was as if… as if she knew what his father was going to say and knew he wasn't going to like it.

More secrets?

The glow from their lovemaking dimmed and he wasn't sure he wanted to hear what either one of them had to say.

But he was going to.

"Fine." He grabbed the car keys off the hook by the wall. "I'll be back, Jules. And then we'll talk." He brushed past his father without looking at him. "Let's go."

Juliet watched them drive away. Watched her future go with it.

It would come out. The money for the mortgage.

She should have told him right away. Should have called him. Something so important shouldn't have had to wait.

When would she learn that the truth had to come out? That there was nothing to be gained by holding back and everything to lose?

Once more, she was going to lose Tanner.

She sucked in a painful breath. Once more, she was going to have to pick up the pieces and go on. Alone. And this time, really alone. Her father had been right. Much as she'd hoped Sandy and Nana had—

Nana.

Oh, God, Nana.

Juliet had to tell her. Now. Before she heard about it on her own.

She had to come clean. Tell Nana why this had happened. Assure her she would be okay. That they'd all be okay.

She settled a hand on her abdomen, trying to calm her breathing. She could do this. She'd had enough practice. It wasn't he end of the world. Her world, yes, but not *the* world.

She grabbed her keys and her purse. Nana deserved the truth.

They all did.

Chapter Twenty-Seven

low down, Son." His father braced his hand on the dash.

"Don't tell me what to do." Tanner almost gunned the engine more, but that would be even more childish than that response. One he wasn't going to apologize for.

"Never could, could I?"

"Are you kidding me?" He glanced at his dad. "You were always telling me what to do. What plays to throw, how to up my workouts, what I should eat, how much sleep, when I could and couldn't go out—"

"I was trying to get you in shape for a career in football. You were the one who wasn't as serious as you should have been."

Tanner gripped the steering wheel until his knuckles turned white. "I was plenty serious. Got that scholarship, didn't I?"

"Which you then lost by being more interested in getting laid than making a name for yourself."

He counted to ten before answering. "You're just pissed because you couldn't bet on my games anymore."

"That was a low blow, Tanner."

"If the shoe fits." Apparently, low blows were what his father associated with his name. Great. This ought to be a banner of a conversation. Talk about going from the highs to the lows… Making love to Juliet one minute then being belittled by his father the next. "What are you doing here, Dad? What did you want to talk about?"

"Go to Missy's Diner. We shouldn't have this conversation while you're driving."

"And having it in public is so much better?"

"I'm not here to fight with you, Tanner. I'm here to apologize."

"For what?"

His father waved his hand toward the strip mall on the left. "Go to Missy's. I could use a cup of coffee."

Gripping the wheel, Tanner made the left a little too aggressively. He hated when his father ordered him around. Especially when *he* was going to be bailing him out.

He pulled into the parking space right by the entrance, slammed it into Park, and got out, clicking the fob to lock the door almost before his father had a chance to shut the door.

He strode to the booth farthest from the door. The less people to hear this conversation, the better. Luckily, Missy's wasn't crowded at this time of day. It'd be nice if they could turn up the Muzak to muffle the conversation, but Tanner couldn't control everything.

That was what was bugging the shit out of him. His father was calling the shots. Just like always. It'd been the one thing he hadn't missed when he'd moved away.

Juliet *hadn't* been one of those things he hadn't missed, no matter how much he'd tried to convince himself she had been.

Missy came over to their booth with a coffee pot in each hand. "Decaf or regular?"

Her father flipped his mug over. "Regular."

"None for me, thanks." He was wired as it was.

Missy poured then gave them the menus.

"Not hungry." Tanner set the menu on the edge of the table.

His father took a few seconds then handed it to her. "I'll have a grilled cheese. American, no pickles."

"Sounds good." Missy smiled at him. "If you change your mind, Tanner, just whistle."

She hadn't changed in all these years. It'd been the same thing she'd said to him when he'd been in high school when her father had run the place. Thankfully, she was only about four years older than him, so it hadn't been inappropriate. But he wasn't anymore interested now than he'd been back then. He would never want any other woman but Juliet.

And he wanted to get the hell back to her to tell her so. "So what is it, Dad? What's so important to say to me that I had to interrupt my time with Juliet?"

"About that…" His father steepled his fingers and took his time before answering him. "I'm sorry for what I put you through growing up. With my gambling. I know the stress it added to our household and I know you resent me for it. Rightfully so."

Tanner sat back. He hadn't expected this. He'd never thought he'd see the day that his father would apologize. Dad had always said he didn't have a problem. Had been adamant about it. Had said that things would turn around. *And* that it was none of Tanner's business.

Technically, that was probably right—until the day Burt Chambers had had the means to force him to marry Juliet.

"Mom said you're in therapy."

His father nodded then took a sip of his coffee. "I needed help. I was so depressed over Burt having the mortgage and forcing you to marry Juliet that—"

"You knew about that?"

"Of course. Burt made sure I did."

"Why that son of a bitch—"

"Calm down, Tanner." His father held up his hand. "Burt had every right to be mad at me. I almost cost us the business. Or, at the very least, his reputation by putting it at risk. He told me that he'd bought the mortgage to salvage it, but he wasn't doing it out of the goodness of his heart. Said some pretty on-point things about me that I didn't want to acknowledge at the time. So then he threw in that he'd blackmailed you into marrying Juliet. But since I knew how you felt about that girl, I didn't think it was a problem."

"Nice. Me not being able to decide the course of my own life isn't a problem. Glad I'm so important to you." Tanner wished he'd ordered coffee just so he'd have a mug to slam to the table because it hurt his palm.

"You are important to me." His father looked away and cleared his throat before looking back. "I know this is too little too late, but I want you to know I'm sorry. For putting all the pressure on you and for screwing up with the gambling. And for giving Burt the means to blackmail you. You didn't have to do it, Tanner. I never expected you to. Made me feel both proud and ashamed, to tell you the truth. But I thought you loved Juliet so it wasn't a problem."

Missy showed up with his sandwich then.

"Thanks, hon."

"Sure thing, Mr. Wentworth. Tanner? You sure you don't want something?"

Her hip was cocked to the right and the look in her eyes…

"Thanks, Miss, but I have what I need."

"Well, you know where to find me." She shrugged with a half smile before walking away.

"That girl wants you," his father said. "Always has."

"Not interested."

"You never were."

"Can we get back to the matter at hand?"

His father took a bite. "It's kind of the same thing."

"I don't know what you mean."

"Juliet. You. You two were always going to be together, so that's why I didn't think it was such a big deal that Burt forced the marriage. But when you stayed away and didn't come back, well, reality set it. It opened my eyes.

That's why I got into therapy. You shouldn't have to bear the brunt of what I did. So I had to do something about it." He took another bite.

"What. Did. You. Do?" Tanner was dreading the answer.

"Nothing illegal." His father set the sandwich down and wiped his fingers on the napkin. "I got a couple of Wagyu. Got into a breeding co-op and sold off enough to keep enlarging the stock. Two days ago, I had a buyer contact me for the whole lot."

Wagyu cattle weren't cheap because their meat, the Kobe beef people were so hot for these days, garnered good prices.

"How'd you afford the first pair?"

His father grimaced. "I, uh, had a buddy who owed me a favor."

Of course he did. And Tanner knew just what kind of *favor* he was talking about. One that involved cards or sports or horses. "Hell of an expensive favor."

"I'm out of that way of life, Tanner. I knew I was getting out. He owed me some money that he didn't have, so I took the stock instead. I had a plan that could get me out from under. Took me some time—not enough time to help you—but as of today, the mortgage is paid off."

"You paid off Burt?" Tanner sat back as the ramifications ran through his mind. Juliet couldn't give him the mortgage back because it was a non-issue. He liked that; it wiped the slate clean between them.

"I would have loved to, but the bastard refused to see me. Told me I had to take it up with Juliet. So I did. Went to her office and gave her the cash. She didn't tell you?"

And just like that, with a couple of sentences, Tanner's happiness came crumbling down.

She'd taken money from his father and hadn't told him. Had let him think she still had a hold over him. She'd been manipulating him again to get what she wanted, and he'd walked into her shower and given it to her, no questions asked.

God, he was such a fool. She hadn't changed. She was still the same conniving spoiled liar she'd been eleven years ago.

"I gotta go." Tanner planted his palms on the table and shoved himself to his feet. "Can you get a ride back?"

"Sure. You gonna go celebrate with your girl?"

"Uh, yeah. Something like that."

Celebrate was not the word Tanner would have chosen. At least, not for this. He would, however, celebrate his freedom when he got back home. *His* home. Nine states away from Juliet.

***

The divorce papers arrived three days later.

Juliet had known they would. Tanner hadn't even come back for his stuff after the conversation with his father.

She'd spent a lousy weekend trying to talk to him, but, of course, her calls went to voicemail. She'd left messages, but by virtue of these papers, he obviously hadn't listened to them.

Or he hadn't believed her.

She spread the papers out on her kitchen table, blinking through the tears. *Dissolution of marriage…*

The thought was just too painful.

"Meow." Houdini shuffled over the papers, little paw prints dotting them from where she'd stepped in a drop of Juliet's coffee on the table.

Juliet scratched her ears. "He made a quicker disappearing act than you did, Houdini." As she'd known he would.

She should have called him before she'd left the office. Should have told him the minute she'd seen him.

Shoulda, woulda, coulda… But she hadn't.

Once again, she'd been so afraid of losing him that her actions—or, in this case, her *non*-action—had led to it happening.

But Nana had forgiven her; why couldn't Tanner? Especially since she was only guilty this time of not acting immediately. She'd been going to tell him.

Juliet took another sip of her coffee, looking at the pages but not seeing any words other than *Dissolution of marriage*.

She'd almost had it all. She'd come *this* close… All it would have taken were a few sentences and this wouldn't be an issue.

If that's all it is, then why is *it an issue? Tanner needs to hear the truth.*

Which was all fine and good, but he wasn't returning her calls.

So? You went to see him once? Why not go again? What do you have to lose?

She sat back. Yeah, why not? What did she have to lose?

Her heart was already broken.

Chapter Twenty-Nine

The following Saturday night

S hake it, Tanner!"

The woman next to Juliet cupped her hands around her mouth and let out an ear-splitting whistle.

Up on stage, Tanner smiled and bump-and-grinded some more.

Juliet wanted to scratch the woman's eyes out.

Her *husband*—no judge had declared them divorced yet—worked his hips like he'd worked them in her shower.

Those were *her* hips, *her* sexy moves. If she had the guts, she'd jump on stage and rustle him out of here.

She gulped some more of her soda—*sans* alcohol. If she were just a wee bit tipsy she actually might do that, but she'd wanted a clear head to talk to him after he was finished.

God, it was going to kill her to get to the *after* part. This past week had practically killed her, but she hadn't been able to leave the office, even staying late last night to finish some negotiations Jim had needed her to handle.

She'd caught the first available flight this morning and gotten here as fast as she could.

The show continued, the other guys taking their turns center stage, but Juliet couldn't stop watching Tanner gyrating in the background.

Hadn't taken him long to get back into the swing of things.

She looked around the bar. How much *swinging* was he doing? Did he think they were divorced? Did the fact that he'd served her those papers mean he was a free man to him? Was he dating anyone? Sleeping with someone?

God, it hurt to think about.

Finally, it was over. The guys left the stage, and the house lights came up a bit. Juliet gulped the rest of her drink, then made her way through the crowd toward backstage.

A good-looking guy in a cowboy hat—that ought to be Tanner's costume but it wasn't—was coming out of the back, his vest open across a broad set of shoulders and flat abdomen, none of which did a thing for Juliet.

She grabbed his arm. "I'm looking for Tanner Wentworth."

The guy tipped his hat back and stared at her. "We have a no fraternization rule."

"I'm his wife."

She couldn't tell if the guy's shock was because she was here or because Tanner had a wife.

Frankly, she didn't care. She *was* still his wife and she wanted to see him. "Is it okay to go back there?"

The guy scratched his eyebrow. "Uh, yeah. I guess. But if the door's closed, knock. It's a shared dressing room."

"Okay. Thanks." She scooted around him—and could feel his eyes on her the entire way until she rounded the corner.

The door was closed.

Taking a deep breath, Juliet knocked.

Another massive guy answered the door, the same one she'd seen the last time she'd been here.

"Well hello, darling. Nice seeing you again. Please tell me you aren't here for Wentworth this time."

She tried to see around him, but his chest and shoulders were almost as big as Tanner's. "I *am* here for him."

"Damn." The guy sighed and shook his head. "Yo, Tan. Babe here for you."

"Busy."

Her body trembled at the sound of Tanner's voice.

"I don't think you're gonna want to be."

The big guy didn't take his eyes off her as he tossed the words over his shoulder.

"Still busy, Markus."

Markus smiled and shrugged. "You heard the man. He's busy. But me, I'm free."

She so wanted to shove him out of the way, but she had a feeling that for all his friendliness, he'd be on Tanner's side.

Until he heard who she was.

"I'm his wife."

Yup, the look on his face said she could knock him over with a feather.

He stepped aside.

Juliet didn't waste any time getting past him. "Hello, Tanner."

Tanner's gaze shot up. "Damn it, Markus, I told you I was busy." He stood up and turned around, giving her a perfect shot of his jeans hugging his backside beneath his shirtless chest as he bent down to get something from his locker. "Go away, Juliet."

"No."

He straightened, but didn't turn around. "I don't want to talk to you."

"Too bad because I want to talk to you. You don't get to run away again."

"Uh, Tan, I'll catch you later." Markus made a quick exit.

Tanner exhaled and pulled a t-shirt over his head, then ran his hands through his hair before turning around. "I can do whatever the hell I want, Juliet, now that you don't have the mortgage to hold over my head anymore."

"I know."

"Yeah, I know you know. My father told me all about it. Unlike you."

The look in his eyes…

No. He didn't get to think awful things about her this time. This time, she was only guilty of not saying something immediately. But she'd been planning to tell him. She'd just gotten… sidetracked. Which she could argue was his fault.

"When was I supposed to, Tanner? The second you stepped into the shower? Excuse me if I wasn't thinking about your father at that moment."

"Not funny."

"I'm not trying to be. Seriously, Tanner, when was I supposed to tell you? Between the times you put your tongue in my mouth? When you hiked me up against the wall? During your orgasm? You didn't give me a chance."

"That's easy to say now that you've been found out. Just like all the other times. Were you ever planning to tell me the truth about Keegan's conception if everything had gone smoothly? Or why your father *just happened* to show up at just the right moment to catch us when he was supposed to be gone for the night? Or was that a lie, too? I can't trust you, Juliet. Not this time. It was too convenient for it to all work out this way. I should have suspected you'd pull something like this when you lied to your own grandmother to get me there. God, I'm such an idiot."

"Stop it, Tanner!" Juliet put her hands up to her ears. "Just stop it, okay? I can't take it anymore. Yes, I lied to you and manipulated you when we were in high school. Yes, I set it up so my dad would catch us in bed together after college. I knew exactly what I was doing both times and I have apologized to you more times than I can count for them. I was afraid of losing you. I'd already lost my mo—one person who'd said she loved me; I couldn't lose you. It's not an excuse but it was my reasoning. But trust me, losing you, our marriage, Keegan… they were enough. I learned my lesson. I even came clean to Nana about what I did to get you back home. I'm not that same person I used to be."

The tears started and there was nothing she could do to stop them. "How much more do I have to pay for those stupid mistakes? I never did them to hurt you; I did them because I loved you, and in my immaturity and insecurity, I thought it wouldn't matter because we'd be together.

"I know now it was foolish and unfair to you, but I can't go back and erase it." She slid her arm under her nose to stop the sniffles. "And you know what? I don't know that I'd want to. I know it was wrong, but something so right came out of that. Keegan. For all that I shouldn't have done what I did, I did have Keegan. Even for that tiny amount of time, I had a son. Our son. Our child. I see him every day and I miss him every day. Just like I miss you. When you came back this time, I swore I wouldn't do anything to jeopardize it. I knew the minute your father gave me that money that I had to tell you. But you didn't give me the chance."

She swiped the tears from eyes with the balls of her hands. "I wouldn't have withheld that information from you. You deserve the truth. Just like you did back then. I'm sorry for what I did and how I did it, but the universe or karma or whatever you want to call it paid me back, didn't it? I lost both of you. So you don't have to keep punishing me, Tanner. I wake with that knowledge every single day. But I'd never do something like that to you again. You—"

The tears and emotions were choking her so she couldn't finish. But then, what more was there to say? Tanner would either forgive her or he wouldn't. But at least he'd know the truth.

Tanner didn't think, he just went to her and wrapped his arms around her and held her. Dropped his chin onto her head while she sobbed against him; hearing her in such pain shredded his heart.

And then he was crying.

And not just a few tears, no. Big, aching shudders ripped through him, and he wrapped his arms around her and held on, needing her to hold him as much as he needed to hold her.

They hadn't cried together back then. No, he'd been numb and she'd been inconsolable and all he'd been able to do was hold her and try to breathe.

He could barely breathe now. The pain… dear God, the pain.

This wasn't about the money. Not really. It was about them. Their past. Their pain.

Their loss.

They'd lost so much and he'd needed the time to deal with, well, everything.

Juliet's arms crept around his back and she bunched his shirt in her fists as she dragged him closer to her.

He needed to sit. His legs wouldn't hold him, let alone both of them.

He wrapped his arms tighter around her waist and sat on the bench, pulling her into his lap and burying his face in her hair.

She brought her palm to his cheek and stroked it.

Tanner took a huge shuddering breath trying to get his emotions under control.

"Tan…" She whispered his name against his cheek, her skin so soft against his.

God, he'd loved her once.

He still loved her.

"Tanner?"

Her voice, so soft, slid beneath his pain and he wanted to reach out. To take the solace offered in that one word.

He pulled back and blinked, the tears making her face fuzzy. Not that it mattered, he'd memorized every dimple and curve and twitch of her lips years ago.

"I'm so sorry, Tanner. For everything. For the lies, for losing Keegan—"

"Shhh." He put his fingers to her lips without thinking it. For her to think she'd had to pay for Keegan's death… He couldn't bear for her to carry that. "You couldn't have known, Jules, what would happen. It's not your fault."

"But if I hadn't gotten pregnant—"

"That time. There's no guarantee it wouldn't have happened another time. Condoms aren't a hundred percent effective. It could have happened without help from you."

She blinked, her beautiful eyes looking like the ocean at dusk. "Does that mean… Do you forgive me?"

He stroked the hair off her face and cupped the back of her neck. He looked at those beautiful, tear-filled eyes. The quiver of her lips. The tracks of her tears down her cheeks. She was in so much pain. And for what purpose? It wouldn't change things. It wouldn't bring Keegan back and, honestly, losing Keegan wasn't her fault. Juliet had loved being pregnant and had been so careful with what she ate and drank and made sure she'd exercised. She'd wanted their child, not because it was a means to keep him with her, but because Keegan was *theirs*. Made of the love they had for each other. She was suffering every bit as much as he was.

They hadn't healed separately; maybe, together, they could.

His thumb stroked the tears from where they slid beside her mouth. "We can't keep looking back. Can't keep blaming. If he'd lived, he would've been the best thing that'd ever happened to us. And just because he didn't doesn't make it the worst. We found out what it was like to love a child. All that selfless, fierce battling to keep him safe. We lost that battle, but we came out ahead for knowing him. I'll always miss him. Always wonder what he would have been like, but I got to hold him, Juliet. I held my son. For a few brief moments, I was a father with my son. I consider myself lucky for having found out what that kind of love is like."

"Lucky? You hated me for getting pregnant with him and then when I…" She took a deep shuddering breath. "When I lost him, it was like I was taking more from you. Again."

He pulled her into his arms. "You didn't lose him. For whatever reason, he wasn't healthy enough to survive. You can't blame yourself for that, Juliet. I never did."

"You didn't? You blamed me for everything else."

"Maybe I was afraid to look at myself. If I'd loved you more, or shown you that I did better, maybe you wouldn't have felt so insecure. I didn't realize what losing your mom must have been like. How tenuous you thought love was."

"No. You can't blame yourself."

"Then let's both stop blaming each other—and ourselves."

Her eyes searched his and Tanner just wanted all the pain to go away. He just wanted what should have been theirs from the very beginning.

"I love you, Juliet. That's why you have the power to hurt me. But I do know that you love me, too. And now, now that we have this perspective, now that we're older and have this perspective, we can make it work."

"Make it wor… Tanner? Do you mean it? Do you really mean it? You want to stay married?"

"*Stay* married?" He chuckled. "Of course you didn't sign the papers. I guess I shouldn't have expected it."

"Actually…" She licked her lips. "I did. I just didn't send them."

"You signed them?"

She nodded. "They're at the hotel. I didn't want to just sign them and send them back without talking to you. Without you knowing the truth. Then, if you still didn't want to work things out, I would give them to you."

"I still want you to."

She stiffened in his arms and he realized what he'd said.

"So I can burn them, Juliet. I don't want a divorce anymore. I want a wife. You. And I want the life we should have had. The family. It's not too late."

"Does that mean you believe me?"

"I do. And I forgive you for the past. I understand why you did it. But I have to take some of the blame for not being how you wanted me to be. How you needed me to be."

"Oh but Tanner you were. You are. You're everything I've ever wanted."

"For not being enough *then*. But know this Juliet Chambers-Wentworth. You are my wife and I'm never letting you go."

Epilogue

Six weeks later

Penelope sipped her wine. She really liked this grape. Niagara, it was called. Fruity and sweet, just the thing for a happy wedding day—or vow renewal as Juliet and Tanner were calling it.

Whatever they called it, she was just tickled pink that they'd finally worked things out.

She was also tickled pink that Juliet actually thought she'd carried one over on her. The poor thing had been so apologetic when she'd explained how she'd gotten Tanner to come home.

Had almost made Penelope come clean.

Almost.

"Nana! Come dance with us!" Juliet waved her over.

Penelope raised her glass. Wine had just been added to her list of approved items, thanks to Dr. Jackson. His condition for his silence was that she abide by his rules for recovery. He'd said he didn't want to see her again for another stroke, so she was going to have to take care of herself.

Now she had the incentive.

She glanced out over the dance floor and fanned herself. Tanner's co-workers were there and even though they had all their clothes on, there was no hiding those dance moves. The single women here tonight were lucky indeed.

All of Juliet and Tanner's high school friends were there, too, all a little older, some heavier, some balder, but it was the same crowd she remembered when they'd hang out at the pool during the summers. And all of them were having a great time.

Well, that Delia girl was on the prowl, but that was nothing new.

She looked around the room. Tanner's parents were at their table, chatting and smiling. It did Penelope's heart good to see them here. Tanner had had a reason to be angry with his father, but what he hadn't realized was that he hadn't had to bail Palston out. That'd been his choice—and it was a good one.

Penelope took another sip of her wine. Life was good.

Well, hers was. Her son's, on the other hand, could use some improvement. He was in the corner alone, surveying the room, a look on his face that was far from a smile. Penelope hadn't seen him crack one all day.

It wasn't the cost that was getting to him—Tanner had been adamant that he and Juliet would pay for the day and wouldn't take a dime of Burt's money. Penelope liked that about Tanner; the boy wanted to stand on his own. That's why he needed a woman who could, too, and Juliet had become that woman.

But Burt… He was burrowing into his den and tuning out the world. Hopefully, Juliet would have a baby soon so Burt could go back to running the company—and she didn't care how old-fashioned she sounded. Juliet wouldn't want to leave her child for hours on end; the company would still be there when she was ready to go back to work. And Burt really needed something to focus on now that she was "better."

She smiled and took another sip of her wine.

"Feeling good about yourself?" Ermalinda took the seat beside her, *chinging* their wine glasses.

"I'm feeling good about them."

"Are you going to tell them?"

"What? That I wasn't as bad off as I'd let them believe? Now why on earth would I do that? That sort of thing is what got them in this position to begin with."

Ermalinda sat back and raised her eyebrows. "That apple doesn't fall far from the tree."

"I hate when you learn new idioms."

"You hate when I'm right."

Penelope sipped her wine and took her time before answering, her focus on her son. "True. But it worked."

"The ends justify the means?"

Penelope set her wine glass down and it was her turn to raise her eyebrows. "My, my. Aren't you the studious one?"

"I am." Ermalinda tilted her wine glass toward Burt. "Take a look."

As Penelope watched, a woman walked up to her son. Nancy Hillson.

And this time, Burt actually talked to her.

"Well played, Ermalinda. Well played."

"Just taking lessons from the master, *Señora*."

***

Juliet tugged Tanner onto the bed in the honeymoon suite. He'd insisted they have a real church service and reception this time, and she'd been more than thrilled that he'd wanted to make such a public declaration. He'd even flown his friends from Beefcake, Inc, in for the occasion. Well, the northern location of Beefcake, Inc. because the ones from the Texas branch could drive in for their boss's vow renewal ceremony.

"My, my, Jules. A bit eager are we?"

"Can you blame me?"

"Hardly." And he kissed her to prove it.

Well, more than kissed her.

It was a while before Juliet could think clearly, but she had something on her mind that he needed to know.

She ran her hand over his chest. She'd always loved Tanner's chest.

There wasn't much about him that she didn't love.

"You know, Tanner, for all your big production about honesty, you lied to me."

He raised his head to look at her. "I've never lied to you, Juliet."

"Yes, you did. That first time we made love after you came back. You told me it wasn't a happily-ever-after. That you were going to make love to me and then leave. That it wasn't forever." She snuggled into him and patted his heart. "See? You lied."

He smiled and it was a good smile. "Well, maybe I just gilded the lily a bit."

"Gilded the lily? Isn't that like saying you're a little bit pregnant?" She worked hard to keep the smile off her face.

Tanner rolled his eyes. "Juliet, you can't be a little bit pregnant. You either are or you're…" His smile tightened. "Juliet?"

She couldn't keep him waiting any longer. She slid her fingers from his, grabbed his wrist and laid his hand across her belly, hers on top of it.

"Uh, Tan? I have something to tell you…"

~~~

Thank you!

Thank you for reading *Beefcake & Retakes*. If you enjoyed this story, please help others find it by posting a review on Goodreads, Amazon, Apple Books, Barnes & Noble… wherever you bought it. Feel free to share a link, tweet about it, Facebook it… All efforts are greatly appreciated.

I love to hear from my readers so check me out online and feel free to friend me!
~~~

www.JudiFennell.com
https://www.facebook.com/JudiFennell.Author/

Sign up for my newsletter at:
http://JudiFennell.com/newsletter-signup/

Turn the page to read an excerpt of book 4 in the series, Gina and Darien's story, in *Beefcakes & Snowflakes*.

BEEFCAKE
& Snowflakes

JUDI FENNELL

MERJINN PRESS

PHILADELPHIA, PENNSYLVANIA

Chapter One

He's at it again."

Gina Taormina wasn't even going to look at *it*, the yet- another-giant-basket filled with things *he'd* chosen. "Send it back," she said to Candy, her spa receptionist.

"Gina, come on. The guy just wants you to notice him."

Gina grabbed the stack of bills instead. Which was saying something. "Send it back."

"But, Geen, it's a really great—"

Gina smacked the granite reception counter with the edge of the bills. "I don't care what it is, Candy."

"Sure about that?"

Hellyeahshewas. "Send it back."

"Aw, come on, Gina. Give the guy a chance."

Gina rolled her eyes and shook her head as she pulled her cardigan closed and walked around the reception desk to Candy's side which was where the nuts-and-bolts of the spa were located: appointment book, credit card swiper, computer, printer, and yesterday's receipts. "I don't do strippers."

"Now that's a damn shame. I'd do a stripper. In a heartbeat."

And he'd be gone the next. Gina had learned that the hard way. Exceptions were few and far between, and given that she was related to one exception and friends with another, her chances of finding a third were close to non-existent. She'd tried and, *whoa*, had it backfired.

Thank God she'd never acted on her crush on Gage. Especially now that he was with Lara. No one had ever known and it'd never gotten weird with her cousin—and Gage's business partner—Bryan.

She yanked open a drawer for a pen. "Send. It. Back. Candy. Now."

Candy set the basket—they were always really nice baskets—on the appointment book. Probably just so Gina wouldn't miss it. "Can I keep it?"

"No, because then he'll think *I* did and that's the last ego stroke Froggy needs."

She slammed the drawer shut with her thigh and got out from behind the desk, as if the basket was made of kryptonite.

For her, it was.

"Fine, but what about any other strokes he needs? And why on God's earth are you calling that hunk by his middle school nickname?"

Because that's how she'd first met Froggy, aka Darien Foster, back in the day, and six years of being humiliation by him hadn't given her reason to think him any less of a jerk. Even if he now looked like a romance novel cover model.

Gina raked her curls off her face. "Just get rid of it, whatever it is. Maybe he'll finally get the message that I'm not interested."

Candy tapped a candy-apple red—her signature color—nail against the fancy bow on the basket. "You might want to take a look at this before you go all not-interested. It's sweet."

That was the problem; Froggy—Darien's—little "gifts" were getting sweeter. He'd started out with flowers, then chocolate, then a single rose with the chocolate, but then he'd gotten smart and started sending her products to give away in her salon. It was a double-edged sword; she'd used all her cash to get the spa up and running with necessities, but extras would take a while since she wanted to grow her staff to offer more services before giving away free lotions or creams to her clients.

But Darien had started dropping off baskets of the stuff. Assortments, as if he was giving them to her, but one woman could only use so many lotions, and three baskets of different scented lotions and oils would take that woman more lifetimes than Gina had.

She hated that he was trying to get to her through her business.

She hated that he was trying to get to her at all. "Just send it back, Candy." Out of sight, out of mind and the sooner, the better. She didn't need to think about Darien Foster anymore. It was bad enough that he worked for her cousin, Bryan, but that was the closest he was going to get. "And let's take a look at next week's appointments. I think we should be okay staff-wise with what we have now."

"Um…" Candy twirled a long blonde corkscrew curl around her fingers in the quintessential "ditz" look the girl had perfected when she wanted something to go her way. Or had bad news to impart.

Too bad for Candy that Gina knew that, behind the stereotypical blonde exterior Candy assumed to suit her purposes, lurked the brain of a Mensa member. Hence the reason Candy was here; she'd set that brain in motion and had made a fortune in the market. She worked for Gina because she wanted something fun to do with her day, not because she needed the money. Which was the only reason Gina could afford a full time receptionist.

"Um, what?"

"We have a bridal party booked for the twenty-third. For a full spa treatment."

Normally, a bridal party was a good thing. But Gina

had just approved two of her three massage therapists for a vacation at that time since the weeks between Thanksgiving and Christmas weren't turning out to be such a hotbed of requests for massages. Gina didn't understand why; the cold weather seemed to be the perfect time to get all oiled up and rubbed down—not to mention a great holiday stress-reliever—but bookings were slim. Didn't these ladies plan on the rigors of last-minute Christmas shopping?

"How many people are we talking?"

"Twelve."

"*Twelve*? Who has a bridal party that big?"

"Sophie Cavanaugh's sister."

"*The* Sophie Cavanaugh?"

"There's only one Sophie Cavanaugh."

True enough. Sophie Cavanaugh was an anchor on the local news affiliate who'd garnered national news during local storm coverage when she'd saved a child from being swept away in a flooded road—as the cameras were rolling. It didn't hurt that the woman was gorgeous, had an actual brain in her put-Barbie-to-shame body, and no one had—so far—turned up one skeleton in her closet since the story broke. And now she was coming to Gina's spa for her sister's bridal party gathering. If Sophie liked it… The word-of-mouth could be worth more than Gina could ever hope to be able to spend in advertising.

"Okay, start calling. We can rotate the guests between all the stations, so I need at least two more massage therapists in here."

"Did that."

Of course she did. Because Candy wasn't as brain-less as she liked people to think. "Who'd you line up?"

"Well…"

"What, Candy?"

"No one."

"What do you mean *no one*? Stacey can't handle twelve women by herself."

"I know that." Candy grabbed a handful of hair. "The blonde comes from a bottle, remember?"

"I wasn't saying you're stupid."

"That's what it sounded like."

"Can we focus on the problem here? You know I love you and value you."

"And when my allotment of free spa services runs out, you're going to pay me what I'm worth, yeah, yeah, I got it." Candy let out a long-suffering sigh and dropped her hair. "The local massage therapist inventory is tapped out. Everyone's booked."

"But our appointments aren't even full so how come no one's available?"

"Where have you been, boss lady? We filled the rest of everyone's schedule on Saturday. Right up until three hours before Charlotte and Tori are catching their planes. That ad you ran a while back must have gone viral or something. Which was what I was going to tell you when you got in this morning before we got sidetracked by Mr. Casanova."

Great. Froggy, er, Darien was upsetting her business operations now. If she could get through the rest of her life without hearing his name, she would be happy. Whether or not the spa was successful.

"You know what, Candy? Don't send his gift back to wherever he bought it. Send it back to him. With a note that says I'm not interested." Gina scribbled herself a note to look getting into a Cease-and-Desist order so the guy would leave her alone. "Oh, and how about if you send a note to the member coordinator at the chamber of commerce? See if any freelance massage therapists have recently joined the chamber. Didn't the local business school recently graduate a bunch?"

Candy pulled a pencil from behind her ear, a testament to its thickness that Gina hadn't even seen the pencil there. "Check. One note that you're not interested, and another that you are."

"Just don't mix them up."

"Now, boss lady, would I do that?" There Candy went with the hair-twirling, vapid look she'd perfected.

Gina tapped her on the nose. "Not if you know what's good for you."

Candy flicked Gina's finger. "Oh, trust me. I know what's good for everyone."

Which was *exactly* why Candy switched the notes.

Here's Judi!

Award-winning, best-selling author Judi Fennell loves to laugh and loves love, so it's no surprise there's a little bit of each in every book she writes. Check out her fairy tales with a twist for a taste of her light-hearted, tongue-in-cheek paranormal and romantic comedies. From mermen off the coast of the Jersey Shore, to genies with magic carpets, to male strippers à la Magic Mike, and manly maids whose motto is *Satisfaction Guaranteed*, there's always a laugh and love to be had.

And, in her copious (?) amounts of spare time, she helps authors with all aspects of writing and indie-publishing with her formatting, cover and promotional design, editorial, consultation, and audiobook company, www.formatting4U.com.

Judi lives in suburban Philadelphia with a menagerie of four-legged friends, and the minute those creatures start A) singing, B) sewing clothing, or C) cleaning the house will be the day she retires from writing…!!

Books by Judi Fennell

Royally Sunk

In Over Her Head

Reel's a merman without a tail, and Erica's terrified of the ocean. Only one thing could get her into the water: a gun. And only one thing could keep her there: the sexy merman who saves her life, only to risk his own.

Wild Blue Under

Valerie's a mer princess landlocked in the middle of the country. Rod is the prince who sets out to rescue her. But can they dodge a usurper's plot and make it back to the ocean before his tail—and his claim to the throne—disappear forever?

Catch of a Lifetime

Logan ran *away* from the circus; all he wants is for his life to be normal. The naked woman who shows up on his boat is anything *but* normal. Especially when Angel turns out to be a mermaid—with an angry sea monstress after her.

Love on the Rocks

Princess Mariana isn't a poser; she really is an artist which she's about to prove with the statue she's carving on a deserted island. Problem is, Jace is hiding out there so the one thing that will set Mariana free from her royal prison is the one thing that will get Jace killed. Romance is rough enough, but when there's a tsunami in the weather forecast, love is on the rocks.

Making Waves ~ outtakes compilation

Read about The Incident that made Erica terrified of the ocean, the reason Valerie, the lost princess, was found,

and how Logan's young son Michael found a mermaid
The stories *before* the stories.

Bottled Magic

I Dream of Genies

Matt's luck has finally changed when genie Eden
escapes her bottle and lands in his lap. Literally. And
she vows never to go back in. Unfortunately for both of
them, the guy who put her in there wants her back and
he'll stop at nothing to get her.

Genie Knows Best

Samantha inherits her father's estate, complete with a
genie who has one last master to serve before his
indentured servitude is up. Sam's more than willing to
set Kal free—until her greedy ex has decided that if he
can't have Sam, no one can.

My Fair Genie

Zane's inherited the family mansion which he can't rid
of quick enough to put the rumors of his family's crazy
history to rest. Too bad the genie who's been the cause
of those rumors has been set free to run amok once
more. Only this time, it's his heart she's messing with.

Your Wish Is His Command ~ outtakes compilation

Find out how Kal came to be imprisoned in his lantern
and why he needs to serve 1001 masters. It's the story
before the story..

Once Upon A Time Romance

Beauty and The Best

Jolie is a personal chef by day and a romance writer by
night. So when she gets a gig for the hot reclusive artist,
Todd, she has the perfect hero for her book. Until Todd
finds out and kicks her out of his kitchen, his home, *and*
his heart.

If The Shoe Fits

Once upon a time, a long time ago, in a land far, far away, there lived a girl by the name of Cinderella. This is not her story. *This* is the story of Lucinda Isabella Casteleoni, who, like her namesake, has a wicked stepmother, two tacky stepsisters, and countless hours of hard work to (not) look forward to. But unlike that fairy tale princess, Bella's Prince Charming is nowhere to be found. Until a little old man with sparkling green eyes opens a shoe store down the street. Then the magic begins...

Through The Leaded Glass (prequel)

An accidental trip to medieval England has ad exec Kate scrambling for a way home… But can she bring the hot knight in shining armor she's fallen in love with back with her?

BeefCake, Inc.

Beefcake & Cupcakes

Lara wants her cupcakes to be a success. Exotic dancer Gage wouldn't mind sampling them, but his work schedule to pay off his nephew's hospital bills doesn't leave him time to do so. Until a party where beefcake meets cupcakes and, *oh*, is it delicious!

Beefcake & Mistakes

When Bryan mistakes Jenna for a hooker and she realizes he's her adopted son's father, the mistakes and misunderstandings start to grow. But something else is growing between them, too. Sometimes, one wrong turn can be oh so right…

Beefcake & Retakes

Tanner his ex-wife to be out of his life forever, but when her grandmother has a stroke and he has to pretend to still be in love with Juliet, can he risk a retake on the one woman who never stopped loving him?

Beefcake & Snowflakes

Gina's had a crush on Darien since forever—until the day he humiliated her in school. Fifteen years later, he leaves her cold. Exotic dancer Darien has come back to town to set a few things to rights. One is the mess he made for Gina years ago… and *maybe* rekindle the flames they'd once had. But the only way to melt the snow around Gina's heart is to turn up the heat, both on the job… and off.

Manley Maids

What happens when three irresistibly sexy brothers lose a poker bet to their enterprising sister? They get hired out for her housecleaning venture. Now, the Manley Maids are at your service. Satisfaction guaranteed.

What a Woman Wants

Resort owner Sean plans to buy an historic estate, making a name for himself and making millions, so he moves in under the guise of cleaning the place to thwart the one condition of the inheritance. But heir Olivia and her menagerie get under his skin, and he finds that the poker bet that got him into this mess isn't the only game-changer.

What a Woman Needs

Movie star Bryan wants fame and fortune, not a repeat of his penny-pinching "normal" childhood. After the publicity surrounding of her husband's death, Beth needs is a normal life for herself and her children, and the movie star who lost a bet to clean her house—with paparazzi in tow—isn't it. But as flirtation turns into seduction, Bryan needs to convince Beth he's more man than a maid. Or actor. Because he's playing the lead in a reverse Cinderella story, and it might just be the role of a lifetime.

What a Woman Gets

Liam has no patience for women who spend a man's money without giving a thought to any actual work. But to make good on his bet, Liam must not only tolerate socialite, Cassidy, he'll have to clean up after her when her father cuts her off. With no money and no home for Liam to clean, Cassidy has no choice but to accept a job offer—as Liam's new maid. But when sparks fly between them, will it be true love or just another messy affair?

What a Woman

MaryAlice Catherine is all set to clean her grand-mother's friend's house, only to find the woman's cocky grandson whom she'd had a crush on growing up—and he'd known all along—is living there and she's mortified. Jared remembers it differently; Mac was always a bossy little thing, but he's not going to let her call the shots now. But with the two of them living in one house, there's no telling who's going to come out swinging.

What A Guy Wants

Beckett is ready to pay up for his lost poker bet. He just didn't realize he'd have to do it with his heart. Jennifer is the one who got away and now she's right here in front of him. In her house. That he's here to clean. Jennifer can't believe the bad boy from high school she'd had a major crush on is in her home, but if there's one thing her ex-husband taught her, it's that she can't count on the bad boy. Until Beckett lays all his cards on the table and he turns out to be someone Jennifer can bet on after all.

www.JudiFennell.com

He took a few photos of the makeshift outline on the floor just to get his mind back on the job. Then he grabbed a few more of the ceiling and its ductwork, then took one of the bar area before aiming his phone around the rest of the place.

He stopped when he was facing the front door.

Jules was leaning against the crossbar on the glass, her body silhouetted by the sunlight.

Her hair fell below her shoulder blades, curling at the ends away from where her back curved in before it reached her backside.

Juliet had an amazing ass. Tight, firm, rounded… Small enough to get his palm on, but big enough to fill it.

His fingers twitched at the memory.

Something else did as well.

He snapped the picture. The last photo he had of Jules—

Actually, he didn't have any photos of her. She'd been the keeper of their photo albums when they'd been together and when he'd left… When he'd left, the last thing he'd wanted was a reminder of her.

He took another. And another. Couldn't stop taking them, though it wasn't as if she was moving.

Tanner did, though. He stepped to the left. The angle changed and he caught the curve of her cheek.

It reminded him of Keegan's.

The blow to his gut wasn't as harsh as usual.

She scraped a hand through her hair and tilted her head, sending the waves cascading down her back.

He loved Juliet's hair. Loved the feel of it, the texture, the way it glided between his fingers. The way it felt trailing over his skin. The way it looked fanned out beneath her on his pillow.

Or hers.

He took a few more shots. He'd love one head-on in full sunlight, but he couldn't ask her for that. It'd open the door to too many questions. Ones he didn't have any answers for.

She moved then and waved to the real estate agent, presumably, outside.

Tanner glanced at the time on his phone. They should get going. It wasn't as if there was a ton of stuff to look at in the place, just a bunch of discarded construction paraphernalia and a couple of metal barrels that he hoped were empty but whose removal would have to be part of the deal. They didn't need to worry about the EPA on top of zoning.

"Tanner?" Juliet turned toward him. "I think the real estate guy is finished with his calls."

"Yeah, I'm about done, too." He shoved the phone into his back pocket.

"So? Are you going to rent or buy this place?"

He shrugged. "Have to hear the terms first. I'm not sure if Gage and Bry have the cash so it can't happen until I'm in."

Juliet exhaled. Deeply. "Right."

She wrapped her arms around herself, looking small and vulnerable.

Dammit, he didn't want to feel sorry for her. Didn't want to… to regret that he was going to leave.

Didn't want to hurt her.

"Come here, Jules." He tugged her into his arms because he just *had* to, tucking her up against him like he always had, and resting his chin on her head.

She unwrapped her arms from her body and wrapped them around his.

He felt her sigh deep into his soul.

"Hey, are you guys—oh. Geez. Sorry." Pfeiffer had the door open then closed and himself back outside in under two seconds, but they were enough to shatter the mood.

"I… I'm sorry." Jules stepped back and brushed her hair behind her ears, her arms going around her midsection again. Classic hurt pose—draw in the limbs to protect the core. "I shouldn't—"